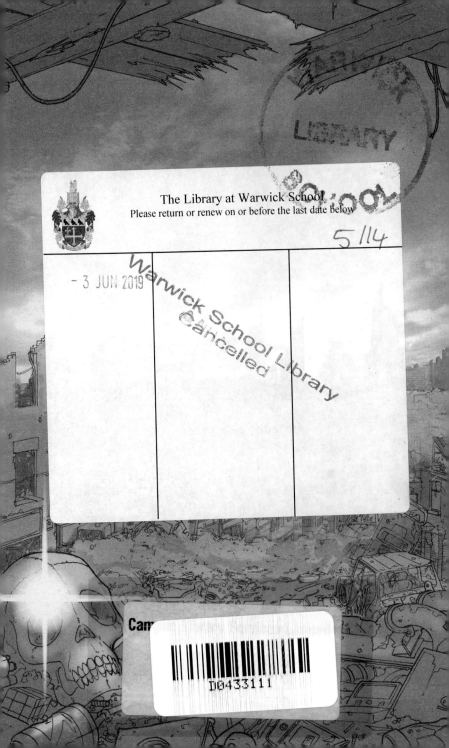

From The Chicken House

This is blistering science fiction at its very best.
It's packed full of amazing ideas, brilliant
characters and a plot you'll need to work out
with your mind's eye. Come on, jump in!
We're on a deadline to save the world!

Barry Cunningham
Publisher

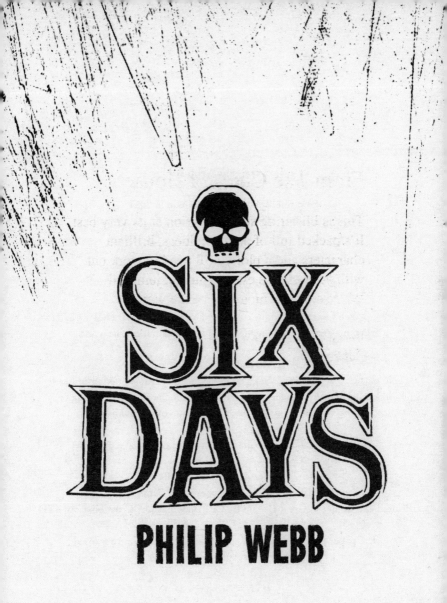

SIX DAYS

PHILIP WEBB

2 Palmer Street, Frome, Somerset BA11 1DS

Text © Philip Webb 2011

First published in Great Britain in 2011
The Chicken House
2 Palmer Street
Frome, Somerset BA11 1DS
United Kingdom
www.doublecluck.com

Jacket design www.crushed.co.uk
Cover illustration Alun Edwards
Interior design Steve Wells
Typeset by Dorchester Typesetting Group Ltd
Printed and bound in Great Britain by CPI Bookmarque, Croydon, CR0 4TD

The paper used in this Chicken House book is made from wood
grown in sustainable forests.

1 3 5 7 9 10 8 6 4 2

British Library Cataloguing in Publication data available.

ISBN 978-1-906427-62-7

For Mum

DEFINITELY NOT SCAV MATERIAL

SO I FIGURE IT'S JUST ANOTHER DAY RIPPING DOWN LONDON FOR US SCAVS, BUT I'M DEAD WRONG COS THIS IS THE SHIFT EVERYTHING GOES BALLISTIC.

First up, our crusher goes kaput, and that's a proper hassle cos we've got to de-clog the filters, which is *the* worst job, and we don't get a bean for it cos we ain't doing real scavving. And guess who's buried in the intakes up to their elbows in concrete powder with a glorified bog brush? Yep, when you're fifteen and a girl, you get all the plum jobs like that cos there ain't no one else on the team can fit in the damn intakes. Well, there's Wilbur, my kid brother, but he ain't in the frame. He'd probably just crawl up here and go to sleep. Bright as a pin, but anything scav-related goes right over his bonce. Anyhow, I'm trying not to think what would happen if the crusher was to crank up again right now, when the old man pipes up from outside.

'Where's Wilbur?'

And you know what? That don't even deserve an answer cos how the hell am I supposed to know?

But then he crams his head into the intakes and even through all the gunk on my goggles I can see he's looking jittery.

'There's been no sign of him since the crusher went down,' he hisses. 'Did you see him?'

I make a show of scanning the tiny space round my head. 'Dad, I ain't seen nothing but the end of my nose for the last hour. He's probably parked on his chuffer somewhere reading a comic.'

'I checked on all the floors. He's not there.'

I don't say nothing then, cos Wilbur's got previous on this. First chink of downtime and he's off nosing about on his tod instead of staying put like he's been told a million times before. And that's bad news on this side of the river.

Outside I can hear the gangmaster barking at everyone to get a lick on, even though there ain't nothing to do till I get these filters clear. He's narked cos every minute the crusher's out of action, he's losing, too. It means we'll be working double speed to play catch-up. And if we're shorthanded there'll be hell to pay.

Dad drags me out by the ankles just as the gangmaster disappears behind the crusher's tracks. 'I'll finish up here. You go and rustle him up. I can make out like you're still inside. And, Cass, don't hang around. I can't stall them for ever.'

'But—'

'Don't argue with me, Cass. Just do it.'

I suppose it makes sense but I don't like it cos we can't afford for the gangmaster to get wind of this. He's always on the look out for an excuse to ditch us from the crew cos we're slower than the others after Dad bust his leg in an accident and it set bad. So we could really do without my useless brother going missing . . .

I sneak into the gaff we've been scavving since the shift started.

'Wil-bur!' I call out – sing-song with a touch of the evil I'll do to him when I find him. I'm still hoping he's just holed up in a cupboard reading from his extensive collection of cartoon cobblers . . .

But it's kind of creepy quiet, like you know there ain't no one there.

And then it hits me where he's gone.

I grab up my gear – ropes, backpack, helmet – cos I'll stick out like a sore thumb wandering off-site without it.

By now everyone's crowded round the busted crusher – guards, boffins, scavs – so it's easy slipping out the far end of Little Sanctuary back across the wasteland towards the river.

Wilbur, what a right royal pain in the bejesus. He's been on about it for weeks, though I ain't paid it one ounce of attention. Cos it was just him blathering on. But I remember he was gutted when we wasn't detailed to be on the Parliament crews.

Luck loves me in one way cos it's the third morning of smog on the trot, a real snot-gobbler as they say, green and sopping from the dust and the fumes. Which means full mask and goggles is the order of the day, so no one clocks that I ain't meant to be there. 'Specially as demolition's at full pelt. This is the face of the scav-zone north of the river and there's got to be a thousand crews working the streets from Millbank to Embankment. But if you ask Wilbur (and I ain't asking), they're all wasting their time.

I hurry down Bridge Street, ducking between the pillars of the old shop fronts, blending in with other crews as they queue up to offload into the crusher chutes. If a gangmaster spots me I'll be in it up to my neck, but everyone's so pooped and bent double with their bins I don't get a second glance.

Man, Wilbur's got some explaining to do. Right after

I spiflicate him. See, he's got some notion he knows where the artefact really is.

Which is nuts.

Cos ever since the end of the Quark Wars, our lords and masters, the Vlads, been forcing scavs to tear down London to find it. A hundred years we been on the case! The Empire of New Russia, the conquerors of the world, with all their fancy machines, can't figure out where it is. But Wilbur thinks he's gone and figured it out just by reading some comics!

Course, the destination keeps shifting. A few months back it was in Churchill's bunker, down on King Charles Street. He was ready to bet his life on it. Till we heard that got picked clean without so much as a murmur.

Now he thinks it's in Big Ben.

It's quiet when I get there, what with the crushers out of earshot. I'm all knackered from the running so I spend a minute getting my breath back, just staring up at the lone tower. And I get a funny feeling about the place, the way it looms above me in the lime smog, caught in the river searchlights, looking spooky and proper lovely. Shame it's gonna be brick-dust inside a couple of months. I rip off my mask and goggles cos they're steaming up big-time. The rest of the Houses of

Parliament is just a honeycomb – scavved out to the bare bones and surrounded by mud canyons and mounds of slag. There's just a couple of teams at the far end ripping down the masonry. In a few days, they'll be ready to prep the tower. That's how it goes. Like starving ants we swarm into every nook of every building, one by one, from your garage to your palace.

Big Ben is gonna have its day.

But not today.

There's some old Portakabins and scaffolding round the base of the tower, and one of the first-floor windows has been busted in, which is probably Wilbur, so I climb up the scaffold and go in the same way past bits of glass. It's dark inside cos all the windows are coated with smog dust.

'Wilbur, you berk!' I yell.

Nothing.

'Wilbur, stop messing about!'

Silence. Just my boots scuffing around in the grit.

'The old man's gonna go mental if he finds out, so you better get down here pronto.'

My voice goes echoing up into the tower. I pull the torch out my pack and switch it on. There's a gloomy hall up ahead, pretty much empty apart from a few benches, and the start of a spiral stairway. Great.

Doesn't take much to figure out he's gone to the top, to the clock. Probably a hundred metres, and then some.

I tighten the straps on my pack and start up the stairway. For the first couple of floors there's landings with mouldy carpet going into the wreckage of the Houses of Parliament.

'Wilbur, you waste of space, I'm gonna burn every one of them damn comics when we get back, swear to God.' But I don't yell this, cos I'm done with yelling. And I don't mean it neither cos Wilbur's head's in the clouds, that's all. He don't mean no harm.

But then my heart just about jumps through my gob.

Someone's standing in the shadows right in front of me.

I stumble back against railings and my pack nearly tips me over the stairwell. I swing up my torch.

It ain't Wilbur staring back at me.

And that freaks me out even more. Cos why would anyone else be here?

It's a boy. Tall and wiry and wild-looking. His eyes blaze at me. And that's weird. He don't squint or shield his face – he just seems to soak up the torchlight. I hold the beam there, like it might hold him at bay. Cos I ain't sure what to make of him. Them eyes – green and clear and unblinking. Like a cat giving you daggers. And he

– 7 –

don't look like any boy I ever seen around London. Definitely not scav material. He's got this crazy hair with clumps chopped out – done in a hurry. By the village idiot. With a blindfold on. And he's so clean you can see the black of his hair and even his eyelashes. I'd have to have a month of baths to look that shiny. His lips are pink and his hands . . . His hands are practically *royal* next to my scabby mitts. You never seen such beautiful hands, like on a statue. Still, the strangest thing is his threads, like military get-up but flimsy, more like a kid's idea of a uniform. About as useful for scavving in as a pair of pyjamas.

'Who the hell are you?' I go.

He don't answer. Maybe he don't speak English. Maybe he's a Vlad or a boffin. Except what's he doing here on his tod, creeping about in the shadows? And suddenly I remember about Wilbur and my hackles go up. Cos scavs have got all kinds of tales about survivor-mutants that creep about in the Underground tunnels, snatching kids and that. Or wanderers from the Northern Wilds. And I always figured them stories was cobblers but look at me now, trying to stop the torch from shaking. Except, the more I look at him, the more I calm down. Cos he's just too flippin' clean to be a baby-eating Feral.

'You seen my brother? Kid, so high, bit gormless.' I stop myself, realising this description is a tad pointless. 'Look, you seen *anyone* around here?'

He steps back, looking like he might make a run for it.

'Hey, slow down. I ain't gonna hurt you. You just scared the crap out of me, OK?'

He keeps his distance and steals a glance over the stairwell. Then he's straight back to me with his wary eyes, shivering a bit now in his bonkers outfit.

'It's just me. There ain't no one else . . . Look, do . . . you . . . speak . . . Ing . . . ger . . . lish?'

'I understand you,' he goes. He's got the queerest accent – *clean* you might say, like he's picked English up from a book. 'There's a boy. I saw him pass. He went higher, up there. I was going to call to him but I didn't want to scare him away . . .'

He trails off, probably cos he's twigged how dodgy that sounds. I'm thinking, *Yeah, but you didn't mind giving me the fright of the century, did you?* I turn to go, cos this is about the weirdest conversation I've had in yonks and it ain't helping me track down Wilbur.

'What are you all looking for?' he blurts out. It's like the words don't come natural to him, like he ain't done no speaking for a long time.

'What?'

'All you people. What are you searching for?'

I'm thinking, *Are you kidding? Surely everyone knows about the lost artefact* . . . But I ain't got time to answer him cos from way up above us in the tower comes the smashing of glass and a muffled cry. Wilbur!

I whirl away from the boy and charge up the stairs, three at a time, my pack slamming up and down with each stride. After a few flights I snatch a glance back and I see his shiny face staring up at me, then he starts following.

I bound up till it's two-at-a-time, then one-at-a-time, tripping, scrambling, then practically crawling on all fours. By the time I reach the top my blood's pumping so hard I'm seeing stars.

There's a bell. The biggest bloody bell I've seen ever, green with age, and if it was to sound off now I reckon it'd kill me stone dead.

'Wilbur?' My voice wheezes out like the last gasp of a mouse.

There's this passageway past all the cogs and innards of the clock, and it leads out onto the back of the clock face. And I can see grey daylight through it, the black numerals and the hands, and a hole near the spindle at the centre. But no Wilbur. I throw off my pack.

The boy stumbles into the space behind me, gasping and retching.

'Give me a leg up,' I go.

'What?'

'Jesus, do you speak English or don't you? Give me a bunk up!'

I show him how to link his fingers into a step, and he hoists me up the wall opposite the clock face where these old pipes and light fittings are. Somehow I scramble up the pipes onto the spindle, then inch to the hole in the glass. I see shreds of green smog, glints of the Thames, the last stumps of Westminster Bridge, far below.

My stomach goes to water. Wilbur's gone. Dear God, no. He's at the bottom now, and I've got to go down and find his body, what's left of it. And I've got to tell Dad . . .

And then I hear a whimpering cry. 'Cass?'

I practically slip over the edge with shock. Then, slowly, I lean out as far as I dare.

And right at the end of the minute hand is Wilbur, clinging on with everything he's got.

WHEN BIG BEN STOPPED

HE'S HUGGING THE OUTSIDE OF THE POINTER, STARING UP AT ME WITH A LOOK OF PLEADING TERROR.

'HURRY, CASS! I'M SLIPPING.'

My first thought is to lump a hole through the glass where he's at and drag him to safety. But the glass is pretty thick and I could end up knocking him off if I do that. Anyway, there ain't no easy way to reach him from the back of the clock face. He's too high up from the floor.

'Cass!'

'Hold on now, Wilbur. I've got to figure out a way to get you, OK?'

'Hurry!'

'It's gonna be OK,' I go. But is it? Is it *really*? *All right, get a grip, think, think . . .*

The only way to rescue him is on the outside. My scav sense tells me that much. I've got to use the clock hands somehow . . . And that's the problem right there, ain't it? Cos first up, I ain't too clever at heights. And second up, what bloody time was it when Big Ben stopped? Twenty to four. Quarter past nine would've been just peachy. But twenty to four means he's sloping down on the minute hand and the hour hand ain't any flipping use at all cos it's too far away.

But then I remember I've got my pack, with ropes in. And the Little Lost Lord of Parliament. So things are looking up a tad.

'Right, Wilbur, listening?'

His eyes are closed tight but he nods.

'Here's the plan. I'm gonna get a rope to you but you've got to hang on a bit longer, all right?'

And what do you know? When I look back inside, Pyjama Boy's already looped one of the ropes over the spindle and he's nearly up to me with the pack over his shoulder.

'Hey, you ain't as useless as you look.'

He casts me this grim, wild-eyed look when he gets up, like he can't quite believe he's here, like all of this is one nightmare he can't wake up from. I know how he feels.

In a jiffy I've hitched up a makeshift harness between me and the spindle, so I can step out safely onto where both hands join at the centre of the clock face. Now it's just a case of sending a separate loop down to Wilbur and hauling him up. But then I cotton on that this ain't gonna be so easy.

'Wilbur, the rope's coming but you got to let go enough to grab it, OK?'

'I can't!'

'You can. You've got to.'

'I can't!'

'Here it comes.'

I swing the loop over, but he ain't letting go for love nor money. Can't say I blame him.

'Come on, Wilbur. If you got out there on your own, you can do it.'

The loop slaps him in the shoulders, but now he's closed his eyes again.

'I'm slipping, Cass!'

I could abseil straight down from the spindle but then I'd never be able to reach him – at number six on the clock face I'd be too far from number eight where he's hanging. There ain't nothing else for it. I've got to back down the minute hand to where he is and grab hold of him. I pay out some slack on the rope and step off the spindle to test my weight. So far so good.

But then a few more steps along the hand jolts and notches down. Wilbur screams. Twenty-*five* to four. Bleeding hell-fire! I scramble back up to the centre.

Wilbur is yelling his head off, crying now, too.

Pyjama Boy pokes his head out next to me. 'You have to go and get him before he falls.'

And right there I lose it. 'Look, you might be master of the bleeding obvious . . .'

But he ignores me and points to the hour hand. 'Going out on that one might be safer . . .'

I don't even wait for him to finish. Genius! The hour hand – if I get the run-up right, I can launch off it in my harness and swing up to where Wilbur is. Though if I even think about it for a second more I know I'll never have the guts to pull it off.

I toss Pyjama Boy the spare rope.

There's a screech from Wilbur. He's just got two arms levered over the minute hand with his legs scrabbling against the glass. This is it. There ain't no more chances. No more thinking things through. I pay out the harness – maybe six metres of slack. It's got to be right but there ain't no time for measuring. It's a guess and that's that.

I swivel to face the end of the hour hand. Away from Wilbur.

Deep breath.

One more for luck.

And I go.

My head ain't really coming with me on this one cos with all that slack in the harness, the drop has become pretty bloody real, all one hundred and something metres of it. Two, three, four strides out onto the hour hand, speeding up as I go, out towards the grubby gold of the rim. All the sky of London surrounds me. A swirl of pigeon wings disturbed from the eaves of the tower. And a fearsome pug-nosed dragon with bat wings leering down at me, its stone eyes bulging. I plant one boot down hard on the fat arrow point of the hour hand. And I feel it give as I leap out.

Then I'm twisting in the air, with the numbers and glass panes rushing past me.

Thwack!

The harness snaps taut and stamps out my screams.

And as I open my eyes again, I'm swinging up towards Wilbur.

He's seen me now, and I don't reckon I ever seen anyone look that scared. Cos he knows what's gonna happen next.

I'm sailing so fast I'm gonna knock him off no matter

what. So, I either catch him, or I drop him. Simple as.

I reach out.

And I'm that close to him I can see the smudges on his specs and two yellow lines of snot.

He lets go.

And when I clutch hold, I can feel him gasp and go limp, like I've squeezed all the life out of his bag-of-bones body. But I've got him. And I ain't never letting go.

We swing gently to a stop. And I can't speak for a bit. Cos I'm just hanging from the clock face of Big Ben with my dopey brother in my arms, facing out east where the smog's lifting a bit now and the sun's getting up and there's the maze of slag pits and sludge where South London used to be before it got scavved out. And there's the Thames looping round towards Blackfriars, and way in the distance I can just make out the smoke trails of the power stations where the Great Barrier holds back the sea.

A loop of rope drops on my head. I slip it round us both and under my arms, and give it a tug. Then, inch by inch, Pyjama Boy hoists us up. I can see his shadow behind the glass right about six o'clock, using the spindle above to take the strain. And he sure don't look like much but he knows ropes as good as any scav. Or he's a quick learner.

When we get back through the hole, Wilbur goes, 'It wasn't there, Cass.'

Then he bursts into tears.

And I don't know whether to shake him to death or hug him.

THE LUBBER

ACTUALLY I DON'T DO NEITHER OF THESE THINGS. COS HE'S GOT TO BE KIDDING, RIGHT?
I JUST GAWP AT HIM AND GO, 'OH, NICE ONE, CASS — THANKS for bailing me out. Sorry for just swanning off mid-shift on a whim. Without telling a soul. Then winding up on the outside of Big Ben with no back-up and no ropes. I mean, what was you gonna do if it *was* the damn artefact, eh? You'd've been a hero for what, five minutes tops, before plunging down to the pavement with a loony smile on your face?'

'I slipped! I never meant to go right out. I just wanted to touch the clock hands, see if I was warm.'

'What?'

'You're supposed to know if you touch it. You *feel* the artefact. That's how you know.'

'What kind of cobblers is that?' I huff at him, trying not to lose it completely.

'It's hidden, but if you hold it, you'll know.' His voice runs out of steam and he gazes at his boots dangling off the spindle. 'That's what I heard.'

'Who from? The king of the fairies?'

'It's not like other things, not ordinary!' he pipes up. 'It's got to be different.'

'Well, thanks for pointing that out, Wilbur. I'll be sure to make a note of that killer fact. And what are you supposed to feel exactly? You know, when you grab hold of this not-so-ordinary bit of poke?'

He don't answer.

I pluck out one of the comics that he's stuffed in his coat pocket and make a show of flicking through it. 'It's all written in here, is it?'

'Hey, give that back!'

I boff him round the head with it and toss it over my shoulder.

'It's not like that,' he mumbles.

'So what *is* it like?' I go, and my voice winds up softer now. Cos I can see how upset he is.

'There's clues in them. It doesn't say exactly. You have to figure it out.'

'Except you didn't figure it out, did you?'

He shakes his head and sniffs.

'Oh, Wilbur! You've got to see how crazy this is! You're trying to tell me that whoever dreamed up the adventures of Captain Jackson and his time-travelling galleon knew where the artefact was and left riddles for us to follow?'

'It's not a galleon, it's a brigantine. And it's Captain Jameson.'

'Johnson, Josephine, Jamboree. That ain't the point! The point is you going out on a bonkers hunch and nearly ending up dead!'

'You're not telling Dad, are you?'

I lift his face to mine. 'You ain't listening to me, Wilbur. I need to know you ain't going on any more solo goose chases.'

'It's not a hunch – the clues *are* in the Captain Jameson adventures,' he insists.

'How do you know?'

'When I'm reading them I can *feel* when a clue is right. It's like an itch inside my head, like the artefact telling me I'm getting warmer. Like it's mine.'

That stumps me and cos I don't answer, his face brightens up. And that's the spooky thing about Wilbur. Cos he's a kid that does stupid kid things, but the clap-trap he comes out with . . . Well, it's clever claptrap. You have to give him that. But he ain't putting my mind at ease, is he?

'I've found a load of clues now. Not just about where the artefact is, but what it's like. Look, these are my reminders – things that help me think about it.' He pulls out all these bits and bobs from his pockets and shows them to me one by one with a look of total wonder in his eyes.

A pack of plasters. 'This tells me it's for helping people, protecting them. Or maybe it can heal you.'

A floppy spring. 'And it can change shape – but it can go back to the way it was too.'

A whole bunch of old tickets and scraps of paper. 'Lottery tickets, scratch cards. I found this one today at the bottom of the stairs – sudoku.'

'Soo-doke who?'

'Like a crossword but with numbers. Numbers are important, Cass – I know they are. I just don't know how yet . . .'

A glass bauble, like from a chandelier. He holds it up to his eye. 'And it can change what you see.'

A conker. I've had enough of this, so I finish it for him. 'Don't tell me – it grows on a tree? Or how about it's brown and shiny like a sheep turd?'

He looks hurt. 'No, it's alive.'

'Riddles, Wilbur. You're seeing what you want to see . . .'

I take a deep breath cos I've got to give him a rollicking now. Except my heart ain't in it no more.

But then a voice pipes up from below. A voice I've clean forgotten about. 'Why does it mean so much to you?'

Pyjama Boy's standing half in shadow, holding the comic I just lobbed over my shoulder. With his sticking-up hair, he looks like he's waiting for the maid to bring him his breakfast. And it ain't that he's been hiding exactly, but it bugs me that he listened to all that without making a peep.

Wilbur gawps at the stranger so hard I reckon his eyes are gonna start swivelling in their sockets any second now.

Pyjama Boy riffles through the comic like maybe the answer's gonna fall out. Like a free gift. The silence is so deep it's embarrassing.

'I mean, you risked your life just then. Why do you want to find it so much?' he asks again.

'Don't you?' goes Wilbur. 'Doesn't everybody?'

'So it's precious then – this thing?'

Wilbur whispers, 'It's more precious than anything . . .'

Pyjama Boy shuffles closer, and I can see the pages of

the comic trembling in his hand.

And that sums up the weirdness, right there. *Yeah, precious about sums it up, when you got close to ten thousand scavs and an invading army looking for it. But how come he don't know this stuff?*

'The Vlads came back to London looking for it after the Quark Wars,' blurts Wilbur.

'Why here?'

'Because London was one of the last cities still standing – most places were turned into dust by Quark bombs. The Vlads already knew it was here somewhere. That's why they only sent bio-weapons to kill people and leave buildings standing. They didn't want to destroy it.'

'But how did they know it was here?' Pyjama Boy's got this scared look on his face now, like he don't want to believe any of it's true.

'The artefact is special,' whispers Wilbur, like there might be Vlads listening. 'Before the Quark Wars began, Vlad hunters came to look for it cos they found clues about how it was hidden in a London building. But they couldn't find it in time before the first bio-attacks.'

Pyjama Boy kneels down to face Wilbur. 'And why is it . . . special?'

'Cos it's got powers more than all the Quark bombs in the world put together. And secrets—'

'There ain't no time for a history lesson,' I go. Best to nip these things in the bud before Wilbur goes off on one. 'Anyway no one knows what it is or what it can do, so it's all hearsay, just a bunch of olden-time stories.'

'But if the Vlads are here looking for it,' pipes up Pyjama Boy, 'they must know something about it. I mean, they must be sure it exists, that it's buried in this city somewhere.'

'Except they ain't found it in a hundred years of trying, so maybe it's all just cobblers.'

'It's not, Cass!' cries Wilbur, getting all fired up.

'Yeah, well, like I say, we'd love to gasbag on, but you know what, the old man's gonna go ape if we don't get back pronto. They're bound to have patched up the crusher by now and if we ain't feeding London into it nineteen to the dozen pretty damn soon then we don't get paid.'

I start fetching up the ropes and hustling Wilbur off the spindle.

'Who is he, Cass?' goes Wilbur. Like Pyjama Boy's deaf.

Down on the deck, I stuff all the ropes back into my pack and slip the comic out of Pyjama Boy's hand. It feels rushed and wrong, but what can I do? I ain't got the time to get into someone else's problems. I'm already hard pressed to think up watertight excuses for how come we've been gone so long as it is.

Pyjama Boy looks gutted.

I hold out my hand, like that's gonna make things better. 'Hey, thanks, you know, for pitching in,' I mumble.

He don't take the hand, so I pat him on the shoulder as I go past.

Wilbur hangs back. 'Cass!'

I chivvy him towards the stairs. 'Not a word, you hear? I ain't even decided if I'm gonna spill the beans on you yet.'

'Where are you going now? Wilbur's only just got here,' goes Pyjama Boy. Like we're leaving his birthday party early. 'Wilbur, you were sure the artefact was here, weren't you? Maybe it still is. We haven't looked properly . . .' There's strain in his voice now, like he's somehow tied to the place, like he's scared of being alone here.

I stop by the bell, but I don't have the heart to look at him. Cos it's wrong. I know it is. But I can't pick up no stray. There ain't nowhere for him to go. Nothing I can do.

'Take me with you,' he goes.

'Look, I ain't got the foggiest where you racked up from. But that's the problem, see? Where I'm going to there ain't no time for answering questions and holding your hand on things you don't know nothing about.'

'He helped us,' goes Wilbur.

'I kind of know that!' I snap. 'But what's he doing here, eh? All on his jack.' I face Pyjama Boy. 'You ain't gonna tell us in a hurry, are you? Cos if you're on this side of the Thames creeping about like a ghost, then you're bound to be in seven different kinds of trouble. And you probably don't even know that if the Vlads catch you on this side of the river after the shifts are done, they'll shoot you.'

He dumps all the colour from his face at that, but still his voice is firm. 'I just need to get back across the river. There's someone waiting for me there.'

I look at him, trying to weigh it up. I shake my head. 'How d'you get here in the first place?' I try.

His lips clam up. Which ain't that much of a surprise.

I give him a shrug. 'There ain't no way back across the river, 'less you're a scav that's come over here on a shift in the first place. Gangmasters clock you in and clock you out again. If they don't know who you are, you'll have to explain yourself to the Vlads. That'll be one conversation that's over in a flash.'

He frowns then. 'These Vlads – what do they know, that makes them so sure the artefact's here?'

'Gramps says it's got to be something to do with the old computer machines,' goes Wilbur. 'They've been broken or switched off for a whole century. Only Vlads can see what's inside them with their scanners . . .'

'Who's Gramps?'

'Enough yakking, all right?' I give Wilbur daggers. Cos this stranger could be a spy for all we know – plonked here in his jim-jam outfit to wheedle stuff out of gullible scavs, like my brother. Except he don't seem tough enough for a spy . . .

'There's got to be a way to help him,' Wilbur whispers.

Then I think about what would've happened if this boy hadn't showed up. Even if I'd figured out on my own how to snatch Wilbur off the clock face, we'd just be dangling there with no one to haul us to safety. Waiting. Till maybe the Vlads used us for target practice. But then I think about what he's even doing here – maybe he trailed Wilbur to Big Ben in the first place. His words rattle around in my mind. *Wilbur's only just got here*, like he's been waiting for him to show up . . . Which is suspect. So maybe it's best to keep this stranger close, find out what he's up to. But what am I thinking of? Helping him is too risky.

I gaze at him then and he's just so out there – like he's just stepped out of one of them pictures of olden-time London, all dandied up and innocent-looking. Clueless about the disaster that's just about to wipe him out. Cos he don't seem to cotton on that he ain't gonna last much more than a week around here with the Parliament crews closing in.

'Thing is, look at you,' I go. 'You're a lubber. You ain't got a clue. We'd be rumbled at the first hurdle. If you was a scav then it'd be a start.'

'So make me into a scav.'

WINGING IT

I MUST BE MAD.

BUT THERE AIN'T NO TIME TO FART ABOUT. IF I'M GONNA LET HIM TAG ALONG, IT HAS TO BE RIGHT NOW. COS THE LONGER I leave it, the harder it's gonna be. He pitched in for us, so I'm returning the favour, though God knows it'll be the undoing of me. I know it. I ain't even got the shadow of a plan, but you've got to start somewhere. And that'd be with the pigging pyjamas.

He holds out his hand this time, all hopeful and grateful and eager-beaver. But there ain't no time for meet-and-greet right now. I plonk my helmet and coat on his arm like it's a rack.

'Stick these on. You won't last five minutes in the scav zone looking like the prince of ponce.'

Then I'm racing down the stairs, dispensing advice

over my shoulder, trying to think of the next thing, the next thing . . .

'You stick on my shoulder. You don't gawp about like a tourist – all this is same old, same old to you, right? And you don't open your cake-hole for nothing. These are the rules, OK?'

'What?'

'Jesus. Do like I do and keep your gob zipped. Comprehend-day?'

Wilbur goes, 'Copy us and don't say anything.'

At the bottom of the stairs I inspect him. And it ain't filling me with hope and sunshine.

'His shoes,' goes Wilbur. And he's right. Moccasin affairs with no tread to speak of. They're a proper give-away.

I peel off a clod of mud from my boots and smear the silky shine off his slippers.

'First chance you get, go knee-deep in crud.'

I plant the rest on his chops. He grins at me and rubs it in his hair, up his nostrils.

'There you go. You'll pass muster.'

So it's out onto the scaffold and the Portakabin roof and into the streets. We skirt round Big Ben and head towards the roar of the crushers. And would you credit it? The smog's really lifting on account the wind's picked up, and it ain't so simple to blend in now cos it's masks off. So folks are starting to cast odd looks our way. Like we don't belong. And down the end of Bridge Street, coming towards us, is a Vlad guard patrol – five soldiers with black armour and headsets and machine-guns. This ain't no stroll in the park neither. They're in formation, checking down alleyways. Stop 'n' search.

My apprentice scav stops dead in his tracks.

'Ain't no time for the jitters!' I hiss at him. 'Stay cool.'

'We have to hide,' he mutters, all the while darting his head about like a spooked squirrel.

'What's your name?' I go.

'What?'

'Your name, bonehead. They give those out where you come from?'

'Peyto.'

'Well, listen up, Peyto. If you head for the hills now, they're gonna clock you bang to rights. You run, you've got something to hide. Which is why we're gonna stay put, see?'

'But—'

'But nothing. Wilbur, get on the deck and look injured.'

Wilbur lies down and starts groaning, a bit too loudly.

I give him a kick. 'Hey, tone it down! This ain't the village show. Just play dead.'

The soldiers are closing in. I can hear the crackle of their radios, the bark of Russian orders.

'Peyto, don't look at them. Look at Wilbur. And let me do the talking.'

We kneel down to Wilbur and I cradle his head to give him some water. At the last minute I dab a bit round my eyes.

The boots stop and shadows close over us.

'You there! Stand clear. Hands on heads.' Cocking of safety catches. 'NOW!'

I stand up, giving it all shaky and lost. Actually the truth is, I *am* pretty damn shaky, cos all five guns are pointing at me.

'Please sir, help us. My brother—'

'Hands on heads! Crew number?'

'He got caught in a cellar collapse. Please, you can take him! He ain't gonna make it if you don't. Please!'

The officer stares at me through his visor. I might as well be a woodlouse, cos behind the dust and reflections there ain't one jot of mercy for me. He looks whacked and tensed up at the same time. Which is weird cos most times the Vlad soldiers just look bored. I figure it's touch and go whether he pulls the trigger to let off a bit of steam. But I've got to carry on playing the card I'm playing or we're done for.

I crumple up my face and reach out to him. 'You've got to help us. We carried him this far but he ain't breathing so good now—'

'Crew number! What zone?' Spit flies out of his gob with the shouting.

'Please.' I sink to my knees.

Some Russian commands come screeching out of his field radio. He swings up his gun and hoofs me out the way. He don't even glance at Wilbur or Peyto. Then the patrol is past us.

Scavs who stopped to watch start picking up where they left off. Way too scared to come over. I'm so fried I can't even move for a couple of minutes. Peyto comes to help me up, and he's all goggle-eyed and shivery.

'They were going to kill us,' he breathes.

'Welcome to London.'

'Why didn't they?'

'Fifty-fifty, I reckon. Bigger fish to fry, I don't know.'

'They were looking for someone.'

We watch the patrol head back towards the river.

'Yeah,' I go at last. 'Looks that way. Looters maybe. Man, they was pretty jumpy, though, eh?'

'Looters?'

'Unofficial scavving. If you're over here you've got to be under a gangmaster, numbered crew. Else you're dead meat. Probably let us go cos we're kids, and they figured Wilbur was on his way out anyhow, not worth the bullet.'

Talking of Wilbur, he's still spark out.

'Hey, they've gone now, you numpty. Show's over.'

Wilbur scrambles to his feet.

'What about those people?' Peyto nods towards the scavs still eyeing us over.

'They won't dob us in, but we'd better get a lick on. Trouble for us is trouble for them if we hang about.'

We head on, eyes peeled for more patrols, past the edge of Parliament Square where the main scav action's taking place, crushers full swing and gangs swarming all over the roofs, picking the rafters clean. A quick shifty at the north end of Little Sanctuary and it's as I thought – our crusher's cranked up again, spewing fumes and chugging out a stream of brick slag into the road.

We swing round and approach from the quieter south end of the street. I still ain't sure how this is gonna pan out. We can't just waltz in there. There'll be soldiers stationed somewhere near the crusher and then there's explanations I need to find for the gangmaster, not to mention the old man.

There's a tunnel through the rubble to a little cobbled courtyard at this end of the street. We slip in. Inside, the old garden's gone to jungle. Trees and vines are growing into the walls, brushing up against the second-floor windows. I start to clamber my way up the branches.

'What you doing, Cass?' goes Wilbur. He sounds worried, like I've lost the plot.

'Winging it. You two just gonna stand there like a couple of prize turkeys?'

I boot through one of the windows, and wait on the landing till they catch up. Then it's up to the top floor, onto Peyto's shoulders and through the hatch into the loft. Torch on. Just a load of mouldy junk and boxes. But as I was hoping, up here there ain't no partitions between any of the loft spaces – it's just one clear run across the rafters to the far house where the old man'll be, slaving on his tod, cursing the day we was born, no doubt.

One quick sprint over the beams and we're there. Except I can't see no hatch for all the rolls of insulation. Ain't nothing for it. I find a soft bit between the rafters and give it a good stamp. Actually, it's a tad softer than I figured. We go through it like a horse 'n' cart through a cake. The whole ceiling. Plus chandelier, by the sounds of it.

When I look up through clouds of plaster and wads of yellow fibre, the old man is standing at the doorway.

And he don't look best pleased.

A SCAV'S LIFE

FOR A WHILE, AS THE DUST SETTLES, IT LOOKS LIKE THE OLD MAN AIN'T GOT THE WORDS FOR HOW FURIOUS HE IS. BUT SOMEHOW HE KEEPS A LID ON IT.

I start to say something. I ain't sure what, except that it ain't the truth. Cos how's that gonna help things?

But he holds up one hand and he's *trembling* with anger. The scav dust draws black marks in all the creases in his face. And there's more of them creases than I remember even since this morning.

'No lies,' he warns. 'Not this time.'

Then Wilbur steps forward. 'It was my fault. I went to Big Ben. I thought it was there.'

The old man looks to one side, and I know it's cos he can't bear to look at us right then.

'For Lord's sake, why, Wilbur? I mean, you know

how dangerous it is to leave the crew. How many hundreds of times have I told you? *How many?*'

'I thought I could find it.'

'But you could've been killed!'

'I was sure!' insists Wilbur, but his voice is a whisper now.

Dad limps over and takes hold of Wilbur's coat lapels. The grip is so tight I can see his knuckles shaking, but he only moves Wilbur gently.

'You can't do that. You can't leave the crew. Promise me.'

Wilbur is set to cry but he sticks to his guns. 'I thought I'd found the artefact. For everyone. And then we wouldn't have to look any more. We could stay at Elephant and Castle. We wouldn't have to come here again.'

'Wilbur, I can't lose you. Do you hear me? I can't lose you. *Promise me.*'

'We have to find it soon,' Wilbur sniffs. 'We *have to*, Dad.'

Wilbur's been in trouble for not listening about scav matters more times than I care to remember. But usually, when he's in the dog-house, he clams up. I ain't sure if he's being brave or dense. It's like finding the artefact has just become his personal mission. Like the

– 39 –

rest of us just ain't trying hard enough.

I squat down to face Wilbur. 'You ain't listening –
you've got to promise us you ain't gonna wander off just
cos you get some *fancy* to.'

'It's not a fancy!' he snaps. 'Scavving the whole city
isn't the way to find it. It's too slow! Don't you see? You
have to *think* to work out where it is.'

'Wilbur!' barks Dad. 'I don't care about the artefact!
I care about you staying alive! Promise me!'

The lad flinches with each shout, but inside he ain't
budging. He sticks out his jaw.

Then he goes, 'What for?'

I figure that's torn it. Dad's ready to blow. But then
Peyto steps in.

'Wilbur, you don't have to go alone. Why don't you
just tell someone next time?'

Wilbur drops his head. 'Cos no one listens.'

Peyto looks at me. 'Well then, it's easy. If people
promise to listen, then you promise not to go off alone.'

Wilbur considers this. Then he closes his eyes and
nods.

It's simple and I feel *that big* for not realising it. He
ain't trying to be a hero. He don't want to go it alone.
He never did. All he wanted was for someone to listen
to his nutty trail of comic clues.

'I'm sorry,' whispers Wilbur at last.

Dad drops his hands from Wilbur's coat, then he gathers him into his arms and squeezes him.

I shuffle about during this bit, cos it ain't so often that we Westerbys see eye to eye about anything, let alone reach the hugs-all-round stage, especially in front of a stranger. Peyto raises his eyebrows at me and I've gone that red it's a good job I'm wearing most of the ceiling. But then I hear the slow stomp of hobnails up the stairs which signals that loving times is over, cos that's our charming gangmaster come to check on productivity. Which means I've got about ten seconds to win Dad over.

'This is Peyto.' I shove him forward. 'He helped us, Dad. You don't need to know the details right now, but let's just say it was touch and go. He don't belong to a crew right now – he ain't got no one, except us.'

The old man looks at Peyto properly for the first time since we crashed through the ceiling. And just when I need him to be normal, Peyto only goes and plants his fist across his chest like he's giving Dad a salute or something. Like he's a flippin' Vlad. Dad just stares at Peyto's hand what ain't seen a day's graft in its life.

At last he turns to me, like he's figured out already that it ain't worth talking direct to Peyto. 'Cass, what am I going to tell the gangmaster?'

'It's just for this one shift, I swear. After that he takes his chances at getting picked like everyone else. Anyhow, we could really do with the extra muscle if we're gonna catch up lost time. Just vouch for him. He ain't looking for pay, just passage back with us . . .'

I guess Dad catches a look in my eye – the desperation after everything that's happened already today. He nods just once and goes to head off the gangmaster. I hear them talking for a while one flight down though I don't hear the words.

They both come up at last, and there's an awful smug look on the gangmaster's jowly mug. He's one sly operator. We all *love* the way he lords it over us. You can tell there ain't no grafting for him with his clean trenchcoat and his pinky ring.

'All right, kit up!' he barks. 'I want the place stripped and the roof off by sundown.'

There's a smirk on his lips, and I just know it's about earnings. We ain't getting a bean on this shift. Still, I give Peyto a wink. Cos after what we've just been through, the rest of the day's gonna be a doddle.

I haul him downstairs for his crash course in scavving. The crusher's hammering at full pelt, gnashing up a bunch of concrete joists. A fountain of dust spews out the funnels.

First up I take him onto the gantry by the blades. 'Right, the main thing is, everything you bring down has to get scanned before it goes on them chutes into the crusher. See them tubes waving about? They're the scanners.' One of them sways over to us and starts sniffing my face till I cuff it away. 'When you're up here, one of them'll check out your bin. It's what the boffins use to look for the artefact – it's hooked up to a load of screens in the control deck. Chances are you'll get a green light on the scanner head. That means you've just got common-or-garden scrap in your bin and it can all go down the chute. If you get a red light – the blades shut down and the alarm goes off. That means jackpot, rare poke that the boffins want to take a closer look at. Don't get excited – it's only happened three times my whole life. Chances are it ain't the artefact anyhow.' I gawp at him then – he looks like a tourist, all wide-eyed at his first scav shift.

He points at the cables that snake out the engines at the back. 'What are those?'

'Power lines. The crushers run on 'lectric. Course there's other gubbins like pylons 'n' that along the way but if you go far enough they all link up to the power stations by the Great Barrier.'

'The Great Barrier?'

'Blimey, it really is back to school for you, eh? Ain't you heard of the bloody big wall that pumps the river out and keeps the sea back?'

He just gawps at me.

'Most of London would be sitting in the drink without it. It's on account of the sea levels rising, innit? Full-time job keeping this city dry – Vlad engineers are on the case 24-7 otherwise there ain't no scavving to be done.'

Then the crusher starts really shuddering and screeching, and Peyto jumps out his skin.

'Don't panic – that's normal. It's just straining on the metal rods inside them chunks of concrete that's just gone in,' I yell. 'The blades'll chew up most stuff but it ain't so clever at steel. Anything solid metal is meant to go in there.'

I point at the molten glow of the furnace hatch. 'Don't get too close. It's liable to blow nuggets of lava in your face.'

Right on cue, the crusher lurches forward and dumps a steaming block of fused metal on the road. It looks like a giant radioactive turd.

'Yeah, and watch out for them. They take about a week to cool down.'

I swing him past the control deck where the Vlad

boffins check the screens for signs of artefact. I nudge Peyto along by there, cos they never check us out and we never check them out – it ain't really the done thing. A case of we're scavs and they're boffins.

'Right, that's the tour over. You know everything I know. Let's get started.'

I kit him out with a spare bin, then we traipse up to join Dad and Wilbur. It's good when the building's fresh cos there's pickings to be had, but it's also the worst cos you've got to start at the top where we crashed in from the loft – six floors up. It's a scav's life. Still, at least it ain't a skyscraper.

The look Dad gives his new recruit ain't that promising. He changes the straps on his bin for him. 'Start with all the loose stuff, son. I'm putting you on the floor down from here.'

That don't register with Peyto but I know Dad's given him the fifth floor out of pity, cos he's pegged him for a lubber. One extra flight of stairs don't sound like much but on an eleven-hour shift it's murder.

Peyto goes, 'What if things are too big to go in my bin?'

'That's what this is for, sunshine.' Dad chucks him a sledgehammer.

Don't get me wrong, I hate scavving, but I always

love a new building what's been untouched for years, 'specially if it's a residential. You get glimpses of the people that lived in London then, our ancestors. Well, sometimes you get more than glimpses. Sometimes you get a full-on view of their rotted mugs.

Sure enough, when Dad shoulders in the door to one of the fifth-floor flats we get that lovely bottled-up mummified smell of the previous owner. Course, the meat's long gone by now, but the bones ain't exactly picked clean, neither. The black skin is all shrivelled and tight on the skeleton, pulling the whole thing up like it's hugging itself. Old dear, I'm guessing, by the necklace. Wilbur, being eight, gets spared this sight. Dad stands him out in the hall. But the truth is it ain't that gruesome, just a bit sad, that the old girl has been huddled up like that all this time with no one to bury her. You see them propped up on the khazi, or lying on sofas, or curled up in cupboards – the exact position they was in when they died. When the bio-weapons fell. And you get to thinking about that moment, when they're croaking their last – how their world's just caving in round their ears.

Still, there ain't no time to mope about.

I catch Peyto gawping at me as I crack the ribcage into my bin.

'Look, it ain't your regular Christian send-off, but needs must. Everything goes in the crusher. They don't let you bury the dead on this side of the river.'

'Why not?'

'That's just the rules. Stiffs get scanned like any other poke. Olden-time Londoners had machines in them sometimes – metal bits and pieces. Maybe the Vlads reckon the artefact could be hidden inside a body.'

He just stands there while I cram the leg bones in.

'Chop-chop, mate. We ain't got time for a poetry reading. She won't mind, she's been dead a hundred years.'

I grab the skull by the eye sockets and hold out the white wisps of hair. 'Least she had a decent innings, eh?'

THE NEXT BEST THING

THE ONLY WAY TO HANDLE A SCAV SHIFT IS TO PACE YOURSELF. TOO SLOW AND THE GANGMASTER GETS ON YOUR BACK. TOO FAST AND YOU CRASH BEFORE LUNCH. I TELL PEYTO TO TAKE IT EASY cos he's going at it like ten men.

'Must show the gangmaster I can do it,' he wheezes. 'Or he won't hire me tomorrow.'

'Listen, mucker, there ain't gonna be a tomorrow for you at this rate. One hour at a time, yeah? Snatch breathers when you can.'

He shrugs at me and carries on down the stairs with his bin way too full to manage. I'm peeved cos I know how to handle the work and I'm only trying to help him out.

Anyhow, sure enough, come noon he's spent out. We sit on the top landing and divvy out our bread and gravy and apples. After twenty minutes he goes all shivery and spaced on us and I figure he's going to crash for sure. But then Dad gives him a nip of the old home-cooked gin and he perks up a bit.

Course, I'm full of questions now like, where the hell has he racked up from? A place where they wear pyjamas and ain't heard of the artefact. I ain't the only one with questions. Most times Wilbur sits in a corner with his head in a comic. But today he just gazes and gazes at Peyto. And I'm sure the old man's just as curious as we are, but he's of the thinking that what you don't know can't hurt you. Anyway, as a rule lunch is a proper serious affair – fuelling up, no chat except for the scavving at hand. You don't sit around long enough to seize up and anyhow the clock's always ticking. Twenty minutes is your lot.

Halfway through the afternoon, Dad tells me to go and gee up Peyto with clearing the fifth floor. The poor lad is really flagging by now. I catch him staring at a picture on the wall – a photograph of some princess in a flimsy dress, and paint on her face, and them spiky shoes that tilt your toes forward. She's striding through olden-time Piccadilly Circus at night and it's a pack-out in the streets with people and cars and doubledeckers. Peyto looks like he's under a spell.

'What happened here?' he asks at last. 'I mean, these bio-weapons – how did they . . .'

'You really don't know, do you?'

He shakes his head.

'Germs,' I go. 'It was over dead quick. Enemy planes over London dropped all these canisters loaded with disease and that. There was a few survivors on the outskirts but most folks died in the first wave.'

'What was it about – the war?'

'Look, how come all this is news to you? Ain't it time for you to come clean with me?'

'What?'

'Where you're from, what you was doing skulking about in Big Ben.'

'I . . . can't tell you.'

'Hey, that ain't good enough. I bailed you out, remember? Least you can do is cut the mystery cobblers and get to the point.'

'You wouldn't believe me even if I told you.'

'Shut up. There ain't no secrets between scavs.'

'So, I'm a scav now, am I?'

'Well, I'm sticking my neck out to make you into one.'

'I'm sorry, Cass. It's best if you don't know.'

'Oh, yeah? I reckon I'll be the judge of that.'

'You don't understand!' he goes. 'I'm grateful you

helped me, but then I helped you and Wilbur, so that makes us even—'

He stops mid-flow, cos Wilbur's suddenly popped up out of nowhere. 'Dad said to come down and hurry you up, that's all.'

Time to change the subject. 'So anyhow,' I go to Peyto. 'How come you ain't got yourself any decent threads yet? First thing I'd do if I was chattering me teeth out on the job.'

'Huh?'

They both follow me into the bedroom as I start emptying cupboards.

'But I thought we had to put it all in the crusher,' goes Peyto.

'Nope. You can take what you like as long as you can carry it.'

'I like books,' says Wilbur, all helpful-like.

'You think we'd do this just for the measly moolah?' I show him my chunky watch. 'Cost thousands back when London was capital of the free world. Rollicks.'

'Rolex,' goes Wilbur.

'But the soldiers—'

'Vlads ain't interested in this old junk. Course, you've got to stand on the belt and get scanned at the end of the shift just so they know you ain't got the artefact, but if you get the all-clear then it's yours.'

Peyto has gone paler than at any time in the whole day. He slumps onto the edge of the bed.

'You OK?' I go.

He looks at me like I've just dealt him the Death card. 'I'm just tired.'

I collar Wilbur and we go in search of old-school threads. Ten minutes later we've kitted Peyto out in a rain jacket, neck-warmer, knitted hat, water-resistant kecks and an unused pair of them rubber shoes with the tread.

I dust him down a bit. 'You won't freeze your nuts off now.'

'We're definitely coming back here tomorrow, aren't we?'

'If you get the nod at crew pickings, yeah. Blimey, there's no stopping you, is there?'

'And nobody else will come here while we're gone?'

'No. Why, you worried someone's gonna walk off with your poke? Forget it – all our lot's done places like Dulwich. That's what you call quality pickings.'

'What about those boffin people?'

'Nah, they ain't fussed about any of this clobber. They never come on site – it's back to a fancy Vlad compound for them come the end of the shift.'

He don't say nothing to that but I can tell he ain't sure whether to believe me.

'Look, you've got your eye on something you can't carry today, just stash it, but you want to start getting choosy. Unless it's proper useful, don't bother. Scavs what hoard stuff for the sake of it tend to get a bit of stick.'

We crack on and the day passes without further drama. Come six o'clock we're all done and dusted. Literally. Peyto takes his turn to get scanned on the crusher belt, and he looks proper guilty clutching a bag he's stuffed with extra clothes. Anyhow we get the all-clear, then it's down to the truck for the off.

There's a hold-up on Blackfriars, some kerfuffle with Vlad troops searching one of the lorries up front. As we're waiting, I clock Dad gazing upriver. Whenever we get to water he always gets this faraway look, prob-ably dreaming about boats or something. He ain't from scav stock originally. His family are fishermen and traders, sea people, from up past the Great Barrier. Something happened for him to leave them little places up the coast, though he's never said what. When Mum was alive, he used to go on about scraping the pennies together to go back to that life, but he ain't brought it up in a long time. Scavs is what we are now – that's what you hear from him these days.

Back on the south bank, the journey home is always more lively. A couple of the old 'uns sing songs and everyone's thinking of the hot nose-bag waiting for us back at Elephant and Castle. Wilbur gets press-ganged into reading out loud from an old magazine – something about a girl who's worried she's too fat to bag a mate.

'Week's scavving would sort her out,' mutters some toothless codger.

I go, 'Why don't you write in, gumbo? Tell her she ain't never gonna be too fat to land you!'

They all start chipping in then. I don't know – it's easy to make everyone laugh about the old-school Londoners. They just seemed so pampered, like everyone was royal. But they had their worries, too, I suppose.

I catch Peyto looking at me then. His face is knackered and serious, all lit up in the last rusty glow of the sun.

'Thank you,' he goes. 'For looking after me today.'

'No bother. Like you say, we're quits now.'

He looks like he's about to say something else, but Wilbur butts in and lands a comic on his lap.

Peyto holds up the front cover – an olden-time sailor swinging from the rigging, staring out at the ocean. 'So is this Captain Jameson?'

The way Wilbur beams at Peyto right then gives me the shivers. Cos my kid brother might not have landed the artefact at Big Ben but you can tell that finding Peyto might be the next best thing . . .

'And his ship travels through time?' asks Peyto.

'Yeah, see, he's sailing in the Indies and it's 1709, and there's this storm and next thing, all his crew's drowned and he's the only one left alive, and he has to sail single-handed, but when he gets to the Americas, it's not 1709 any more. It's 3709! He's washed up into the future!'

'Two thousand years,' goes Peyto, and there's this weird look on his face that I can't quite read. Like Captain Jameson has hit a nerve. 'Then what happens?'

'Well, it's a comic, he has different adventures. He helps people out, but even if a lady goes soppy for him, he never sticks around. He always gets on board the *Vanguard* and sails off with his latest crew. But the thing is, every time he sets sail he goes back in time a hundred years so he can't change his mind and head back to the last port, cos everyone he knows there won't even be born yet. He has to keep going.'

'But one day he'll make it back to 1709?'

'I suppose. I just haven't found that comic, yet. But I've got loads. My favourite's 2009.'

Peyto leafs through the comic then he asks, 'Have you ever heard of a character called Halina?' It's odd cos his voice catches on the name, like it means something to him.

'No, who's she? Have you found any Captain Jameson comics then?' Wilbur goes, getting all wound up. 'There's a few ladies in it – the best one's a pirate who can't decide whether to love him or kill him . . .'

Peyto smiles. 'No, she's not a pirate. At least, I don't think so.'

Wilbur blathers on fit to bore a statue to death. But it ain't boring to Peyto. And just like he promised Wilbur this morning, he listens.

It's dark by the time the truck gets us back to the hiring point. We all offload, and Dad mumbles at Peyto to join us for some grub at the Elephant and Castle meeting house.

'Thank you, but I should be getting back.'

He jumps off the truck and turns to me to do this crazy half-bow – the prince of ponce again. 'Thank you, Cass.'

He glances away towards a girl who's hanging back from the crowds at the hiring point. She's about my age, tall and skinny. She looks proper lost, shading her eyes from the glare of the truck headlights. And guess what?

She's wearing pyjamas. My heart sinks a notch to see her, cos even from here I can see she's a looker. But then she's got the same bonkers hair as Peyto – shining black and sticking up all over the place. So maybe she's his sister.

'Your mate's welcome, too, ain't she, Dad?' I pipe up.

But Peyto is already backing away. 'Maybe another time.'

He jogs over to the girl and starts yanking out the clobber from his bag. It's sweet cos he's gone for enough layers to truss her up for Pass the Parcel. The tartan fleece ain't a bad option, cos it's got detachable sleeves. But what she's gonna do with them fluffy ear-muffs I ain't so sure. Typical lubber choice. Still, the way he greets her and helps her into the gear, it gives me a feeling. Just of loneliness. Like they're just gonna slip into the byways and I won't be seeing Peyto no more.

'You could've invited him like you meant it,' I go to Dad.

'Leave them be. They're not our kind anyhow.'

'What kind of talk is that? He did his graft! For nothing. He's got every right to tuck in same as us.'

'Enough of your lip, Cass. I offered and he said no. You want me to go on my bended knees?'

I give him the daggers he deserves. 'Scavs don't cold-shoulder people. He binned up till his hands bled, and that *makes* him one of us. He just don't know the score, that's all.'

I'm all hot under the collar as I storm off towards Peyto. But as I get closer, I can hear they're having a right old to-do – all hissing under their breath and looking over their shoulders. Peyto starts to point but drops his arm. I figure he's looking over at me. But he ain't. He's looking at Wilbur.

'What do you mean, you left it there?' The girl's nearly in tears. She rips off her ear-muffs.

'I told you, I had no choice. I can find it again tomorrow.'

'And then what? Hide it again the next day and the next and the next?'

'What do you suggest, then? I couldn't have brought it back with the soldiers there! They'd have found it for certain!'

'But what if we lose it? We can't afford to! What if I lost mine, too? We'd never get back to the ship then.'

I'm thinking, *ship? What ship?* There ain't no ships in the Thames, 'less you count the Vlad ones . . .

Peyto holds his hand out to steady her down a bit cos she looks set to lose it big-time. 'Look, it's fine. We'll think of something, I promise.'

'It's not fine and you know it!'

At last they spot me hovering and they clam right up.

'Sorry,' I go, like I ain't heard a sausage. 'But I ain't gonna let you miss out. Wednesday's meeting night and the grub's free. You're both welcome.'

I put my hand out to the girl, and she just holds it like she's never shaken no one's hand before.

'You're Cass.'

'Hey, word gets round—'

'Cass,' she blurts out. 'We need your help.'

Peyto grits his teeth. He looks set to blow his top. 'Erin, we don't even know for sure if he's the . . .' He trails off, reining in his anger.

'He was there, wasn't he?' goes Erin. 'Where he was supposed to be?'

'Yes, but we can't involve other people till we're sure. It's not safe!'

She turns on him then. 'Safe? In case you've forgotten, we don't have any time for playing it safe! How are we ever going to be sure if we don't take a chance and ask?'

I've got a million questions, but out the corner of my eye I see Wilbur running over, and it's time to wind things up before they get out of hand.

'Whatever you want to ask me, be my guest,' I go. 'Straight talking never did no harm. But it's got to wait just one hour cos there ain't nothing as important right now as some good scoff.'

The two of them look set to take lumps out of each other, but good old Wilbur puts paid to all that.

'Come on,' he pipes up. 'Mabel's done pork and we've got to be quick to get first dibs.'

BAD BLOOD

OUR LITTLE SETTLEMENT AT ELEPHANT AND CASTLE AIN'T MUCH MORE THAN FORTY HUTS, A PATCHWORK OF ALLOTMENTS, THE MILL WITH ITS FLOUR STONES AND MULE TEAM, A FEW SHEDS for the livestock, and, in the middle, the meeting house. The closest proper settlement is Greenwich but there's dozens of places, mainly scavs and farmers, as far east as Dartford and as far south as Purley.

The meeting house don't look much from the outside – just a stockade of railway sleepers dug into the clay, then a pitched roof with a hole in the top to let the smoke out, no windows. But inside, on a wintry night, with everyone in there, it's my favourite place in all the world. The walls are lined with straw and clay, and there's all nice old-school paintings hanging up. Gramps says they're priceless, which means they've got the biggest price of all. Some of them are a bit manky now, what with the steam and the smoke, but there's loads of museums north of the Thames we ain't even reached yet, so no one's that fussed. By the flickering light of the main fire you can see the ring of tables and benches, and the cauldrons and the spit, and the old dears who knock up the grub. Today, it's honey-roast hog with an apple in its gob.

I'm right curious about Erin's plea for help, but there ain't no time to chat in private cos it's a pack-out already, and the world and his wife want to say hello.

The shout goes up for first sittings so I get the two of them in line, but when their turn comes, they shake their heads.

Mabel's a feisty old mare and she takes it personal.

'Been slaving over this porker all day. What's the matter? My cooking ain't up to scratch, huh?'

'I can't,' says Erin firmly. 'It's a dead animal.'

Mabel pokes her carving fork in the pig's snout. 'Well, I hope it's dead, girl. It's been turning over this fire for the best part of six hours.'

'Is there anything else?' goes Peyto.

I slap a couple of slabs of bread and a wodge of honey on their plates instead. 'There you go – no dead animals in that. Unless you get a weevil. In which case it's probably alive, so best spit it out.'

'All right, move your fussy mates along, will you? I got a hundred-odd mouths to feed and I ain't got all night to do it.'

I nudge Erin. 'So, what, you ain't partial to meat then?'

'It's not *about* the taste . . .'

I think she's about to explain but then she looks at Mabel hacking away at the hog and she clams up.

Back at the bench, they both get serious about tucking in. Erin sets to like she ain't eaten in a week. I get them both to go back for seconds. Mabel loves that.

After the grub is done and the pig's just a charred backbone and ribs, it's time for the meeting. Our Elephant and Castle chief, Gus Turnley, stands up on a barrel and calls for hush. There's general groans all round cos Gus is a stickler for meetings and everyone knows he's just in love with the sound of his own voice. Still, rules is rules, and Turnleys, over the years, have made decent enough chiefs, so people put up with the meetings even if they do break into everyone's drinking time.

'I'd just like to thank Mabel and all her fine helpers for putting together such a grand Wednesday feast—'

'Get on with it, Gus, you old windbag!' someone shouts from the back.

It's pretty funny watching Gus looking for the culprit as he clatters a spoon against his flagon for silence. Half-cut, he teeters on his barrel, his bleary eyes scanning the crowd, his top lip plastered with beer foam.

'First item of the evening is the urgent and ongoing matter of latrine maintenance. What's the point of having a rota if no one is going to adhere to it?'

'How come you're not on the rota, then, Gus?' someone pipes up.

''Specially when you spend the most time filling them pits up!'

That kicks off an uproar that flusters Gus so much, he nearly topples off his perch.

Right at that moment there's a blast of cold air as the door slams open and in marches Elephant and Castle's resident maverick and doom-monger. There he is – all wild-eyed and nutty, his hunched back jutting higher than his white-whiskered face. He bounds in with that strange sideways loping and everyone hushes up in a way they never do for Gus Turnley.

'Who's that?' whispers Peyto.

'That,' I go, with a touch of pride, 'is my gramps.'

'Still banging on about the state of the bogs, Turnley?' growls Gramps. 'How come no one ever talks about what *matters* at these meetings?'

He rounds on everyone then, taking centre stage. 'As long as there's meat 'n' beer, you lot don't give a damn, do you? Well, how much longer are you going to bury your heads in the mud?'

'Give it a rest, grandad! We been graftin' all day . . .' cries a voice from the back.

'Just like I did for fifty years or more, and my father before me and his father before that!' snaps Gramps. 'And for what? A crippled back and a handful of olden-time coppers.'

Dad walks stiffly over to face Gramps. 'It puts food on the table, doesn't it? You know same as everyone else, we need the money for trading out of England.'

'Slave wages! Before the Vlads we had a whole city full of treasures for trading with the Gallics – now we've just got half of one. And soon we'll have nothing!'

'That's right!' cries Dad. 'You've got the answers, eh? Chasing your dreams and your rumours! That won't keep the fire stoked!'

Dad is proper riled now. But Gramps ain't never one to back off from a scrap, certainly not in public, and certainly not with my dad. As far as he's concerned, Dad, being from Gravesend, is an outsider – not a proper scav. Must have caused a few ructions when Dad tied the knot with his precious daughter. Plus there's the small matter that Dad wasn't on the shift when Mum died . . .

Gramps flobs a greenie onto the floor. 'I know about the day-to-day like nobody else under this roof. That's how these Russians keep us down – paying us just enough not to rebel, never enough to get ahead. But this was our city once. We should reclaim it. Those bones north of the river are our dead!'

Dad goes, 'Still peddling the same old lines. Might be news to youngsters but the rest of us have heard it all before. Think we're stupid? Vlads have got all the guns and power. Reckon they're gonna take notice of a rabble of scavs armed with kitchen knives and rocks?'

Dad and Gramps stand face to face for a few moments, breathless and seething. That silence says plenty – the bad blood between them ain't exactly a secret. Wednesday meetings ain't never been this riveting, ever.

Dad is the first to blink. He chucks his hands up and turns to the crowd. 'What choice have we got? We can't exactly down tools, can we? How do you think that would pan out? Reckon that'll just give them the excuse they need to turn really nasty.'

'But what if we find the artefact before they do?' Gramps says. 'We'd have the upper hand then. They'd have to settle with us. And we *can* find it, if we organise, if we're clever, if we use our brains instead of our strength. We're scavs, aren't we? Rooting through this city is what we do best. But grinding every building down piece by piece isn't the way to do it! There aren't enough Vlads to police us if the men take to the tunnels and buildings north of the river. Send the women and children into the Wilds . . .'

'You're crazy, old man!' cries Mabel. 'We won't survive five minutes up north! Berserker tribes, Blue-faces, Ferals!'

Gramps fixes her with a furious eye. 'Those are just fireside stories. None of us really knows what's outside of London . . .'

'I ain't going nowhere Vlads are scared of going to!' another woman shouts.

'What about west, in the Waste Mountains?' goes one of Turnley's sons. 'I've heard the people there are like us, like scavs . . .'

'Mutants, more like!' puts in Mabel. 'The dumping grounds of the world. Who'd want to scrape out a living there in all that filth? I'll take my chances in London, thanks very much! Least the soil ain't poison here.'

Fred Cowan the pigherd steps into the fray, and this is pretty strange, cos old Fred don't say much to no one except his pigs. I never heard him pipe up at a meeting before. The hall goes quiet for him. He looks nervous as he speaks.

'We got to do something.'

Everyone waits.

'I saw things. Two nights back. Late, when folks was kippin'.'

'Prob'ly on the drink!' shouts someone. But there ain't no one laughing.

Fred shakes his head slowly. 'Light in the sky. Not copter or an airplane. Like furnace sparks comin' fast. It went into the water 'cross from Tower walls. Sploosh.'

'What was you doing up there?' goes Jacob Armitage, our preacher. 'That's miles away!'

Couple of folks snigger, but you can tell they ain't that tickled.

Fred shrugs. 'I just go where them pigs go.'

People start gabbling but Jacob hushes them up. 'Go on, Fred.'

'There's bubblin' and steam off the river. I wait a bit but nothin' comes up again. But then, on the north stump of the Tower Bridge, I see these soldiers comin'. They got search torches but they ain't no soldiers I seen before.'

'What do you mean?'

'They're machine-men.'

'What?'

'They come out of Vlad trucks, but they was made of machines. Legs and arms like . . . scaffold. I don't know.'

He hangs his head, and a few folks start laughing for proper now.

Gramps holds up his hand. 'This is what I mean. The Vlads are losing patience, sending in new weapons. We've got to find the artefact a different way, then hand it over while we've still got the chance to salvage something of our lives.'

Mabel pipes up. 'Come on! You just fed him that claptrap to back you up!'

A few murmurs of agreement.

Gramps whirls to face her and points a shaking finger. 'Fred Cowan's his own man. He's got no reason to lie for me or anyone. I promise you, scavving will be the death of us. The sooner the Vlads get what they want, the sooner they'll be gone from here. Think about it!' The sight of him hopping up onto a table hushes the crowd. 'The artefact must have knowledge. Secrets from another age. And they won't leave us in peace till it's found.'

'Stories and rumours!' cries Dad. 'You've looked for

it so long you're believing in your own made-up dreams! You don't have any idea what this artefact is. No one does.'

'I know this much – it's got a *soul*.'

Gramps lets that hang and no one breathes a word. But next to me Wilbur begins to fidget.

Gramps looks around at us all, milking the moment. 'It's *alive* and it *watches* us.'

Gus takes centre stage for the first time since the barney started. 'Whatever the artefact is, I don't care.' His voice is all shaky with feeling as he stares at Gramps. 'We've survived as scavs for a hundred years – all this talk of change is madness. The Vlads will crush us if we throw down our tools and go looking for it alone.'

Nobody speaks for a few moments. Gus Turnley might be a coward, but he sums up the feelings of most people.

Gramps rounds on him in a fury. 'Well, you're a fool, Gus Turnley!' he spits. 'Don't you want to be free? We need to find the artefact before the Vlads, and there's clues in this city, for those who care to look.'

Everyone starts putting in their two-pennyworth then, and crowding towards the chief's barrel.

And that's when Peyto stands up. I can't believe it cos

youngsters ain't supposed to do speaking at meetings.

He just walks into the centre of the room and, in a clear voice, speaks out to everyone. 'So, if the Vlads had the artefact,' he asks, 'wouldn't that just make them even more dangerous?'

A gobsmacked silence drops over the meeting house. It ain't something I reckon anyone's thought about. We're so busy scavving all day every day, no one really thinks they'll live to see the day it gets found.

Gramps leaps down from the table, his rags all flapping like crows' wings.

'And who are you, young sir?' He jabs at Peyto. 'Who are you – in our meeting hall? A stranger. Asking questions about the artefact . . .'

A few nasty murmurs bubble up from the crowd.

'A Vlad messenger maybe. Or a spy?'

I feel Erin start forward and I snatch her arm.

I keep my voice low. 'Go to the well. It's at the far end of the street.'

'But—'

'I'll meet you there in a minute.'

She tries to read me, wanting to trust. But she ain't sure.

'Go!' I hiss.

As soon as she turns for the door, I break towards the

middle of the hall. It ain't even like I've got a clear idea what I'm gonna do. All I know is I've got to mix up some kind of trouble. Right now.

I leap onto the serving table, hurdle the hog spit and charge towards the fire. At the far end of the table is a whopping great cauldron of water for the washing-up. I jump into the slide, feeling plates and knives skid out from under my buttocks. And wallop! Feet first into the cauldron. It takes about ten years to tip over, then a great wave of soapy water heaves into the flames. Steam rushes into the dark.

Just before it goes totally black I eyeball Peyto, so I know exactly where he is as I grab hold of his hand – soft like no scav hand ever would be.

And I yank him through a circus of yelling and shoving. Through the door and out into the night.

THE FLINDER

WE RUN, HAND IN HAND, AWAY FROM THE HALL, STUMBLING IN THE POTHOLES. THE WELL IS JUST UP AHEAD, AND I CAN JUST MAKE OUT ERIN CROUCHING IN THE SHADOWS. WE HUDDLE DOWN next to her, our breath smoking hot and fast.

Erin flashes Peyto a filthy look. 'What were you *thinking* of? Things are bad enough as they are!'

'I'm sorry. I just wanted to know what they'd do if they really found it—'

'Haven't we got enough to worry about without the whole village chasing after us? We have to go, right now.'

'Settle down,' I go. 'You ain't in danger. Things'll blow over. They ain't a bad lot, trust me.'

Erin pulls away. 'You don't understand, Cass. We have to go.'

'We can't. It's far too dangerous—' starts Peyto.

'We can't leave it there,' cries Erin. 'We've got days, Peyto! Days! Not weeks! And now you've gone and lost—'

'Calm down, I haven't lost it. I know exactly where it is. At least I found Wilbur – he was right where he was supposed to be.'

'You don't know if he's definitely *The One*.'

'Wait a second – what about Wilbur?' I go. 'He's the one what?'

But they're so mad with each other they ain't listening.

'It's all right for you,' goes Erin. 'If the ship crashes it's not your family . . .'

Peyto leaps up. 'Don't you ever say that – that it's all right for me!'

Erin's pacing about now, fit to explode. 'Tell him! Tell him he's got to listen!' she pleads to me.

'Whoa!' I go. 'Rewind! Lost what? What ship? What's too dangerous? And what's this about Wilbur? You knew he was gonna be at Big Ben?'

Peyto slumps against the edge of the well. 'There was meant to be someone at the clock tower – someone to . . . help us. Wilbur was there. He has to be The One. He came there to look for the artefact of his own accord. It makes sense.'

'OK, look, you've got that wrong,' I go. 'Wilbur ain't got no more clue where the artefact is than any other scav. He's just a kid with bonkers ideas, all right? He's had more guesses where the artefact is than he's had hot dinners. And they've all been dead ends, believe me. It's a game for him. Anyway, who told you there'd be someone at the clock tower?'

'It's a long story,' mutters Peyto, looking away from me. 'There's something we need to find. And there's someone we need to find, too . . . a woman.'

I want to ask him how come this is all connected to the artefact when he didn't know a damn thing about it at Big Ben, but he's closed off from me, still seething at Erin.

'The point is, we're in even more trouble now,' goes Erin, glaring back at him.

I glance between them. 'Why?'

'I left something back where we were scavving,' mumbles Peyto.

'So? Get it tomorrow.'

'You don't understand. I *had* to leave it there, or the Vlads would have found it when I got scanned at the end of the shift . . .'

I shake my head. 'Ain't you had enough for one day?

I told you already. We ain't allowed that side of the river till it's been cleared. They see you, they shoot you.'

'I'm going,' says Erin, and she means it.

I back-pedal in front of her, trying to smile. 'Slow down, lady! You ain't even gonna make it across the river.'

Her eyes sparkle with tears as she tries to look through me, all hell-bent on marching to the edge of the world. At last she stops and hangs her head.

'Bejesus, and I thought Wilbur was stubborn! What's going on today? What's so precious you can't just pick it up tomorrow?'

And that's when Erin brings something out from under her collar.

It's such a shock, I figure I'm dreaming as she cups it in her hand to show me. First off I think it's an animal. Long tentacles, thin as fishing wire, are waving about where it was clasped around her neck, and then they just disappear into the rest of it, like when you touch the stalks on a snail. It ain't much bigger than a chestnut shell but it's an odd shape, a sort of knot with bulges and stalks and creases. And it's glowing with the faintest of lights – a shimmer of faraway blue and green, with hairline streaks of cream drawn across its surface in patterns, like the grain of bleached wood. Except it's much finer than that – all the detail is sharp and layered and sunk down deep inside. And as I gaze at it, I could swear them patterns are moving about, very slowly shifting and mixing. It's the most weirdest, most stand-out beautiful thing I've ever clapped my eyes on.

'What . . . the hell . . . is that?'

'It's a flinder,' says Peyto. 'Erin's got one and I've got one – that's what I had to leave on the other side of the river. But there are others, and . . . well, one of them is lost. Here. In this city. We think. I don't know what the Vlads are looking for, but this missing flinder, it could be your artefact.'

Gently, almost reluctantly, Erin hands it to me.

And as soon as I touch it I *know*. This is what we're all looking for. The artefact is a flinder, just like this one.

I think about what Wilbur said – *'If you hold it, you'll know . . .'*

It feels like . . . a sleeping heart, filled with wrestlings and yearnings, sparking out echoes that snatch away before I can hold them. Like the scraps of dreams when you wake up. Like ghosts stirring, flinching from my touch. I come back to the here and now slowly, flutters in my skin. The stalks unfurl again, like moth feelers, gently reaching out to touch my fingers.

'So, will you help us?' asks Erin at last.

Her manner ain't pleading – she just lays it down like the quietest of challenges.

I don't say nothing, and I can see her sucking in her temper, then, writing me off. She takes the flinder back.

I feel suddenly lost, like the thing's swiped a warm bit of my soul. The tentacles reach out to embrace her.

Up the street I see the meeting breaking up – everyone standing in huddles arguing. We can't stay here. Awkward questions are coming our way . . .

But you know, I've seen crews march out of buildings just cos the floorboards creak a certain way, and ten minutes later the whole street comes crashing down. It's that feeling that bugs me now – my scav nose for trouble. And what else? It spins in my head like the beacon on a moving crusher. I could take it, this flinder. I could give it to the Vlads and maybe they'd just pack off home and leave us in peace. It's what Gramps would do. Peyto looks uneasily to the ground. He knows what I'm thinking.

But it ain't as simple as that, is it? Cos I ain't gonna sell them out after what's happened today, am I? Thing is, these two strangers from God-knows-where are both ready to lay down their lives rather than lose their flinders. Question is, why?

Just right then, Erin puts on her kiddie ear-muffs,

like she's shutting me out, moving on. And they'd be ridiculous on anyone else, but somehow she carries them off, cos she ain't got a clue that they're in any way wrong. She don't even know they was meant for little girls. To her they're just ear-cosies, and that's when I warm to her. So I smile.

'Lord only knows I must be bonkers, like I ain't already had a gutful of trouble today. But I suppose you'd better count me in.'

Just right then I spot Wilbur trotting up towards us, and I hiss at Erin to tuck her flinder away.

'We'll have to start pretty soon,' I go. 'It'll take us at least an hour to reach the river even if we go in the cart. Don't ask me how we're gonna get across the water but we'll figure something out.'

I listen to myself as I'm whispering all this, and I can't believe it's coming out my mouth.

'Cass, what's going on? You're planning something!'

Sharp as a tack, my little brother.

'What makes you say that?' I go, all casual.

'I can always tell. Just the way you poke your tongue in your cheek when you're thinking hard.'

There ain't no point in trying to deny it. I make my mind up right there to include him, else he'll just blab something to Dad. But there ain't no way I'm gonna let on any more than I need to, least till I figure out just how dangerous this whole escapade is. When in doubt, orders.

'Right, Wilbur. Listening? Go and fix up Sheba to the cart, and do it nice and quiet. Meet us up at the head of the north track in ten minutes. Make sure no one sees you. And, Wilbur? You goof and we're gone without you, all right?'

He scampers away towards the animal sheds.

My head's going frantic with the details. Course, I suppose I could still bail out. But somehow, now I've taken charge, I know that ain't gonna happen.

'Thank you, Cass,' Erin goes at last.

'Not a word about any flinder malarkey to him, yeah? Kid's got enough spooky ideas as it is, and I don't want him getting hurt, all right? But listen up, I swear to God, when this is over tonight, you tell me the whole shebang. Agreed?'

Peyto smiles. 'Agreed.'

IN THE FOOTSTEPS
OF LOOTERS

WILBUR SHOWS UP ON THE NOSE OF TEN MINUTES, AND WE ALL CLAMBER INTO THE BACK OF THE CART. BY NOW I'VE FIGURED WHAT TO SAY TO MY BROTHER ABOUT THE MISSION. HE SHOVES the bridge over his specs further up his nose, and his excited little face is hanging on my every word.

'Now, listen up. Peyto's gone and dropped his cash bag on the job and we're gonna get it back.'

Wilbur searches my eyes. 'How come we don't just get it tomorrow?'

'Cos it's too risky! It's everything they've got, and if we ain't careful some nosy gangmaster doing recce first thing's gonna snaffle it up.'

He nods, but I can tell he's seeing right through me and out the other side. Cos Peyto and Erin ain't the sort to even have a cash bag. They've never grafted for money their whole lives. Still, Wilbur takes it on board, even gives me a cheesy grin.

So I gee up Sheba and we're off. It's a windy night with no clouds to spoil the moon. The stars swim and hover when you squint at them, like the sparkles of coins at the bottom of our well. But I clock that Peyto and Erin ain't interested in any of that. They spend the journey glued to Sheba's swaying flanks, the flick of her tail, her wheezy progress along the north track. At one point, Erin reaches out and touches the old nag's rump – just gently, like a kid does. Sometimes in the distance we can make out other villages – huddles of lamplight and the faint burble of people rabbiting. No one says a word. There's something about this caper that makes me think it's just a game – that we'll only get as far as Blackfriars or one of the other bridges, and it'll dawn on us that it's nuts to go any further.

For the last few hundred metres before the river we leave Sheba and go on foot, away from the track and up onto one of the slag mounds. All along the dark reach of water we can see the still-standing bridges picked out with searchlights. To the right, the remains of the old Millennium Walkway and Southwark. In front of us, the arches of Blackfriars. And to the left, as the river swings round, Waterloo. Even from here, I can make out the figures of Vlad sentries moving about near the busted railings of the bridge ahead.

'Ain't no good. We'll never get past them guards.'

'What about a boat or something?' goes Peyto.

'Nah, there ain't no boats here. People ain't allowed on the river this far up.'

'Maybe we could swim,' goes Erin.

I look at her like she's lost it. 'You seen the current? You'd be down to the Dogs soon as you dipped your toe in. Anyhow, even if you was a decent swimmer, it's way too cold. You wouldn't last five minutes.'

'Just an idea,' she goes, all sulky.

'The tunnel,' whispers Wilbur. 'You know – the Jubilee one.'

'Nah, it's got to be flooded. The tunnel's lower than the river –'

'No, the water's drained away – not completely, but there's like a gap near the roof.'

'What kind of cobblers is that, you spod? How can it drain away? There ain't no tides no more with the Great Barrier holding the sea back.'

'It's not a tide that does it. It's the pumps – there's loads of them on the north side dredging the old Underground tunnels. They run all day but they work much harder at night when all the crushers are shut down.'

I look at him. 'How on Earth d'you know all that?'

'Heard Gramps say once.'

He's all shy then. Wilbur's so quiet most of the time, you forget he's there. But when people are yabbering, he never misses a trick.

'Makes no odds,' I go at last. 'If it ain't drained away the whole hog then it's still gonna be too deep for us.'

'If Wilbur thinks there's a way across the river, we should at least look,' says Peyto firmly. 'We said we'd listen to him.' The way he glances at me, his eyes all fired up, I feel on edge all of a sudden.

Wilbur looks gobsmacked cos no one ever listens to his hare-brained schemes usually. I give him evils, just so he knows not to get too cocky on all the attention. But I can tell none of them is gonna back down. So I lead the way through the trenches towards the big old crater that marks where Waterloo Station once stood. It gets sludgier as we plough on, till you can see water pouring into the entrance where the old tracks dip underground.

'See?' goes Wilbur.

'See what?' I snap back. 'Anyone got a submarine handy?'

'We've got to go deeper, follow where the water drops,' says Wilbur.

'Wilbur, you crack-job, this ain't like paddling up Blackheath. Check it out!'

But Wilbur ain't looking at me. He's looking at Peyto, who's forged on ahead, clambering down bits of broken concrete at the edge of the tunnel wall. I'm pretty much done with the whole adventure, but I don't want to waste the I-told-you-so speech that's brewing in my head. So we carry on.

And guess what? Wilbur's right – where the tunnel starts proper, the roof is a good ten metres clear of the water. It don't exactly look inviting, though – the tunnel mouth has all these rusty rods poking out of it, all covered in gunk like mucky fangs. And course, we ain't thought to bring a lamp or nothing.

We edge closer and look at the darkness, which is about as total as it gets. In the distance, you can hear the rushing echoes of water, and what sounds like a right downpour – probably leaks in the roof. Me and Peyto squelch down the slope together, leaving the other two behind. Peyto spots it first – an old steel ladder fixed to the wall. It leads to a platform cut into the concrete and there's something bulky stashed up there.

We look at each other. I know what he's thinking. Everything round here has been scavved out, so whatever it is has to be stashed here on purpose.

I volunteer to go up first but pretty soon I'm cursing that blinding idea, cos the rungs are all slimy and I get the horrors about three-quarters of the way up. Somehow I hold it together enough to reach the platform. The thing is lashed really tight to the wall with rope and tarpaulin, but at last I manage to squeeze under the cover.

Whatever it is, it's sopping wet and stinks of old rubber, and I'm squitting it cos I can't see a thing. Then my hands land on what feels like a bag and inside it something solid, plastic maybe, long like a tube. I try to drag the bag out but I lose my grip and drop it. Then my heart nearly gives out cos a light beam shoots right into my face. Slowly I calm down and realise what I've done. The bag is see-through and inside it is a torch – old-school 'lectric with a battery. Me dropping it has switched the damn thing on.

All the stuff inside is bone dry. Apart from the torch there's half a dozen street maps torn from a book, a notepad, a pencil and a compass. In the notepad it's just diagrams with no writing, and what looks like numbers, but I can't read so it's cobblers to me. I pan round with the torch. And find myself sitting in the bottom of a dinghy. It's pretty big – enough room for six or seven people, I reckon. Parked on the sides there's two paddles and a grapple hook on a cable.

Next thing I know, there's a pale face staring up at me from the edge of the tarpaulin and I just about freak.

'It's me!' goes Peyto.

'Yeah, you wanna give me some warning next time? My ticker's gonna give out any second!'

But he's just grinning at the boat. 'There's a winch here, see? Give me a hand.'

I show him the notepad and the maps, but he can't suss them out either.

'It looks like code, or a checklist. I don't know.'

'This is looters' stuff,' I go. 'Maybe we should just get the hell out of here.'

'We're just going to *borrow* it.'

I shine the torch at him and he's beaming from ear to ear. He really is enjoying all this, but then, I have to admit I am, too.

Ten minutes later we've got the dinghy lowered into the water.

Erin and Wilbur are both speechless – Erin through fear, and Wilbur . . . Well, Wilbur don't exactly look scared, but it's kind of funny that he doesn't 'ooh' and 'ah' like I'd expect. In fact, he never says much at all, right up to the point when I say he can't come.

'Cass! Oh, please!'

'I'm crazy even to let you come this far! If Dad knew, he'd clout me into next week!'

'It was my idea to come to the tunnel!'

'So? This ain't a game!'

'I can help!'

Wilbur's on the verge of tears but then Peyto squats down and puts an arm round him.

'Of course you can help,' he goes. 'See, someone has to stay and look after Sheba.'

'That's right,' I go. 'Gonna have to be one brave soldier staying here in the dark to keep Sheba company.'

Wilbur ain't too happy about it, but least he stops snivelling.

'Can't Erin stay with me?' he whimpers.

We all look at Erin.

'I don't think we should leave Wilbur here on his own,' she goes at last. 'Can't we all go together?'

'I told you he ain't coming with us.' I'm all spoiling for a fight, cos we just sorted the question of Wilbur.

She throws a pointed look at Wilbur, who's getting all hopeful about tagging along again. 'But what if the Vlads come here looking?' she goes.

'It ain't no crime to be this side of the river. All he has to say is he's digging up bait for fishing or something.

But they ain't gonna be bothered – a kid and a cart horse. It's us you have to worry about. '

'I don't think you realise how dangerous it is over there,' explains Peyto.

'Too right. We ain't got any excuse to be across the water at night. They catch us, it's curtains.'

She gives me a puzzled look then, not angry. 'I don't want to argue with you, Cass. I just didn't want to leave Wilbur alone, that's all. If you say it's safer for him here, I believe you.'

That takes the wind out my sails. 'Fair enough. I think it's me and Peyto on the paddles but someone has to sit up front with the torch – and that's got to be you.'

She strokes Wilbur's head and nods at me, and without the huge scrap I was gearing up for, it's done and dusted.

'Right, Wilbur, listening? Check your watch. We're gonna be gone no more than, say, six hours. If we ain't back by two at the latest then don't hang around, you hear?'

'But then what?' groans Wilbur.

'Well, we *are* gonna be back, I promise. It's just in case we get stranded over there when the sun comes up – if that happens I'd rather lay low till it gets dark again. Look, it's gonna be fine. Get onto one of them mounds and keep an eye out. When we get to the far side, I'll flash the torch a few times to let you know we're safe, then you stick with Sheba till we show up again.'

He nods and watches us as we clamber into the dinghy. It's tragic watching him wave as we undo the winch rope and cast off into the gloom.

It's swirly in places where the water's being sucked deeper into the tunnels – vicious little currents that make the dinghy hard to straighten up. Every now and then water gushes down from the roof and we get a drenching.

The further we go, the stronger the current gets. After about ten minutes I clock a patch of moonlight shining through a hole in the roof. The tunnel branches off here in two directions – up a steep slope to the surface, and off into the rest of the Underground where the old Tube trains used to run. Me and Peyto paddle against the flow, and Erin manages to wedge the grapple hook round a bit of concrete. Which is a relief, cos I don't fancy floating all the way into the West End – them old train tunnels are meant to go on for ever this side of the river. I leave the maps in the dinghy and just take the torch before we head up to the surface.

All's quiet as we climb out onto the north bank – just a few foxes screeching. I spot one of them padding through the river mud, starving and wary. This end of the tunnel has got the same slag mounds and we crawl up one of them for a butcher's. To the south I can't see much – just the leaning wreckage of Westminster Abbey and Big Ben blocking out the starlight. In the west I can make out the swaying tops of trees – St James's Park. North lie the yet-to-be-scavved buildings of Whitehall, shabby and stained but still managing to look important. To the east lies the approach to the river – the ripped-up canyons of mud and the bare stumps of Westminster Bridge, mostly pulled down now.

It's a risk to signal Wilbur, but I can't leave the lad on tenterhooks. He's got to know we're safe, so I flash the torch three times.

'Let's get a lick on,' I whisper. 'And keep your eyes peeled.'

THE SPIDER NEST

WE HURRY UP TO THE EMBANKMENT ROAD AND MOVE AWAY FROM THE RIVER TOWARDS THE OLD ADMIRALTY OFFICES. I WANT TO STICK TO SEMI-SCAVVED AREAS COS OF THE COVER AND COS it's quicker than crossing mud and potholes. I scout out the way where it's open, then give them the signal to follow one at a time. Peyto's not bad at the commando stuff, but Erin's a nightmare – running bolt upright like a goose, and what with her ear-muffs on, her head's about twice as big as it needs to be. Talk about give the Vlads a bit more of a target to aim at. And God, she's clumsy – tripping over her own feet and making a proper racket.

'Can't you get down lower?' I hiss at her. 'Might as well be waving a flippin' flag the way you're prancing about.'

'I can't help it,' she groans. 'I can't see anything!'

'Just go slower then. And d'you reckon you could get through London without kicking every bit of brick along the way?'

'You could plant your feet where I plant mine,' offers Peyto.

'Hey, if I need your advice on how walking works, I'll be sure to ask you,' goes Erin.

'All right, don't flip your gimbals – it was just a suggestion.'

They both eyeball each other and Peyto looks stunned at what he's just said, like he's made it up.

'*Flip your gimbals?* What planet are you two from?'

They go blank as mudfish on me then like I've just badmouthed Jesus. Which is just as well, cos I want to get on with minimum fuss.

It's right creepy round Horse Guards Parade with weeds scraping in the wind and not a soul about. I ain't used to being in the scav-zone at night like that without the crushers going hell for leather and the chock-chocking of picks and hammers.

It's all clear as we creep past the once-grand houses of Downing Street where the Lord President of London used to live. And in the dark and the silence, without the scav gangs swarming all over it, you can imagine this city as it once was. It don't take much to think of the lights and the crowds, maybe folks like the Piccadilly Princess in the picture, rushing off to meet her fella, living it up.

We get to Little Sanctuary safe and sound, and I'm starting to think the whole jaunt is a breeze. Past the silent crusher, up five flights of stairs and into the rooms we scavved earlier.

Peyto scrabbles round in the dark for a bit, feeling along the edge of the skirting board.

'Switch on the torch – I can't find it,' he goes.

'Where d'you stash it?'

'I hid it just here. I'm sure it was in this gap.'

'Come on, Peyto,' pleads Erin. 'Don't play around.'

'I'm not! It's not here I'm telling you!' Peyto's voice is getting panicky.

'Hey, pipe down, will you?' I go. 'You want the whole Vlad army up here?'

I push past him and shove my hand into the hole. At first there's nothing. Just dirt and loose wires. The plaster's so crumbly it comes away in my fingers, and I start to pull at it one chunk at a time till I can see the cavity behind. There's no need for the torch – Peyto's flinder glows blue through churning puffs of dust. He breathes a sigh of relief and reaches out for it, but I hold him back. There's something there, moving in the shadows, and as the dust settles I see it clearly – a whole nest of spiders, big and small, crowding around the light. And they ain't just milling about, they're building a web. Together. Peyto and Erin edge closer.

'That is stand-out weird,' I go at last.

'Why? What are they?' says Erin, her face caught up in the wonder of it.

And it hits me slowly. She ain't never seen spiders before.

'It's like they're trying to hide it,' breathes Peyto.

And he's right – the tresses of the web are starting to cover the flinder like a cocoon. It gives me a shiver to think how long they'd have to be at it to blot out that light. It's the first time for a hundred years anything new's been *built* in London.

'Sorry,' I go to the spiders. Cos it's a shame to break that gorgeous bit of weaving. Needs must. But then as my fingers push through the threads and close on the flinder, them lonely echoes rise up again, tingling through my arm, into my brain. Like faraway voices calling out to me. Not calling, more like singing. It's a shock and I want to let go. But I don't, I can't, cos the touch of it *holds* me. It pulses softly, like Erin's flinder, but it's a different shape, more knotty with a hole through it.

'What's wrong?' goes Peyto.

I realise I must look a bit dazed. I hand it to him.

I feel that wrench again, the same as when Erin took back her flinder. Except this time I'm distracted by a whole bunch of spiders, clinging to the broken trails of web, scuttling to and fro over my hand, up my sleeve. And it feels a strange comfort that they're there, not running away. So I let them be.

Peyto's much more interested in the spiders than the flinder. He smiles at me and tries to catch them as they drop.

'You get the goosebumps when you touch the flinder?' I go.

'What do you mean?'

'Like voices inside.'

They both stare at me.

'No,' he goes. 'But Erin does.'

I shrug. 'Maybe it's a girl thing.'

But straightaway I know it ain't that. I see it in the way he holds the flinder. He don't treasure it the way Erin treasures hers. To him it's a thing he *should* look after, not a thing he wants. Erin would never have left hers anyplace, even if the whole Vlad army was on her heels. And maybe it *knows* that. Cos I reckon Gramps is right. It really *has* got something like a soul.

There's about a squillion questions queueing up in my bonce now, but this ain't the time or the place.

I hurry them both down to street level and peep outside the door. Still all clear. It's all going so swimmingly that I'm starting to reckon we're gonna get away with this. Which is the worst jinx ever.

Cos that's precisely when it all goes pear-shaped.

We turn out of the top end of Little Sanctuary and there, coming from the park towards us, is a Vlad patrol – maybe a dozen soldiers.

We duck behind the skeleton of an old car and I check we ain't being surrounded.

'Have they seen us?' whispers Erin.

The lead soldier makes a few hand signals, then the others peel off either side of him and start advancing up the road from car to car.

'They've seen us . . .' I mutter.

Peyto goes, 'The river.'

'No way! We'll get cut off!'

'We won't. Trust me.'

Before I can hold him back he's off, darting towards the river. The Vlads are closing. I can see the red beams from their rifles and my guts go loose. It's sheer panic that makes me grab Erin's arm and charge after Peyto. Stealth's out the window – we just leather it, not caring about our pounding feet. Peyto's a fast runner and I have a job keeping up with him, but Erin's slow. I keep dropping back to stay in touch with her, and she's stumbling all over the shop. By now the soldiers are shouting – warnings maybe. But we don't stop.

The paving crumbles away into sludge, and all that's between us and the river is craters and rubble heaps. Peyto's bounding over the waste ground ahead and in front of him I can see the water lit up from search beams. There ain't nowhere to go. I'm cursing myself for going after him when Erin struggles up to me.

'What are you stopping for?' she cries.

'We've got to get back to the streets. We can't shake them off here!'

'No, you don't understand. Follow Peyto!'

She lurches after him, practically cartwheeling into the bog. When I look back over my shoulder, I can see swinging torches and then a couple of gunshots crack out. I'm thinking, *They're gonna shoot us down like rats*. I slither into the mud and it drags me down. And I know then I won't even make it to the water. Erin's just ahead, reaching out to help me. Then I see Peyto hold his flinder up high, and he's saying something over and over again. It sounds like a chant.

There's a movement in the water, just a restless

bubbling at first, but the skin of the river rises and parts, and out comes this big black shape, ploughing up from the depths. I cry out and all around me there's these spurts of mud and I realise the soldiers are taking pot-shots from the road. But that seems like the least of our worries cos this huge hump-backed *thing* sends a wave slooshing up to our shoulders. But for the mud holding my legs, I'd have been swept away.

I'm so scared I can't even breathe.

I figure it's alive, the way it surges round in an arc between us and the bank, its bulk all slick and smooth like a giant fish. But then I hear gunfire bouncing off it.

Thunk! Thunk!

And suddenly a hole opens up and a searing light stabs into my eyes.

THE *AEOLUS*

IT AIN'T LIKE WE GO THROUGH THE HOLE OF OUR OWN ACCORD. IT'S MORE LIKE THE THING TIPS US UP AND SWALLOWS US IN ONE GO, MUD AND ALL. I TUMBLE DOWN IN A HEAP WITH THE others and lie there for a moment, not believing any of it, as my eyes get used to the glare. Above me, the hole closes up and we're moving now, fast and downwards. The walls are covered with machines and dials, and in the middle there's a ring of six padded seats. Sludge from the Thames slops about on the otherwise clean floor. Peyto and Erin are glued to a couple of screens flickering with diagrams and weird symbols.

At last I go, 'When I said, has anybody got a submarine, I was joking.'

'Get into one of those chairs,' orders Peyto. 'We're going to launch in twenty-five seconds.'

'*Launch?* Launch where?'

'The *Aeolus*,' goes Erin, like that explains everything.

'All right, I figure we had to get clear of them Vlads sharpish, I get that. And I ain't even gonna ask how come you got a submarine. And how come you never mentioned it when we was risking our lives crossing the damn river in the first place. No problem. But for your information, I ain't *launching* nowhere. You can just steer it back to the south bank where Wilbur is before the lad freaks out.'

'Can't do that,' goes Peyto. 'Please, Cass, just sit in a chair and strap yourself in . . .'

I slip-side over to where he's gawking at the screens.

'You ain't listening! My brother is standing on his tod, freezing his buns off, worrying himself half to death about us!'

'I'm not in control! I can't *steer* it anywhere!'

Erin's is the calmest head. 'Cass, listen to me. We're in an evac-shuttle – it's just an offspring vehicle.'

I gape at her. *Evac-shuttle?* It's like someone's opened this door to where Wilbur's comics are real. I think about old Fred the pigherd. Lights in the sky and machine-men.

She holds up her flinder. 'When you get in an evac-shuttle with one of these, it just takes you back to the mother ship. It's automatic in case you've become injured or you're unconscious. We should be able to override that setting but, well, there's some problems with the ship itself . . .'

'Oh yeah, and another thing, I ain't got a clue what you're talking about.'

'I know you haven't, but you have to strap yourself in or you could get really hurt. It's a short journey. We'll explain everything just as soon as we get out of here, I promise.'

'Explain everything,' I mutter, my voice all shaky. 'Yeah, that'd be just peaches, that would. I want a bloody good *explanation* an' all. With bells on.'

Both of them guide me to a chair and put these padded belts over my shoulders. When they strap in either side of me, the chairs tip back, then the vehicle starts shaking and humming so hard that everything goes blurry. My head slams back and I feel like a wall's pressing down on me and there's this crazy roaring. I yelp out but I can't even hear my own voice. All this spit dribbles out my mouth but I can't lift my hand to wipe it off. Next thing the roaring stops, and I feel all light and woozy. My spit sails past, wobbling around in slow motion.

'What the . . .?'

'It's all right, you're just weightless,' goes Erin.

'You mean we ain't in the Thames no more?'

'No, we're in orbit about thirteen miles above London.'

Then she just leans forward out of her chair and *floats* over to the screens.

'A submarine what can fly,' I say out loud to no one in particular.

It's weird how my voice sounds all dreamy while my heart is thrashing about like a bee in a tin. *How the hell is this even happening?* No one's even been in space since the Quark Wars, or so Wilbur says. Them old rockets and stations in the sky have been empty for years. And there just ain't no way for me to get a handle on this. I think about the run to the river with all the Vlads chasing after us, taking pot-shots – that just feels like it never even happened. But still, the stink from the river is in my nostrils. And I keep thinking about Wilbur, about how he has to be done in with worry by now. He'd have heard the gunfire for sure.

'We've got to get back,' I go.

'We will,' says Erin. 'When we dock up to the *Aeolus*, we'll be free to return to London just as soon as we reset the shuttle . . .'

'And just exactly when's that gonna be?'

'Don't worry,' Erin says gently. 'It'll take no more than half an hour. Plus, going back is under our control – there's no emergency protocol or anything. We can navigate straight to where Wilbur is. We'll be there long before the two o'clock deadline. I promise you.'

I figure I've got to trust her. What else can I do? Peyto has kind of clammed up, but Erin's completely the queen of the flying sub, cos she's suddenly got this air of *confidence*.

And the weirdest thing? I slow right down. Bonkers stuff is happening all around, like floating people and flying ships with mothers, but my brain just freezes over and pretends everything's fine and dandy. Like, that world you knew about all of thirty seconds ago, well that has just gone, so welcome to this new world. Where your spit don't stay on the ground where it belongs.

'Right then,' I go at last. 'I'm just about ready for that explanation now.'

Erin taps the screen a couple of times and the view switches to something floating in the night sky. It's shaped like a bone – narrow in the middle with bulbs at either end – and it's twirling very slowly.

'What's that?'

'That is the *Aeolus*,' says Peyto without much of a fanfare. 'The ship.'

He unstraps me and I float out of my chair. It's like swimming without holding your breath. But I don't like it much – it feels like you ain't really there.

The *Aeolus* gets bigger till it fills the screen. I can't tell how large it is but the surface looks pretty close now, like wrinkled shell, and shot through with pink webs and blue streaks. And then these tentacles peel out of the surface, swaying like reeds under water.

'What the hell are those?'

'There's nothing to worry about,' mutters Erin. 'It's just the ship docking with us.'

There's a soft thump on the roof above us and a squelching noise.

'Them feelers,' I go. 'It's . . . alive?'

'Yes,' answers Peyto. 'It's alive and it's smart.'

'Whoa, that thing's a creature. And we're going inside it?'

'No, not a creature. It's an organic machine for space travel.'

'But you're saying it's got a brain?'

'Not exactly,' goes Erin. 'Its intelligence was designed separately using a machine, then transferred into a living organic shell. The process is like fusing body and mind – we call it birthing.'

I must be gawping like a loon. 'You made a spaceship

what can live and think?'

Peyto tries to explain. 'Not us, our ancestors. Ordinary machines just break down in space. The best way to make a ship really last is to make it alive so it can repair itself.'

'Docking complete,' goes Erin.

Then something grows out of the wall opposite me. It bulges like a giant zit, before popping open and squirting me with a warm gust of cheesy air.

'Blimey, gut rot! Does it usually guff like this?'

Erin ain't amused. 'It's not in prime condition.'

'You can say that again – smells like it's been eating something right dodgy . . .'

'It doesn't *eat* anything,' she sighs.

I suppose that should put my mind at rest a bit, but as we squeeze past the zit flaps into the ship proper there's these ridged walls flickering with bluish light, and I can't help thinking it looks like the inside of a giant gob.

Erin calls out, 'Hello?'

Nothing.

'Should it be saying stuff back?' I go. I psyche myself for a huge, booming voice to reply.

'It should,' mutters Peyto. 'But there's some kind of communication fault.'

'Like what? Is it deaf, or asleep or something?'

'No, the messages are just getting lost in transit, I think. It's just malfunctioning,' goes Erin. 'Communication has been . . . patchy since the emergency.'

'*Emergency?*'

'There's a hull breach.'

'You mean there's a flippin' hole in it?' Even I know that ain't good news. 'Ain't we gonna run out of air or something?'

'Don't worry, we're sealed off from where the breach is in the central shaft. We're safe in here.'

Safe? Inside a wounded space monster? Safe is tucked up in my sleeping bag in our hut . . . in Elephant and Castle . . . thirteen miles away. But it seems to me we're a good deal further away than thirteen miles.

I glance about at the walls like they're all set to cave in. 'What made the hole?'

'I told you, it's *safe*,' insists Erin. 'The Aeolus might not be a hundred per cent but it's not ready to fall apart just yet.'

Neither her nor Peyto seem that freaked out right now by the 'emergency' – maybe it's under control. I try to relax a bit.

The main chamber inside the ship is speckled green and ever so gently it *throbs*. And it's wet – not something you really want to touch, but I ain't got a choice on that front cos the only way to move is to shove yourself off the walls. Waving your arms and legs like you're under water just leaves you where you are. The *Aeolus* walls are warm and stringy – the gunge glues itself to your fingers but that makes it easier to get a grip on things so you can swing from one hold to the next. It don't seem to bother Erin and Peyto but I don't like the way the gunk clings to your skin.

'So this ain't normal then, the way it's all sick?' I go.

'It's not an animal, Cass,' answers Erin a tad wearily. 'It doesn't catch illnesses, it doesn't feel pain, it doesn't get tired or sleep . . .'

'But it has *changed* since we got here,' Peyto chips in. 'It's not the ship we set out in, is it? All perfect and clean . . .'

'What do you expect?' she goes. 'It's damaged so badly it can't self-repair. Its systems are in a critical state.'

Just as I'm poking at the walls I spot a rogue spider that's hitched a ride on me – it spins away from my sleeve, legs akimbo, paying out thread as it goes. And when it brushes the surface of the ship, it sinks in and disappears.

'Hey! I thought you said it doesn't eat stuff!'

But just as suddenly as it swallows the spider, it spits him out again right as rain. I scoop him up and he tethers to my collar. Erin smiles at me then. It's the first time I've seen her do that, and just for a second she's someone else, someone proper beautiful. Then she brushes her ruined ear-muffs against the wall and all the mud from the Thames just drains out of them. They come up fresh as dandelion heads.

We venture further into the chamber, and it's much deeper than I first figured. It's spooking me out cos by now I can't see if I'm facing up or down. Past my dangling feet I spot where the blue light's coming from – there's this diamond shape made from lanterns that flicker together like they're disturbed by a breeze, though there ain't no movement in the air. I count up the lights on each side – seven by seven. Except there's gaps in the grid.

In an effort to get a better look, I lose my balance and end up nudging into Peyto. And that's lesson number two about this new world – once you're moving you don't slow down, you just float onwards till you hit something.

'Keep zig-zagging across the chamber till you reach that square of lights,' explains Peyto.

'Easy for you to say. I'm about as good at this as a pig on wheels.'

I'm putting everything into getting my zig-zag moves right so I don't really get a decent view of the grid of lights till I'm practically on top of it. And so it's a shock when I see what it's made up of.

Each light is at the head of something that looks like a long see-through blister.

And inside each blister, submerged in milky-blue liquid, is a body.

A human body.

The faces are pale and empty. And round every neck is a flinder, twinkles of blue and white light. Somehow I know they're just sleeping, not dead. It's the way the hair's sprouting across their arms and legs. And the nails, curling out from fingers and toes, like ribbons. It fills me with dread to think how long they must have been lying like this, not moving, just growing, more like trees than people. Symbols flicker and swarm over the surface of the blisters, casting light and shadows on the skin below, sometimes spinning, sometimes drawing lines or nets. *Busy. Watching.*

Three of the blisters are open and empty, wrinkled as walnut shells. And then it dawns on me that this was where Peyto and Erin have come from. Except there's *three* empty blisters, not two. And I remember Peyto talking by the village well about a woman they needed to find . . .

Erin comes alongside me. 'This is the sleeper bay. Forty-nine of us in total.'

'You live here, like this, asleep?'

'These are the pods. They're life-support capsules, like a kind of quarantine, so no germs can reach the people inside,' explains Peyto. 'They're more *preserved* than asleep, kept on slow-life —'

'You mean frozen?'

'Sort of . . . It's called stasis. You don't live but you don't die. Like animals that hibernate. That way the ship can replace your cells when they grow old. It's the flinders that make it possible, though we don't really understand how they work.'

'What?'

'The flinders are old, very old,' goes Peyto. 'From a time when our ancestors had a greater understanding. But we lost that knowledge aeons ago. We know they're powerful but they keep their secrets. Some say that each flinder is itself alive, and that it draws the vitality, the soul of a sleeper deep into its core for safekeeping.'

'But how come you're asleep in the first place?'

'Because of the distance we travelled,' says Erin.

'We'd all have died long ago without stasis. It takes so long to move between stars, between galaxies . . .'

I just gawp at them. I want to laugh, I want to scream. But what's the point? I can see with my own eyes that the impossible has become real. My turn to make like a mudfish.

'You ain't from Earth.' Slowly, like a voice waking me up, what that means sinks in. 'There's *people* on other worlds? *Human* people?'

'It's as much a shock to us as it is to you, Cass,' goes Erin. 'We came here looking for a new world, a new home. The last thing we expected was to find people.'

The thought that they was born on a different world is so off-the-scale strange that I can't stop staring at them. How can they be real? Are they *really* like me? Or are they just *acting* human? But maybe that's what they figured when they first clapped eyes on us.

'We're from Homefleet,' goes Peyto. 'It's an artificial colony of different ships all tethered together.'

I'm just gawping so he goes, 'It's like a convoy in space . . . It's in another galaxy. It's taken us about a billion of your years to get here.'

I just look at him.

'I told you you wouldn't believe me,' he goes.

I think about him holing up in Big Ben in his

pyjamas. He's like a regular Captain Jameson. With a time-travelling galleon. And right now I'm wishing I'd taken a bit more notice of Wilbur's comics . . . I feel like I'm one step away from going loopy and all of a sudden I figure I have to bite my lip on the big questions, the really *huge* questions. All I can deal with is what's happening right now.

I look at the sleeper pods. 'So how come no one else is awake? What about the adults . . .' I remember the third empty sleeper pod. 'It ain't just you two, is it? There's someone else, the woman you're looking for.'

Erin glances at Peyto but he just drops his head.

'There was another,' she says hastily. 'But she's . . . not on the ship any more.'

And then, at last, I twig why this woman might be a touchy subject. She has to be the one with the missing flinder. And if her flinder *is* the artefact we've all been looking for over the last hundred years, then . . . by now she's got to be well dead.

Peyto lifts his head at last. 'After . . . Look, the *Aeolus* only resuscitated us – we don't know why. Maybe it can't wake the others. This was three days ago. When we came out of life-support, the ship was in the highest state of emergency.'

'OK, so the ship's kaput, but can't you just try waking

everyone else up yourselves?'

They look at each other all serious, and I start to get an inkling about how desperate they really are.

'It was the first thing we tried, but the resus system doesn't respond,' says Peyto. 'It would take three weeks to revive people manually.'

'So? Rustle up some sarnies and knuckle down. It's only three weeks—'

'We haven't got three weeks. We've got six days.'

'Before what?'

Peyto looks at me helplessly.

'Before the *Aeolus* crashes into Earth. It says the only thing that will save it and everyone on board is the missing flinder.'

THE MISSING SLEEPER

MY FIRST THOUGHT IS, *LET'S GET THE HELL OFF THIS FLOATING PUS-BALL AND GET BACK TO WILBUR.* THEN I GAZE AT THE RANKS OF SLEEPERS — PEYTO AND ERIN'S FELLOW TRAVELLERS — THE ones who ain't gonna wake up in time. And they're probably blood, bound to each other by the journey, as tight as our little scav clan. It makes me see how terrified Peyto and Erin really are, and how well they've hidden it till now.

'We need to get back,' I go at last. 'To Wilbur.'

'Yes, he'll be worried,' says Erin. 'I don't like to think of him alone . . .' There's a hint of fear in her voice and she don't look me in the eye when she says it.

'Look, I know you think Wilbur's *special* or whatever, that he knows where the missing flinder might be. But he don't have no more clue where it is than I do. If he did then he'd be the first one trotting off to claim it.'

'I know,' she sighs. Then she faces me proper. 'It's just he's our only chance. The ship sent us to find the clock tower, to find The One to help us. We didn't even know where it was. We split up to search on different sides of the river. It was a miracle that Peyto found it. And the only one there was Wilbur.'

Just then I remember Peyto asking Wilbur about his comics, if he'd heard of some character . . . Helen, was it? Or Eleanor? But Wilbur had never heard of her.

'Maybe he'll remember something that will help,' goes Erin, but she don't sound too hopeful. 'But before we head back, we have to reconfigure the shuttle.'

'What's that mean?'

'We can't just fly back to London. Normally the ship would do the resetting for us but its navigation systems are damaged. The only way to do it now is manually from the bridge on the far side. It means going along the central shaft where the hull breach is.'

'Where there's no air?'

'We've got special suits.'

'There's only two suits, remember?' mumbles Peyto.

Erin offers to go and I want to tag along.

'No, it's too dangerous. Besides, I'll be quicker alone.'

'Yeah, and what if something happens, eh?'

'She's right,' Peyto chips in. 'It's safer with two. Let her go. Let her see.'

Erin ain't too chuffed but she beckons me away from the sleeper pods. I glance back at Peyto, and he's just hanging in mid-air with his back to me, like someone drowned.

'Is he all right?' I whisper.

'Just tired, I think. We've been going non-stop for days now. And it's been hardest on him . . .'

'What d'you mean?'

'Let me get you into a suit, then I'll tell you.'

She guides me along the main chamber till we reach this big hollow set into the wall. There are twelve slots in it like a clock face, and two of them are taken up with these little puppet things with huge heads. They look a bit creepy, like hanging skins with see-through skulls.

'Take a suit,' urges Erin.

'They're a bit small, ain't they? Like for little kids.'

'That's their default state. When you start getting in one, it'll expand to fit you.'

'Where's all the other suits gone then?'

'Good question. They've just disappeared. The ship said they got lost in the emergency.'

'How come it ain't speaking now?'

'I don't know. It speaks when you least expect it to.

When it's got something to say, I suppose.'

I put my arm into one of the suit sleeves and it swallows my hand, all greasy and slick. It bloats up in some places and goes stiff in others, surrounding and supporting me. Erin helps me with the skull helmet. When that hinges down, I get a misty shrimp-shell view, but then it suddenly goes clear and lights flare up from the collar. It smells yeasty inside. I can feel the lining fizzing and bubbling against my skin.

'Don't worry about that – it's just the air supply coming online. It'll settle down in a minute.' Her voice is all crackly, right with me inside my helmet.

She kits up, too, and then she touches a button on the wall that's dark and rough like a scab, then all this skin shoots out from the edge of the hollow and snaps together like a bubble, cutting us off from the main chamber.

'This is the airlock,' she goes. 'Ahead of us on the far side is the hull breach. You OK?'

I put up my thumbs. The truth is I'm slightly cacking it. But Erin gives a smile to bolster me up. She looks so different to me then – her face so *at home* behind the face-plate. Because we don't weigh nothing, her hair is swaying about inside the helmet doing loops round the ear-muffs like baby snakes, and she ain't all closed up any more.

Up till now, the whole idea that I'm thirteen miles above the ground ain't sunk in. So I ain't really ready for when the airlock bubble spits us out the other side. First, the sound dies, then the crisp shadows of space swallow me up.

When she'd said 'hull breach', I'd figured on a little hole in the wall, not a bloody great crater. The walls of the ship are torn open, layers twisted and shredded into stumps, like shattered bones. A web of loose veins, thin as spider silk, wafts at the edges, and past a cloud of twinkling wreckage all the vastness of the universe sends me into a quiet terror. What strikes me dumb is that there ain't a thing between the ends of my fingers and the next star. Wilbur says that some stars you look at ain't even there no more, cos by the time the light gets to us, they've died out. Thinking about this, I feel like I'm one stride away from being lost for ever.

And then as I'm gazing at this ocean of black, the Earth wheels into view. A blazing rim of blue fire. The sky and the land and the seas are all swirling inside one arc, shimmering bands and storms all caught up in a plate of pearl, turning in the dark. And it's all so silent and terrible somehow. Like it's got a *life* of its own, nothing to do with the tiny creatures that bumble around on its surface. Cos it's hard to picture Wilbur down there somewhere, patting Sheba, and the breath steaming out from both their mouths. He's so out of reach, it gives me the horrors. But, God alive, if he could see me now! This is Wilbur's dream I'm living out – swanning about in a proper space suit!

Erin comes alongside and as I turn, her helmet nudges mine and I see her just smiling sadly at me, like she's guessed what I'm thinking, that up here, far away, the world is a different thing, a stranger to us.

She anchors us both up with a tube like a link of sausages, then she presses something that looks like a hairy mole on the forearm of her suit skin, and this cable shoots out. It spools clear and catches onto the far wall, then she reels it in, dragging us along, away from the breach.

'What happened back there?' I ask at last. 'The hole, I mean.'

'No idea. The one person who would know isn't around any more.'

'From the third empty pod?'

'Yes. Halina – Peyto's mother.'

'His mother?'

My first thought is one I keep to myself – *So you ain't brother and sister, then*.

'All I know is what should have happened. If the

Aeolus finds a suitable planet, then we're meant to terraform it ready for colonisation.'

'Too much boffin-talk. Tell me in English.'

'OK, imagine the ship finds a rock floating in space around a star like the sun – no air, no water, no life. We orbit at a safe distance, start off chemical reactions, make an atmosphere and oceans, and turn the rock into a place where we can grow food and have proper lives. That's what terraforming means.'

'Don't sound that easy.'

'Well, it takes a long time. That's why we stay asleep. We don't know how it works exactly but we do it through the flinders, through our dreams.'

'And the ship's meant to shake you all out of bed when the cake's baked?'

Erin gives me a look like she'd rather go back to the boffin-talk.

'That's right. Except, well, only Halina was woken up.'

'Then what?'

'That's the hazy part. The thing is – if everything had gone to plan there'd be air and water on this planet, but not life yet, not *people*.'

'So your alarm call was a bit late?'

She sighs as if getting ready to explain something

tricky. But right then the ship speaks. And that creeps me out, cos it's like it's been listening to us the whole time. Its voice is deep and soft as it comes to me through the helmet, and I know it ain't even close to being human.

'This vessel needs *all* the flinders with their sleepers or it cannot be repaired. Without the forty-nine, this vessel and all those aboard are doomed. If this vessel perishes, its death will devastate the Earth.'

'Hey, what do you mean, devastate the Earth?' I go.

Erin flashes me a warning look.

'The sleepers and their flinders nurture the Earth, they protect it from harm. Without them, a plague of wars such as this world has never seen will sweep across all lands. You must find the missing flinder. You must find Halina.'

'But how can Halina even be alive now?' says Erin. 'The missing flinder has been lost on the planet for a hundred years or more. Why didn't you speak of this? Why didn't you resuscitate us earlier?'

'Only now is it time for you to wake. The flinder is with her. Find Halina and you will find the flinder.'

'We're still searching. We came to the tower you spoke of, and there was a boy there. But he doesn't know anything.'

'He knows.' The answer comes slowly, from a faraway place.

'What makes you think that?' I go. Erin gives me daggers but I ignore her. 'I mean, why would he know?'

'He is the key. His heart is true. Through the sleepers, I see the shape of *living* minds, *his* mind. His dreams of this flinder are strong. He can sense where it lies.'

I tap the side of my helmet at Erin. 'Wilbur? I think you've got your wires crossed or something. He don't know squat.' But my voice sounds shaky. And I'm thinking about my little brother's artefact clues . . . Erin does a furious hand-chop at her neck to get me to zip it and she's right – it don't make sense to get the *Aeolus* riled. 'Specially when it's clearly as mad as a bag of spanners.

'The flinders must not be earthbound. They are of the sky, of dreaming. Forty-nine flinders for forty-nine sleepers. Together we will watch over the Earth.' It sounds like it's been listening in on old Jacob Armitage's Sunday sermons.

There's a silent question in the frown Erin throws at me, then she says, 'But the sleepers must wake now, mustn't they? This planet is terraformed.'

No answer.

'You have to tell us what happened to Halina,' she

demands. 'Why did she leave?'

But the ship ain't speaking. Which, to me, is a tad suspect. We wait, but clearly the conversation is over. I take a breath to say something, but Erin shakes her head at me.

At last we reach the far end of the shaft where there's another blast hole, bigger than the first. And it don't take a rocket boffin to figure out there's been a struggle here. The bridge itself is a proper maze with loads of tubeways worming past each other, linking up at junctions and bulging with veins.

Bits of debris hang in drifts that get thicker as we delve onwards – lumps of glittery black stuff like coal. They knock against my helmet and shatter into soot.

'What's all this?'

'Frozen flesh – from where the ship was damaged. Some of the navigation equipment has been destroyed. We can't maintain a safe orbit without it. That's why it needs the missing flinder so it can repair properly. Otherwise it'll burn up in the atmosphere and crash into the Earth.'

There's a hairpin bend ahead and before I know it I'm hanging over this whacking great hole into nowhere, all the stars under my feet, which is like *the* worst rush of vertigo I've ever had.

'Whoa!'

'Sorry, I should've warned you. That's the dock for the other shuttle – the one Halina used to get to Earth. There would have been no reason for the *Aeolus* to seal it up because all the air in the bridge and the central shaft was already lost to the breach.'

We squeeze at last into a poky space crusted over with bubble screens all rattling out lines and lines of writing. I can't read but even I can see it ain't alien writing.

'Hey, it's all in English,' I go. 'It takes you a billion years to get here and you speak English?'

'The ship says the flinders equipped us with the language we needed for our mission on Earth. When we woke up from stasis, we couldn't remember any Homefleet words. Your language is the only language we know now.'

I keep looking round over my shoulder cos I really don't like that the ship ain't talking to us no more.

'So how does the shuttle resetting work?'

Erin points at a jagged cut below the screens. It looks like someone's taken an axe to it and there's all this spongy, tangly gunk inside, like sheep's guts.

'All the control centres for the shuttle are severed from the rest of the ship's nervous system.'

'And that means what, exactly?'

She thrusts both hands into the wound. 'I have to bridge the gap. Don't be alarmed – I probably won't make much sense for a while.'

'You ain't making sense right now.'

But then she closes her eyes and starts shaking.

'Erin?'

Her face goes slack.

'ERIN!'

I shake her and try to pull her arms out, but they're jammed in pretty good, all coiled up in the innards . . . And just as I start to panic Erin starts calmly reeling off some nonsense, like 'geo-sink stable' and 'air equal-lies' and 'Anglia moment-tum in hold pattern', all in this flat voice like she's reading raffle numbers, bored out of her box. And then, all of a sudden, it's over and she opens her eyes.

'It's done. The shuttle's re-primed. Let's get back to Peyto.'

I ain't sorry. This side of the ship is giving me the creeps – it's too hemmed in, with too many hidden nooks and turns.

We head back in silence. The shaft has moved and the hull breach is now facing outwards to the bare universe. And the black view is heartless, a place where prayers might get lost. Looking at the emptiness, I'm suddenly desperate for home, and I think about these space travellers, how they set out one day, never really knowing if they'd find a place to settle. Scavving ain't no picnic but it's *something* at least.

When we get back to the sleeper side, Peyto's waiting, but when I get closer I see that his eyes are all red. He looks at us, all quiet and lost, and I know he's been crying.

I give him a hug then, cos it's awful to see him so upset.

He chokes back his tears. 'She's dead.'

And there ain't nothing I can say to that. Cos it has to be true.

'She's dead, isn't she?' he yells at the *Aeolus*.

No answer.

'Maybe there's a way she's still alive,' says Erin gently. 'Maybe she's in stasis or something . . .'

'How, Erin? There's nothing to keep her in stasis on Earth. She's dead. She died years ago while I slept.'

'We can't give up,' she pleads. 'The others need us . . .' She's on the edge of tears now, too.

Peyto takes a couple of deep breaths to get himself under control. 'I knew she was dead. From the moment I woke up. I *felt* it.'

'Oh, Peyto . . .' Erin takes his hand. 'We've got to keep going. We've *got to*. It's not just us any more, it's the world down there too, it's everyone.'

He looks at her at last. 'What do you mean?'

'The Aeolus said if the sleepers die, then the whole world will be in terrible danger.'

PLANS AND LIES

SEEING PEYTO BRINGS IT ALL BACK TO ME, ABOUT MY OWN MUM. I REMEMBER THE FEELING WHEN SHE DIED. YOU SUCK YOURSELF IN, BUNCH YOURSELF UP, BUT YOUR HEAD GOES OUT WANDERING into daydreams and memories, searching for that face you know you won't see again. And when you come back to yourself, you're a bit older, a bit harder.

Slowly, a calm settles down on us all. I check my watch cos I've lost all sense of time up here, and it don't seem possible we've been on the ship less than an hour. Erin hands me something then. It's a silky cuff, see-through and frilly at the edges. The solemn way she hands it to me, it's like sealing a pact.

'What's this?'

'It's a . . .' She pauses, to spare me the boffin term, I think. 'It's like a countdown. You put it on your wrist, like your watch.' She draws up her sleeve to show me hers, close to the skin, and all you can see are marks there like a tattoo. Except the marks are pulsing.

'I've synched yours up to show the same thing as mine and Peyto's.'

I slip the cuff over my hand and it comes to life – coils of ink on the underside of my wrist, itching a bit near the veins.

'A countdown to what?' I go.

'A countdown to . . . well, until it's too late.'

The coils straighten into six bands, each one made up of dots no bigger than freckles. The top band is slightly shorter than the others. As I gaze at it, one of the freckles vanishes. I feel it prick me slightly. And then I get it – each freckle is an hour and I've just lost one. Twenty-four hours in each band. Six bands for six days . . .

There ain't much to say about the journey back. We're all wrecked, 'specially Peyto who did his first ever scav shift on top of everything else. We stash the suits back in the hollow, strap into the shuttle and silently launch off from the *Aeolus*. A few minutes later Erin tells us to brace ourselves for 're-entry', which is thunderous, like we're being shaken to pieces. But then the roar drops away, and the screens show us skimming into the

Thames upriver towards the Jubilee tunnel.

My weight comes back, and it's good to feel my bones settling into place, to be *solid* again. I take a deep breath of chilly London air as the shuttle roof parts for us – just the smallest of openings.

'Won't the Vlads spot us?' I go.

'Get up there,' answers Erin. 'Tell me what you can see.'

Peyto helps me stand on one of the chairs so I'm practically level with the river surface, just peeking over a furrow of water so smooth that it's like a fold of black velvet. No bubbles, no foam. The junk of the river, plastic bags and old buoys, bobs past my face, but the wake of the shuttle is so slight it might as well be a knife drawing through the currents.

Some way ahead, I spot the wide stone arches of London Bridge but they're dark, no signs of movement. Behind me, though, the crumbled stumps of Tower Bridge are clustered with searchlights, trained onto the water.

I duck down. 'It's clear ahead. But there's a load of action on the last bridge.'

'They must have seen us come down into the river,' mutters Erin. 'No way round that.'

I take up my look-out position again, but the way

ahead is quiet, past the broken humps of Southwark, the twisted wreckage of the Millennium Bridge. Even the two standing bridges, Blackfriars and Waterloo, are empty, so I start to breathe easier. Maybe the Vlads are all so caught up with where we came down that they left these bridges unmanned. And it's a shock to be so *glued* to a proper place again, to hear the lap of water, to see the city. Now as I look at the night sky, I know it's the same, but somehow the endless darkness of space ain't such a threat from down here.

Erin goes, 'I've got control to steer now that it's not an emergency. Which bank? North or south?'

'Best to land the same side as the dinghy,' I go. 'Then we can take it back to where Wilbur is . . .'

Peyto just nods. His tears are over, but he looks proper haunted – all the stuffing battered out of him, like going to the ship has brung it all home to roost just how bad things are.

Erin glances at me, then she strokes the right-hand wall of the shuttle, and we veer towards the north bank. We all clamber out into the shallows, near the ruins of Westminster Bridge, then the shuttle closes up and disappears into the river. All's quiet as we scramble up the bank, then down to the tunnel floor, where the water's still low and the dinghy's still tied up, thank

God. I try not to get too chewed up about Wilbur. It's only been a few hours, but what with everything that's happened it feels like a week. The ship don't seem real just then. It's like the stuff of fireside stories.

We paddle like ten men back towards the south bank, which is proper hard work cos we're going against the flow now. The moonlit hole at the far end of the tunnel gets bigger but there ain't no sign of Wilbur.

'Where is he?' goes Erin. 'Surely he'd be able to see the torch.'

'Well, I did tell him to stick with Sheba on pain of death . . .' But the truth is, I'm getting nervy, too.

'I see him!' cries Peyto.

And there he is, leaping up and down like a jackrabbit.

When we reach the far end, I slosh through the shallows and give him a mighty hug. 'How's Sheba?'

'Dozing off. I didn't think you were ever coming back! I just came down for a last look and I saw the torch!'

'Well, you did well holding the fort. We got what we came for, so let's get back now before Dad gets wind, eh?'

Wilbur gives us all a hard stare then. 'You've got to let me in on it,' he goes.

- 133 -

'Hey, ease up, will you?' I glance at the others. 'There ain't nothing to be let in on, you buffoon—'

'I saw it, Cass. I saw it and I *heard* it. A rocket shooting out of the river. It lit up the sky all white.'

'Ah . . .'

'I want to know, Cass. I can help. You know I can.'

I'm too plain knackered to lie.

'We must tell him,' goes Peyto.

'Yes, Cass,' urges Erin. 'Wilbur could know something important.'

I think about where I've been, how it'd almost be cruel not to let him in on it now. And I've got to admit there'd be some kind of relief just offloading what's just happened, though God knows I've tried to keep him in the dark this far.

So after we haul the dinghy back up into its hiding place, we tell him. Everything. Well, nearly everything. Or anyhow Peyto does. And it's like telling the story chivvies him out of his worries, bucks him up. I just chip in at the end making sure to cut out the bit about the whole world going to rack and ruin. Things is desperate enough without scaring Wilbur to death on that score. One sharp look at Peyto and Erin and they get my drift. Wilbur listens goggle-eyed without saying a word for the whole journey back to Elephant and

Castle. Peyto and Erin show him their flinders and he gazes at them, but his face is hard to read. He don't even reach out to touch them which is the first thing I expected him to do. He just leans closer to their haloes of light, staring at all the tiny patterns blooming on the surfaces, gobsmacked but shy. And he just gives this little shiver, and his eyelids flicker, like someone's just walked over his grave.

'How come they're different?' he goes.

He's right, but it's hardly the most staggering thing about the flinders. And yet, it *is* the kind of thing Wilbur would spot about them.

'Well, I don't know,' says Erin at last, as if she's only just realised it herself. 'Each one is a special match for a person. And because each person is different, I suppose each flinder is different. It's said that you don't choose a flinder, it chooses you.'

He just nods at that, like it makes perfect sense.

'Wish I'd been there, on the ship,' is all he says.

'It said you'd be there, at the tower, at Big Ben,' goes Erin. 'How did you get the idea to go there in the first place?'

'I thought the artefact was there, that's all.' From the inside of his coat he brings out a roll of Captain Jameson comics. 'I pick up clues about where to try looking from these.'

'And Halina, are you sure you haven't heard of her?' asks Peyto. 'I know I asked you before but . . .'

Wilbur shakes his head and Peyto looks crestfallen. 'I suppose the ship could be wrong – about Wilbur knowing something.'

'Maybe I just don't know *yet*.' Vintage Wilbur – spooky eight-year-old pronouncement number thirty-one.

'Hang on, you said you found something else at Big Ben,' I try. 'The so-cod-poo or something.'

'Sudoku – it's a number puzzle. Gramps reckons numbers are important, too.'

'You been talking to Gramps? You never said.'

Wilbur looks guilty. 'Sometimes. I go Sundays.' Dad gives him the day off on Sundays, cos scavving the whole time's a real grind for kids.

'You're meant to be sticking in the village!' I go.

Peyto rests his hand gently on my shoulder. 'What else does Gramps say?'

'Just bits and pieces. He mumbles a lot. Forgets I'm there, I think.' He looks up at us more brightly. 'But he collects clues, too. On the other side of the river.' He points at the dinghy we've just put back in its hiding place. 'That's his boat.'

'Bloody hell, Wilbur! Why didn't you tell us that before?'

He picks at his mittens. 'I thought you'd get mad at me.'

'Gramps is a *looter*?'

'Then maybe he's close to tracking it down?' goes Erin.

They all look at me as I think it through. 'He's a crazy old duffer sometimes . . . But still, there ain't no point in us just signing up for another scav shift. So maybe he's right, that scavving ain't the way. It's too slow . . .' I rub at the countdown cuff Erin gave me, thinking of the time draining away, like grains in an egg-timer. 'I reckon it's worth paying Gramps a visit tomorrow.'

Back at Elephant and Castle, we head for the stables. I get Peyto and Erin sorted with some old blankets and set them up a bed on the hay. It ain't exactly the Ritz but with all the animals in there it's pretty cosy.

'You'll come and find us tomorrow?' goes Erin. She sounds on the back foot again, now we're back on Earth.

'Yeah, course. I've got to get out of scavving . . .' I think about Dad struggling alone on the shift with his gammy leg. 'But I'll figure out something.'

I watch them bed down, fumbling with their blankets, and suddenly I don't want to leave them either.

'Toodlepip, then,' I go.

Peyto looks at me blank.

'Goodnight,' I try, and the word sounds all proper – not like me at all.

He grins back. 'Toodlepip.' Like the worst Cockney accent ever.

I let Wilbur unhitch Sheba while I head back to our hut. I'm trying to dream up an excuse for why we've been gone so long but my head's fried. And worst luck, Dad's waiting up, staring at the remains of the fire, his face stewing in fury.

'Where the hell have you been?'

Then Wilbur comes in and, before I can open my mouth, he goes, 'It's my fault. I took an apple to Sheba, but when I was feeding her, I got all dizzy. Reckon I had one of my spells . . .'

I look over at Wilbur then and I'm gobsmacked to see he's clutching his specs, and he's got this whopping black eye and a cut across his forehead.

Dad hobbles over and leads him towards the fire. I hope he's flustered enough not to notice the damage is a bit too fresh to have happened much more than two minutes ago.

Hating myself, I pick up the lie and run with it. 'After the meeting, I went off to look for him. I thought I'd find him easy but I searched all over.'

'And you didn't think to tell me your brother was missing?'

I stare at the floor.

'I never figured on you being so stupid, Cass. He could've been anywhere!'

'Sorry . . .'

He turns to Wilbur. 'You black out, son?'

'Yeah, dunno how long. Had all this froth on my face like that time in the summer.'

He's all wobbly and pale, and that ain't acting, so I figure he must've cracked himself pretty hard back at Sheba's stable. There's a couple of vicious splinters poking out his bonce.

'I don't feel that good,' goes Wilbur, looking all set to pass out on us.

'Lay down here. Cass, fetch some water!'

We bathe his head, yank out the splinters and make up a poultice. Ten minutes later he's out for the count. I'm in shock – I can't believe he'd go that far to cover up for us.

Dad can't even look at me when he speaks at last. 'I want you to stay back tomorrow, keep an eye on him.

No point in him tagging along for a shift, not in that state.'

'All right. Look, I'm sorry, Dad.'

'So you said.'

I want to ask him about the rest of the meeting, about Gramps, but there ain't no point, cos I can tell he's closed me off now.

For a while as I lie down, my head's just spinning, whirring away, thinking about flying ships, and being weightless, and the curve of the Earth with its trapped skies stretching away from me . . .

It feels like I've been out for five minutes when Wilbur shakes me awake. Sunlight is peeking through cracks in the roof.

'Cass, we've got to go!'

Peyto and Erin are hovering warily by the entrance.

'Where's Dad?'

'He went ages ago. There was soldiers up at the muster point checking all scavs reporting for work. Old Fred says they've gone to Lambeth village looking for anyone that's not a proper scav, anyone that's a stranger. They must've seen the shuttle coming back.'

THE FIRST SCAV

I SCRAMBLE OUT OF BED, AND BUNG SOME STUFF INTO MY PACK — WATER BOTTLES, EXTRA ROPE, BISCUITS.

'IT AIN'T GONNA BE LONG BEFORE THEM SOLDIERS MAKE THEIR way here. We've got to make tracks, find Gramps.'

'He doesn't live around here?' goes Peyto.

'Nah, he's got a shack up on the edge of Battersea Woods.'

'What are we going to tell him?' asks Erin. 'About us, I mean.'

'Little as possible, I reckon. Let me do the talking, cos I know how he ticks. He can get pretty worked up about finding the artefact. But there ain't no sense in mixing in things about ships and sleepers and what-have-you.'

I stop for a moment and stare at Wilbur. Behind

the bottle-bottom specs, his eye's gone all purple and yellow, closed in like a fat mussel. I realise I can't leave him here with soldiers coming.

'You good to go?'

He nods too much, the way kids do.

'If Dad could see you now, hopping about fresh as a daisy, he'd be mad. Some casualty you turned out to be.'

He gives me one of his cheesy grins.

'Don't pull any more stunts like that, Wilbur. I mean it. Things is dangerous enough as it is, without you bashing your own head in.'

'It's a beaut, though, eh, Cass?'

'Yeah, real prize-fighter.'

But I don't want to chew him out too much – it ain't often you get spared a scav shift.

Outside, there's a few old dears about but nobody looking our way. The last thing I need is someone clocking us when we leave.

We slip out the settlement and head southwest towards Battersea. It's a clear morning, still and bright, touched with a fur of frost. We scout further south than the crow flies to give Lambeth a wide berth, but we don't see no soldiers. I want to steer clear of the main tracks, and that means trudging over the slurry ground between settlements. It's proper hard work, cos when the rain first hits it, slag dust goes into this claggy mess that glues to your boots. The only thing that grows on it is brambles, which makes ploughing through it ten times harder. It's two hours before we start bending up north again towards the river.

On the way Peyto goes to Wilbur, 'So how did anyone know to ever start looking for the artefact? Back at Big Ben you said Vlads were searching in London, even before the germ attacks. How did they know to come looking here?'

Wilbur skips along to keep up, all perky that Peyto's taking an interest in what he knows. 'Gramps told me it was a man called Morgan Bartlett – the very first scav – who started the search, before the Quark Wars.'

This is a new one on me. 'How can Gramps know who the first scav was?' I scoff.

Wilbur sticks his chin out. 'Not a scav like us, I suppose. Scav's just short for *scavenger*.'

'All right,' chips in Erin. 'But what made him look in the first place?'

'That's what I'm trying to tell you. Morgan Bartlett found a . . . *disturbance*. That's what Gramps says.' Wilbur takes a deep breath and the way he speaks then, it's like he's reciting it word for word, from memory.

'Before the war, there were computers everywhere, and they were connected up with each other. London was like a great sea of light and words and sound. And people relied on their computers for everything, but not a single one of these machines was what you'd call clever or alive, not in the same way as a human being. Then one man, this Morgan Bartlett, came across signs of something living and hiding in the connections between computers – something with a voice and a mind of its own, like a ghost running loose in the electricity.'

I exchange glances with Peyto and Erin, and I think about them echoes I felt inside the flinders, like voices. It's like a kid's story, the way he tells it. Something Gramps spouted off to shut Wilbur up during one of his Sunday visits. But still, maybe there's something in it. We're all waiting for more but Wilbur clams up.

'So, then what happened?' urges Peyto.

'Gramps never said. He had a coughing fit.'

'Bleeding Nora, Wilbur – how come you kept all this quiet? Gramps' dinghy, your Sunday visits, this Morgan flippin' Bartlett!'

'You never wanted to listen before,' he complains.

'Well, we're all ears now,' I go, rolling my eyes at Peyto. 'Any more secrets you want to lay on us, just go right ahead.'

Battersea Woods is all raised up on a wide mound. Like all the old parks, it stands out higher than the wasteground, like an island with its proper trees – oaks and sycamore and hawthorn, winter-bare now. No one's really sure how come the Vlads never sent scavs into the parks. I mean, you'd think the artefact could be buried there just as much as anywhere else, but the rumour is they've narrowed it down to a man-made place, a proper London building. But how they know that is anyone's guess.

Scav settlers tend to steer clear of the old parks. They're untamed, abandoned to the undergrowth, homes to foxes and wild dogs and birds. And the truth is, I've never liked it here, even though I've been to see Gramps plenty of times as a kid. I don't like the branches clawing at my face, or the dead-leaf smell or the startled birds or the fungus. I don't like the shapes of the trees or their roots – naked and old and peeling. And I know Wilbur feels the same way. But our space-travelling pioneers are wide-eyed at it all. I watch them stare at the tree--tops and run their hands over the bracken stumps, the rotting wood of fallen trunks. But maybe if I'd been cooped up in a box for a billion years I'd be spellbound by this manky old wood, too.

We come at last to the lake. Clogged up with weeds and sludge, it's more like a swamp now, but Gramps says this was once a place for pleasure boats and picnics. We circle the bank and come to a sunken clearing, the site of the old pump house, and on the far side is Gramps's falling-down shack of timber and turf. It's got one cracked window and a canvas sheet for a door, and poking out the lean-to roof is a rusted pipe chimney. There ain't no sign of a fire, though, and no one answers as I call out.

Inside there's just a makeshift bed of busted branches and dry grass with a ratty old blanket and some dirty pots. The ashes of the fire are warm, though.

'He ain't gone far. Must've gone to check his traps, or something.'

'He lives here on his own?' Erin wrinkles her nose at the smell, and I have to admit it looks like the old duffer has let himself go a bit.

She stands there, hugging herself, looking warily at all the junk. 'Why doesn't he live with everyone else in the settlement?'

'He fell out big-time with my dad after Mum died. Bit of a long story. He's lived here about five years now, but even before that he had the shack up here for trapping game. In the good old days he used to look after me and

Wilbur in the summer, when we was too young for scavving.'

'And he's searching for the artefact on his own?'

I'm about to answer when we all hear the snick of a gun being cocked.

'And who wants to know?' demands a voice from outside.

We all step out into the light. Gramps is standing just a few metres away, aiming a huge pistol at us. That's a hell of a shock – I've never seen him wield anything more dangerous than a skinning knife. And nobody I know has even got a gun.

'Gramps, it's me. Cass.'

Slowly he lowers the pistol.

'I nearly shot you dead. Thought you were Vlads.'

'I gave you a shout, but there wasn't no answer.'

'What do you want, Cass?' He stuffs the pistol in his belt and glares at us.

'We heard what you said at the meeting,' I go. 'About how scavving wasn't the way to find the artefact and all that. We thought you could do with some help, you know.'

I go for casual but it comes out false, like I've been rehearsing it.

He clocks each of us in turn, lingering most on

Wilbur, though he never says a word about the black eye. It dawns on me that it's been ages since I've spoken to him face to face. He's always been a moody old hermit but he seems more wary now, like he don't even know us no more.

'So you're not scavving these days, eh?' he goes.

'Well, we ain't about to hang up the bins just yet. But we figured your way might be worth a go.'

'Pack off home. It's too dangerous . . .'

'Why don't you listen to us?' goes Peyto. 'We gave up a day's pay to come out here and see you.'

There's a twitch in Gramps' beard that might be a smile. 'Well, I am honoured.' He nods towards Erin. 'The two newcomers at the meeting. And just who might you be, then?'

'Just people who are searching for the same thing you are. Sometimes five heads are better than one.'

'You and your mate not from London, eh?'

When Peyto don't reply, he goes, 'And what exactly do you bring to the search, son?'

'Look, we're offering to help you,' says Erin. 'I don't see too many other volunteers queueing up at your shack!'

'That's as maybe, young lady. But I don't ask the likes of children for help.'

'Is that how come you ain't found it yet?' I go, feeling sore at having dragged everyone out here now.

'You didn't just come out here on a whim, eh? Give me one good reason why I should hear you out.'

'Because we know what it looks like,' goes Peyto.

If that's a bombshell, Gramps don't let on. He just pulls at his grubby whiskers, and sucks his teeth.

'And how would you know that, seeing as no one in living memory has ever set eyes on it?'

'Because I've held one just like it in my hands.'

Gramps don't even blink for a full ten seconds. He just drills his gaze right into Peyto.

Then at last he says, 'So you know there's more than one.'

'There's forty-nine.'

Gramps goes all goggle-eyed for a moment but then he settles himself. 'Well, seems I was a bit hasty, eh? Why don't you tell me some more interesting things on the subject of the *forty-nine* artefacts?'

'You tell *us* something,' goes Wilbur. 'About that voice Morgan Bartlett found in the computers.'

'So, you told them about old Morgan Bartlett, eh?'

Gramps looks suddenly weary then, and he parks himself on a tree stump before going on.

'My father told me about Bartlett, and his father

before him. Just a fireside story passed down. But it struck me as true, because after that I heard the Vlad boffins talking about it once, when some promising bit of poke had been found and our crusher was shut down. They spoke then of a thing living in the circuits of computers, though they never mentioned the name Bartlett.'

'But what did this *living thing* say to Bartlett?' goes Peyto.

'It said it was called the *Aeolus*, the keeper of the winds, and that it held the storms of war in check.'

I snatch a glance at Peyto. I'm thinking, *The ship was able to speak here, on Earth, through computers? How? But maybe it could once, and now it can't cos of the emergency making it sick, or maybe cos all the computers down here are kaput now . . .*

'It said it was trying to find a special object it had lost,' continues Gramps. 'Something trapped here in London. It said this *artefact* was a thing of immense power and knowledge from a far-gone age, and that perhaps it held the key to life itself. It said that without this artefact it would die, and then the whole world would suffer – wars would rage for ever.'

Gramps spots me eyeballing Peyto, but he carries on. 'It warned him that indeed a terrible war was coming that would lay waste to England and all the lands east of here to Russia, and that one day an invading army would come to London looking to use the artefact for evil purposes. So, to keep it out of the wrong hands, it gave him clues about where the artefact could be found.'

'But at the meeting you said you'd just hand it over to the Vlads if you found it, so they'd leave London alone!' blurts Peyto. 'You'd let it be used for evil!'

Gramps flashes him a look of anger. But then his eyes soften. 'Well, son, what people *say* at village meetings is one thing. It's what they *do* that really matters. I was just trying to whip everyone up, to get them away from scavving, to get them using their heads to find it. That lot won't go out on a limb just because I say the artefact is powerful. But they might if it meant the Vlads packing off back to Russia and leaving us in peace.'

'So you lied to them?' goes Wilbur.

'I wanted to spur them on. If the artefact is as truly powerful as the stories say, then it'd make sense for scavs to find it first, don't you think?'

'Wait a minute,' Erin pipes up. 'You said this *Aeolus* only gave Morgan Bartlett clues about the artefact. Why didn't it just say where it was?'

'Good question,' goes Gramps. 'Because it said the

artefact wasn't ready to be found. A special person needed to find it, to make it even stronger, but that person wasn't yet born. Bartlett's job was to listen to all these clues and find a way to preserve them for the future.'

Wilbur's voice is just a whisper. 'So he left those clues behind without ever knowing where the artefact really was?'

'That's right. He may have died in the war like most other Londoners but somewhere buried in London is the trail he left behind – a trail I've been following for fifty years.'

'So you've found Bartlett's clues then?' I go.

'Yes, I believe I've found some of them.'

'So where are they?'

He points to his smelly old hermit gaff with its one ratty blanket and scuzzy pots.

My heart sinks then, cos his eyes have gone all nutty, and how can this falling-down shack lead to anything? I glance at Peyto and Erin to see what they're making of it all but they're just staring at him, all wide-eyed and breathless. And after everything that's happened, I'm desperate for just the smallest crumb of hope, anything.

He strides up to the shack and swishes back the

canvas sheet like he's the king of bonkers. We all just stand there, waiting.

'Well, do you want to see Bartlett's hoard of clues or don't you?'

That's when I figure he's really cracked, as we all huddle together inside his filthy hovel. And I'm about to cry with the sheer disappointment of it, cos how can this be going anywhere?

But then Gramps shoves his bed to one side, and there, set into the ground, is a trap door.

THE AMAZING ADVENTURES OF CAPTAIN JAMESON – ISSUE 13

GRAMPS FLICKS ON A TORCH AND LEADS THE WAY DOWN SOME STEPS INTO A DRIPPING TUNNEL CAKED IN LIMESCALE. FOR A MOMENT I THINK ABOUT HIS DINGHY STASHED AT THE JUBILEE tunnel, the notepad and the maps. Still, I keep shtoom, cos Gramps is bound to go spare if he knew we'd used his dinghy to go on a night-time trip north of the river.

We follow him through the tunnel into a cellar room piled floor to ceiling with crates and tool boxes and binliners. Glinting in the torch beam are all these heaps of old computer bits and bobs – screens and wires and 'lectric boards, printing machines and towers of silver discs, ripped-out number pads and keyboards, and a thousand more gizmos that I ain't even got a name for – a hoard of poke that beggars belief. So all these years he must have been beavering away down here in secret while me and Wilbur played on the grass outside.

'How did you get it all here?' I go.

'I combed the unscavved city at night and hauled it back here piece by piece. I mended the computers, wired them to old batteries and trawled through their memories for Bartlett's clues.'

I can't see his face but I can hear it in his voice – proud of what he's done, but sad, too. Like he's given his life to this hoard of clues, but somehow it ain't exactly worked out.

He moves to the far end of the cellar and there on the wall is a massive map of London. It's plastered with notes and scribbles and photos and arrows, and peppered with hundreds of little coloured pins. Some of the pins make patterns like S-shapes or spirals. It looks like the life's work of a lunatic.

'What's that?' goes Wilbur, all quiet, like he's scared of what the answer might be.

'My incident map. The pins mark the locations of computers where I think the voice guarding the artefact left a trace of its passing. Morgan Bartlett himself probably tracked them down, too. I've checked most of them – they in turn have led to other clues. Anything important is marked on the map – places where the artefact could be hidden.'

We all gaze at it. I can't read the scribbles but there's loads of tiny photos skewered together in little stacks. I reach up and start thumbing through them – there's statues and billboards and plaques on walls and pub signs. Alleyways and stairwells and rooftop terraces and balconies. Graffiti and flyposters, sundials and weather vanes. All the forgotten corners of London.

'Well?' goes Gramps at last.

He's got this fixed grin on his face like he's waiting for me to say something.

'Well what?'

'Well, do you see anything in the clues? There must be something – something I've missed.'

And I'm thinking, *How do you know there's anything here to see, you batty old fruit-cake?*

But to humour him, I go, 'There's a lot here, Gramps.' I turn to the others. 'We need some time to check it all out, don't we?'

They all go mudfish on me, but then Peyto pipes up. 'Which ones are your clues and which ones are Bartlett's?'

It's a funny question, I think, but there's an edge to Peyto's voice. Like his real question is, *Where's the original trail? Cos your crazy incident map's gone and messed it all up.*

Gramps gets a twist in his gob then that ain't pretty to watch. 'What does it matter? Bartlett's dead now – I've picked up his work. Everything you see is a possible lead.'

'Is the trail getting any stronger?' goes Erin. 'I mean, is there a place on here that we can search right now?'

I'm thinking, *Nice one, Erin. Let's boil it down a bit. 'Specially as the clock's running down and we ain't got another hundred years to keep looking . . .*

Gramps squints at the map, flicking through all the little photo stacks, and I can tell he's just winging it. He ain't got the faintest idea.

Then his torch dies and I can't see a sausage.

'I've got spare batteries up top,' mutters Gramps. 'I'll just be a minute.'

After he's traipsed back up the steps I flick out my lighter and gather everyone round the flame.

'What do you think, then?'

Peyto shrugs.

'It's guff, innit?' I go. 'He's lost his marbles. You get more sense out of Mabel reading your fortune.'

'Let's not be so quick to judge,' says Erin. 'I mean, he's spent years gathering all this information.'

'Yeah, but look at it. Every one of them pins is a stab in the dark. And what's he found? He said it himself, he's followed most of them, and all they lead to is another bleedin' goose chase. He's stirred up the biggest nest of claptrap in history. This geezer Bartlett might've been onto something but Gramps muddied up the water years ago.'

'So if this is a waste of time, what do we do now?' Erin sounds panicky.

We ain't heard a peep out of Wilbur, and when I look over at him he's only sat down leafing through one of his flippin' comics.

'Come on,' I go. 'This is a dead end . . .'

But then Wilbur leaps up and stands on tiptoe to point at the board. 'Look, Cass, Churchill's Bunker!'

'So what? There's millions of things pinned up there, Wilbur!'

'And Big Ben, see? Maybe me and Gramps were on the same trail – at least some of the places overlap.'

'Oh yeah? Congratulations! You've both been barking up the same wrong tree . . .'

'No, there's a connection here, I *know* it!'

He goes back to riffling through his comic.

'Come on, Wilbur – we ain't got time to chase down every one of these places. I mean, Gramps has got the whole of London pegged up here!'

'Wait a minute, Cass,' goes Peyto. 'Give him a chance.'

Then Wilbur stops leafing through the comic, and he goes very still.

He looks up at me. 'Cass, I know where it is.'

'You what?'

'The artefact – I know where it is.'

'Wilbur, I ain't in the mood for another Churchill's Bunker fiasco . . .'

'No, I really know this time.' He taps the page of his comic. 'It's right here, in issue 13.'

We huddle round and I hold up the flame so we can all see.

It's a Captain Jameson adventure. There ain't much in the way of speech-bubbles – just pictures. Our hero's standing in a big circular room looking a tad ridiculous in his seagoing clobber – I figure it's a library by the number of books lining the walls. He's studying a chart on the wall. Next frame is a close-up of the chart. That's when I get the goosebumps.

Cos it's only the same chart as Gramps's crazy incident map. The streets of London, the coloured pins, the photos and scribbles – the whole caboodle.

I snatch the comic up and flick to the next page.

'What's he looking for? I mean, does he say where the artefact is?'

Wilbur grabs the comic back. 'It's not as simple as

that! The Captain's just trying to find buried treasure –
it's not our artefact or anything. It's like the clue for Big
Ben. It doesn't tell you the whole story – you have to
figure it out.'

'So how come you're so sure?'

Peyto puts a hand on my shoulder. 'Let him explain,
Cass.'

Wilbur takes a deep breath. 'He's looking for treasure, like we're looking for the artefact. That's the first
link. But this is a fake map made by his old enemy, the
Black Cardinal.'

Erin points at the incident map on the cellar wall. 'So,
this is a false map – we can't trust it.'

Wilbur beams at her like he's just fallen in love.

'Terrific, Wilbur. We get that – the map is
codswallop . . .'

He turns to the next page in the comic. 'So, Captain
Jameson figures out the map's a fake meant to throw
him off the scent of the treasure.'

He lets us follow the scene then – Jameson rips the
map down in fury. And behind it there's a gap in the
wall. Stuffed to the gills with pieces of eight.

I look up again at Gramps's map. 'So the treasure's
right here, behind the cellar wall?' It seems a tad
unlikely.

Wilbur sighs. 'No. Don't you get it?'

'It's not here where we're standing,' goes Peyto. He points at the comic. 'It's in this room – wherever Captain Jameson is.'

'Great. And where's that? Wonderland House, Made-up Avenue, Cobblersville?'

Wilbur holds his comic up and points at the map. 'Look at this page and Gramps' photo clue here,' Wilbur goes. 'They're both the same.'

He's right. Both the comic and the photo show a large circular room with rows and rows of bookshelves, and above them, huge arched windows and a dome ceiling.

Wilbur reads out the caption on the map photo. 'It's the library of the British Museum. It's a real place, Cass – north of the river.'

You have to hand it to my kid brother. He don't say much, but what he does say is priceless.

But then again I've heard this kind of 'rock solid' lead before. 'Come on, Wilbur. We ain't saying you're wrong but it's a bit flimsy, innit? I mean, how do you really know about them connections that lead to this British Museum gaff?'

Erin points at the comic. 'Are you saying someone wrote the story that way on purpose, so you could see all the links?'

'What's so special about the Captain Jameson adventures, Wilbur?' goes Peyto.

Wilbur juts out his chin like we're all ganging up on him. 'I don't know. I just like them. To start with I just collected them cos I wanted to see what happened next.'

I roll my eyes. 'Yeah, but how come you got all those flippin' hunches in the first place?'

Wilbur clams up.

'Where did you find this issue?' tries Peyto.

'In the back of a clock. They're always hidden away like that – up chimneys, in mattresses.'

'So what made you look there?'

'I found the first one, issue 4, by accident. Sort of. I had this funny feeling when I went through the door, so I searched round really carefully. I liked the story, so then I kept an eye out in the next building we scavved, case there were any more tucked away.'

'No wonder you're so bloody slow at scavving if you're turning everything upside down like that!'

'They're always in the same kind of places – you know, where the bed's in the same room as the kitchen, all untidy, usually above a little shop . . .'

'As if it's been the same person living in those places?' goes Erin.

'Yeah. And I always get that feeling when I walk

through the door, like a tingling in my head, like I just *know* there'd be another Captain Jameson adventure if only I search hard enough for it.'

We all give each other a look. Cos this is us just going deeper into the barmy reaches of Wilbur's Special World . . .

'Perhaps it's got something to do with the building where you found this issue,' says Peyto. 'Can you point it out on the map?'

'I remember *every* building we've scavved,' he goes, like it'd be stupid not to. He studies the map for a bit then points south of the river. 'Here, Redriff Road near the park.'

Peyto sticks a pin into the map next to Wilbur's finger. Erin takes the comic and starts leafing through it.

'Then there was issue 18, I found that in John Roll Way near the Tube station . . .'

I hold the lighter up to the map as Peyto sticks in another pin.

'Then Crucifix Lane – just where it bends round . . .'

'This is strange,' mutters Erin. She edges closer to the flame with her nose buried in Wilbur's comic.

But I ain't listening cos I'm glued to the map. And it's starting to look like Wilbur and Gramps ain't so bonkers after all . . .

'Whitefriars Street, just next to Tudor Street. There were three issues right there but that's all I've got so far.'

'Bloody hell,' I whisper. Cos all the pins make a straight line, as the crow flies, northwest across the river. I'm trying to get my head round that, cos we've been sent every which way on scav shifts – there ain't never been rhyme nor reason to it. It's just where the gangmaster lands up. But maybe there's dozens of issues on that line and Wilbur's only chanced on a few of them.

Meanwhile Peyto's taken off his belt and he holds it up against the pin markers to see where the line's headed. He turns to me with a grin.

'Look, Cass.' His finger rests on a spot of unscavved territory. 'It's on the same line. Whoever was hiding the comics would eventually have ended up right here – the British Museum. Wilbur's right.'

'Whoever was hiding them was *making* them, too,' goes Erin.

'Eh?'

'They're not printed, look.'

And she's right. She shows me a fancy bit of writing on the back page where the ink's smudged. It ain't just a throwaway ten-a-penny comic, it's a proper drawing.

'What's it say?' I go.

'It's the artist's signature. Not the full name, just the initials.' She beams at me. 'MB – for Morgan Bartlett maybe?'

That clinches it. I gather Wilbur up and plant a smacker on his forehead. Cos it really does sound like we're on our way this time. But then I suddenly remember Gramps. And he's proper taking his time about getting that spare battery for his torch . . .

I charge out of the cellar and up the steps. The trap door's still open but the hut's empty. Peyto and the others ain't far behind.

'Maybe he just pretended the torch didn't work,' goes Erin. 'Then he just hid by the steps to eavesdrop on us.'

'But why's he just disappeared?' Peyto runs to the edge of the clearing. Where's he gone?'

'He wants to find it first,' says Erin flatly. 'He's gone without us.'

For a moment I'm floundering for another reason why he ain't here no more. Cos I don't want to believe he's gone and pulled a fast one. He might be a nutty old duffer but still, you don't expect your own flesh and blood to carry on like that.

Peyto's voice is panicky. 'But we were helping! We were all figuring it out together.'

'He doesn't know us, don't you see?' goes Erin. 'How does he know what we'd do with it if we found it first? He can't *afford* to trust us. Not after all these years of searching for it by himself. He means to beat us to the British Museum.'

My heart turns cold then. 'Yeah, but what's *he* gonna do with it? Keep it or give it to the Vlads?'

And I'm still trying to figure it out, how he thinks he can outrun us – he's quick for an old geezer but he'd never last the pace. But suddenly Peyto just leaps up and charges off into the trees.

'Hey, wait!' I call after him. 'Where you going?'

He stumbles as he turns round. 'Where do you think? Come on! We have to get to the dinghy before he does!'

NIPS OF TIME

EVEN AS WE HARE OFF I FEEL SOMEHOW IT'S THE WRONG THING TO DO, BUT I'M CAUGHT UP IN THE DASH. I SUPPOSE THE THOUGHT OF GETTING STRANDED THIS SIDE OF THE RIVER SPURS us on. Still, it niggles at me that we ain't thinking things through. Anyway, after charging through the woods we're all strung out and it dawns on everyone that there's a long way to go. So we try and pace it, saving our breath, going at the rate of the slowest, which is Wilbur. I might be a plodder but I can keep going for ages so I end up chivvying everyone along, making sure we stick together.

It must be five miles and then some along dirt tracks from Battersea Woods to the Jubilee tunnel entrance, and we're all done in when we get there at last. But it's a proper relief to see that the dinghy's still there. The water's much higher – just like Wilbur said it would be during daylight – but there's still a couple of metres' gap up to the tunnel roof.

'Man, them Underground pumps ain't working so great now, eh?' I go. 'Let's hope they don't pack up while we're paddling across, or we're kippered.'

'Let's hurry up, then,' goes Peyto. 'In case it rises any higher and we have to wait till it gets dark.'

'Ain't it weird how the dinghy's still here?' I go. 'I know Gramps didn't have that much of a head start – and let's face it, he ain't exactly built for speed, is he? But he must've known he'd never get here first. It's like he's just left us the boat.'

Peyto's already up on the platform, lowering the dinghy into the water. 'What does it matter? Let's just be glad the boat's here. Maybe your gramps has got another way across.'

'But that's what worries me! If he don't need the dinghy then how's he crossing the river?'

I hang back, trying to picture what Gramps would do with the same facts we've got.

'What's the matter, Cass?' Peyto snaps. 'Let's just go! We know where the missing flinder is and so does he – it's a race!'

Peyto glares at me, and I know he's thinking about

his mother, about how this museum might hold the answers for him. And he's got to be desperate to get there, to know one way or another. But this time we're going out on a proper limb.

'If we cross the river this time in broad daylight, then we ain't coming back any time soon. You know that, right? It's all or nothing. On a kid's comic from a hundred years ago.'

And no one's got an answer to that.

Peyto finishes lowering the dinghy in silence. Wilbur's keeping it zipped, too, probably hoping that if he keeps his head down I won't send him back home.

I touch Peyto's arm while he's fussing with the winch ropes, busy avoiding my eye.

'Look, I never said I'm bailing out. I know it looks like we're onto something here, but I just want us to figure stuff through.'

Wilbur gets in the dinghy then and fishes out the maps. He's made his stand clear, and I know he's testing me. And it's probably safer if Wilbur's with me where I can keep an eye out for him. Probably. But the truth is, I ain't got the heart for a scrap. We're in this together now and there ain't no pulling out.

'All right,' I go. 'Fair enough, I'm with you, this museum hunch has to be worth a go. But it's proper dangerous north of the river, so we're doing things my way. Agreed?'

Peyto grins as he hands me a paddle. 'Agreed.'

And so we set off, but I ain't feeling that good about it. There's something about the whole business with Gramps that's still nagging at me, though I can't nail it down. Plus I keep thinking about Dad grafting through his lonely shift. And I think about what he'll do when he finds out we're gone. I ain't scared of the fall-out – things are way beyond that. I just wish there'd been some way to let him know we're all right, but that can't be helped now.

As we get closer to the north bank, the drone of the crushers gets louder and louder, another day of London getting chewed to brick-dust. Wilbur shows me the route he's sussed out from the maps. The museum is just north of where Shaftesbury Avenue crosses Oxford Street.

After tying up the dinghy, we get up on a slag heap near the tunnel mouth to spy out any patrols. And we're in for a shock.

Out on the water towards Hungerford Bridge is a Vlad ship.

It's way bigger than the usual launches, its bows lifting maybe twelve metres from the surface, its decks bristling with gun turrets and missile launchers. Some other dinghies are bobbing about nearby, and I can make out the heads of divers and yellow marker buoys. Troops on the ship deck are using some serious lifting gear to pull something up from the river.

Then we watch in horror as the sleek black shape of the shuttle rises clear of the water.

'Can't we summon it?' whispers Erin. 'You know, get it away from them?'

'What, and let them know we're here?' goes Peyto. 'Anyway, if we summon it, we'll end up back at the *Aeolus* and then what?'

Erin's starting to get all jittery. 'We should never have brought the shuttle back to the same place! The whole army would've seen us launch from this exact spot when we were with Cass. Of course they'd go searching for it here when they saw us splash back down into the river! Why didn't we *think*?'

'Calm down. It's done now,' goes Peyto.

'But we have to do something! What if they use it to get to the other sleepers?'

'They might be able to dredge it up but they won't get inside. Not without a flinder,' says Peyto.

'You sound pretty sure about that,' I go.

'It's practically indestructible in lock-down mode. It's

for scouting planets so it's stronger even than the *Aeolus*. They won't be able to breach that hull. Not without destroying it. Maybe it's a good thing they've found it – it'll keep them occupied for a while.'

'I should have sent it deeper, into the riverbed,' groans Erin.

'No, it takes too long to summon. It only came in the nick of time last night, remember? Look, it doesn't matter right now. Let's worry out about retrieving it when we have to.'

So we crack on. The crushers are going full pelt all the way up Whitehall. We pinch some spare bins, load up with rubble, and wander between crusher queues. Around Trafalgar Square it's just rammed but we slip through OK cos all the attention's on old Nelson, who's nose-down in a crater of his own making. Scavs are swarming all over him with metal cutters, and it looks like he's spurting sparks of fiery blood.

Finally we sneak away from the action one by one into Charing Cross Road. And that's where we hit the first piled-up skeletons in the street.

'Scav prep-teams have been here. We've got to go easy, case there's Vlads about,' I whisper.

'What?' Erin's just gawping at the heaps of bones.

'All these stiffs piled up means the area's getting

prepped. They clear the streets so crushers can get in. Look, we can't hang around, it's too dodgy.'

Peyto takes Erin by the hand to move her on. Wilbur's just staring at his feet – he gets upset when a horse cops it, let alone a person. I chivvy him along, all the while keeping my eyes peeled for troops, but the further north we head, the quieter it gets, till the scav-zone's just a distant buzz. This is where we've got to go careful, cos there ain't no excuse for us to be here.

Up by Oxford Street we come to the limit of the prepping area, where my know-how of the streets drops off. All the way down every road are bushes growing out of drains, and rotting cars, and people lying where they've snuffed it – unscavved territory. It's the kids that get to me. I spot a bunch of them huddled together in the back of a car. Paper skin, hollow faces, falling into their own ribs . . . The driver is face down over the steering wheel – Mum or Dad maybe? Where was they going? Wilbur's gone all still and he's staring at them with tears in his eyes.

'Hey, Wilbur – don't look at them. Come with me, mate.'

It takes a little while to get through to him, but finally he comes to his senses.

'Let's go. Hold my hand and look at the sky, all right?'

Following the map, we skirt round this overgrown square, and find ourselves at last at the open gates of the British Museum. The courtyard up to the steps is clear – no bodies, which is a bit weird. Maybe the museum had been closed on Doomsday. It's a creepy old gaff all right – just these dark windows and columns gone black with ivy. A couple of pigeons break for cover as we hurry across the paving.

I'm counting on having to break in, which ain't that easy for museums what have precious stuff inside, but the front door is all busted in already. And I don't like it, cos that means we ain't the first here. Still, things look quiet as we step into the main chamber with its white marble floors and curved walls. The ceiling's made of these glass panels that probably looked beautiful in their day but now they're plastered with bird crap, and they cast shadows over the place that make it look more like a clearing in a wood. It stinks of cats, and there's a fair bit of bird crap on the inside, too, piling up from a bunch of nests near the roof. There ain't no sign of Gramps, though, or anyone. It's deathly quiet.

But across the marble floor, straight ahead, is the entrance to the circular library room. Wilbur whips out his comic and scurries off.

'Wilbur! Wait!'

I charge in after him. And stop dead. We're too late.

Every single book has been ripped down from the shelves. They lie scattered about, covers open, all over the place. Whoever's been here ransacked the place in a real hurry. Wilbur's hunched over his comic, trying to work out where the fake chart would have been mounted. But it's a waste of time. All the shelves are bare and there ain't no hidden gap.

'Seems like a dumb place to hide the flinder anyhow,' I go.

Everyone just stares at me. Peyto and Erin both look heartbroken.

'Stands to reason. I mean, soon as someone fancies a read and pulls a book down then, hey presto, there it is. As hiding places go, it's rubbish.'

'Now what?' goes Erin.

'Well, someone's got it – maybe Gramps,' I go.

'No one's got it,' says Wilbur.

'You sound pretty sure about that.'

'Look, *all* the books have been pulled down. Every last one. Look how many there are. What's the chances of finding it behind the very last book? It was never hidden here.'

I gawp at him then. Cos this window into the workings of Wilbur's mind is making me dizzy.

'OK, if it ain't here then where is it, genius?'

'Maybe we're in the right building,' says Erin. 'It's just not in this room, that's all.'

And if Wilbur was already in love, he's died and gone to heaven now. Cos Erin's right on song with this clue business. And I have to admit, now we're here it only makes sense to keep looking.

'Wouldn't whoever pulled the books down still be in the building, especially if they didn't find the artefact?' goes Peyto, snatching glances over his shoulder to the main chamber.

He's right. I creep to the edge of the library and peer out, straining to listen. But there ain't nothing except the faint scuffling of cat claws.

'OK, it seems quiet enough but let's scout around first, make sure the place is empty.'

The museum rooms all lead off the main chamber. Wilbur reads them out to me – 'Ancient Egypt and Assyria', 'Oriental', 'African', 'European'. They're even dingier than the main chamber and they swarm with movement when we poke our heads in – troops of cats, skittering over statues and glass cases, mewling in the shadows.

There's a gift shop full of dusty souvenirs and post-cards, some bogs in the basement, and a sweeping staircase that leads up to another level. There ain't no sign of anyone else. If Gramps was here earlier, looks like he's legged it now. My hopes take a nosedive, though, cos this place is huge. If it turns into a straight search for Halina's missing flinder, it could take us weeks. Weeks we ain't got.

As the afternoon shadows draw in, I glance round and everyone's all in. Except Wilbur – running off to read yet another plaque.

'So, whoever was here – looks like they ain't around no more. And even if they're lying low, there ain't no use in us pretending we ain't here – it's too late for that.'

'You reckon it was your gramps that ransacked the library?' goes Erin.

'I don't know – I can't see how he'd have got here before us. It don't make sense . . . Anyhow we need to rest and get some chow down us pretty soon or we're gonna fall asleep in our boots here.'

'No,' mumbles Peyto. 'We've got to keep looking.'

'Hey, sunshine – remember your one and only day's scavving, how you practically crashed before lunchtime? There ain't nothing more important right now than sorting out a camp and some grub, otherwise we're gonna be too knackered to do anything.'

'We haven't got time!' cries Peyto, holding his

countdown cuff up to me.

As he says it, I get another little nip from mine, like a flea-bite – and it's like the ship egging us on. Another hour lost . . .

'Let's not panic. Look, we done well today. We're onto something here, I reckon. But it's getting dark now – we'll have to call it a day till tomorrow.' I trace the bands on my cuff. 'We still got five and a bit days.'

Peyto sighs, fed up from arguing.

'We have to rest sometime,' says Erin gently.

'What about food and water?' he mumbles. 'We didn't bring much.'

'There's always water in these places,' I go. 'Check out the gift shop – the plastic bottles last for ever. And food – well, that's everywhere, running around on four legs.'

'Eh?'

'Shouldn't be too hard to catch a couple of cats . . .' I add, trying to chivvy everyone along.

They both look at me like I've just gobbed on the Bible.

THE GAZE OF THE LAMASSU

TERRIFIC. TWO KIDS FROM OUTER SPACE AND MY LITTLE BROTHER WITH HIS FEAR OF DEATH. NOT EXACTLY WHAT YOU NEED FOR HUNTING DUTY.

'If you're hunting, I suppose I should do that with you,' pipes up Peyto.

'You sure? It could get messy.'

'I want to learn,' he goes. 'If we get all the sleepers down here, we won't have the ship giving us food any more, will we?'

Erin's gawping at him big-time. 'But killing is—'

'It's different now. We've got no choice.'

'So you're planning to butcher a living animal?' She looks at Peyto. 'We can choose not to.'

'And we can choose to do it, too. We'll go hungry otherwise,' says Peyto.

For a moment she looks like she's gonna lose her rag big-time, but then she stares up at the glass roof and takes a deep breath.

'I can't stop you,' she goes. 'But I'm not eating it.'

She heads off towards the library alone, leaving the rest of us standing there.

'Hunting ain't murder,' I go.

'It is where we come from,' Peyto mumbles.

'God, you're as bad as Wilbur. Look, it's probably best I do this alone.'

'No,' he says firmly. 'I said I want to learn. Show me.'

I send Wilbur off to set up camp and get fuel for a fire. And seeing as Peyto's so keen, I take him with me to look for a weapon. I settle for a piece of polished stone from one of the museum displays. I got no idea what it is but it's just right for a throwing club.

I set myself up at the corner of one of the exhibit rooms and wait for Peyto to flush the cats out. About ten of them come haring into the main chamber. I take aim and let fly with the club. It smacks one fat tom square in the bonce and whips out the hind legs of another. I snatch up the club, run up to the injured one and finish it off, then wring both their necks to make sure.

Peyto watches me as I wipe the stone with a rag and it's impossible to know what he's thinking. After about half an hour we've racked up three full-grows and four little 'uns.

We take the kills into the gift shop and I show Peyto how to do the skinning and gutting. He's so careful with the carcasses, as if the cats are just asleep and he don't want to wake them, but he takes it all on, asking the odd question as I prep them up.

'So I take it back at Homefleet, animals just die of old age,' I go at last.

'There's so few of us, so few native creatures,' he says. 'Everything's . . . so precious – water, food, people, animals. We don't kill to eat meat. It wouldn't make sense because it's so hard to keep things alive.'

'But that ship of yours is alive, ain't it? It don't seem to have that much trouble surviving.'

'That's different. It's artificial – it would never have existed without the ancients designing it to thrive in deep space. Real creatures need a natural environment – gravity, light, the right food. That's why we study them, nurture them.'

'Bit different to here, then.'

'You've got a whole planet to roam around.'

'It's your planet too now,' I remind him. 'I mean, this is what you was looking for all that time, eh?'

'True, but I didn't imagine it would be like this.'

He looks at the blood on his fingers.

'But you must've come from a planet like this once?'

'That was thousands of years before we left Homefleet. There's nothing left of that world.'

'So how come you ended up being a sleeper on the ship?'

'You take a test – to see if you're a good match for a flinder. I passed, just.'

'So you *had* to take the test?'

'Yes, everyone does. Most people want to go, to breathe *real* air, to walk on *real* ground. But in any case, if you pass the flinder test then you don't get a choice because a good match is so rare. It usually runs in the blood so there's a good chance families get to stay together. Well, it was always just me and my mother . . . Anyway, she was a near perfect match for her flinder.'

'What was the test?'

'If a flinder can project your dreams while you sleep then you're a match. When we sleep, especially in the deep sleep of stasis, we catch scraps of each other's dreams.'

'How do you know they're other people's dreams, not your own?'

He smiles. 'You just do. It's like . . . you go somewhere to dream in the same place.'

The idea of this is so lovely I don't speak for a bit. Sharing dreams . . .

'But you wanted to come, right?' I go at last. 'On the ship, I mean, as a sleeper?'

He shakes his head. 'That's just it, Cass. I wanted to stay, on Homefleet. I'm not a pioneer, I guess. I was interested in other things – the ancients, all their technology, what's left of it, their libraries and history. Homefleet is the last link with that age.'

'So you'd've spent time in museums like this, then, if you'd stayed home?'

He smiles at that. 'I suppose. Well, I ended up a pioneer, and *this* is my home now.'

And I can see how bitter sweet this is for him. He's made it to a new world, but he's lost his mum. He's busy breathing that *real* air, walking on that *real* ground, but his people are stranded on a doomed ship. I want to ask him loads more, but I figure he's had enough of talking cos he gently gathers up all the cat meat and heads back to the others.

Wilbur and Erin have been busy setting up camp in Ancient Civilisations. There are robes for our beds, and a roaring fire stoked with books and carvings. Wilbur's even rigged up a spit out of bits of old armour and a sword.

While the cats are cooking, Erin walks to the edge of the main hall. I watch her tossing a pebble into the air and trying to catch it. She's rubbish, like a nipper, snatching at it too late. I go over to her with some biscuits from my pack.

'Hey, let's not fall out,' I go.

She tilts her head to look at me, puzzled almost. 'I'm not falling out with you. I'm just not going to eat those animals, that's all.'

She nods towards the edge of the firelight where some cats are straining forward, drawn by the smell of meat. 'It's so strange for us down here. Even *walking* is new. But then you see the things that live here and they're so *balanced*.'

She turns to me again. 'We're strangers, Cass.' Her voice wobbles. 'My parents are on that ship, my brothers, all my friends. And they don't even know we've arrived. They might not ever see this.'

'Don't say that. They will.'

'But don't you see? Even if they do, this might never be home.'

And as she nibbles at the biscuits, trying to catch the crumbs in her mouth, I *do* see. Cos she's a lubber to this life but there ain't no going back for her, not now.

The rest of us eat in silence. Even though the meat's

a bit stringy and sour, it's *heaven* to get some hot food down our necks. Afterwards Erin joins us and we all get togged up in the robes round the fire.

Light from the flames throws shadows against the great statue towering above us. It's a right mish-mash of creatures, as daft as a kid's doodle, but somehow it manages to be all dignified and mysterious. It's got a man's head with a square-cut beard, the body and legs of a giant bull, and the fanned wings of a bird. Wilbur catches me looking at it.

'It's from Nineveh, a city in Assyria.'

He closes his eyes as he speaks, remembering the words he's read. And that amazes me cos he's spent all afternoon reading. He's probably leafed through them books on the fire for all I know.

'Go on then, clever clogs, what is it?' I go.

'It's a lamassu, like a spirit. They put them up to guard doorways and temples.'

'So it'll guard over us tonight,' says Erin.

'Well, just in case it's forgotten how, we'd better take turns to keep watch,' I go. 'Nobody'll see the fire from outside, but still, we can't be too careful.'

Peyto and me take the first stint. We nudge up next to each other, and for a long while we just watch the fire eat up another carving. The elephant god goes slowly, burning first at the ears and trunk, splitting in the heat and sending sprays of sparks over our heads. Wilbur's crashed out next to Erin, both of them dead to the world. And she's got one arm cradled over him, holding him close.

'Tell me some more about Homefleet then,' I go at last, to break the silence.

And so he does. He tells me about the coil habitats, miles-long strips of crops and water, all tethered up to each other, fanning out into space, turning to face whatever sun they're sailing past. He tells me about what animals they saved from their home planet and how they're different to ours, but not that different, so you got things like horses and rabbits and dogs. But they don't do so good in the weightless stakes, cos they've got to live pampered lives all trussed up ready to breed when they find a new home.

Then I ask about the people.

And he tells me about how his ancestors, the first ancients, had to leave their worlds cos of war and how they set out to live their lives without killing. Homefleet got built along the way as they went from star to star, but they couldn't find the right kinds of planets to settle down on, which is how come they sent off ships like the *Aeolus* in all different directions, hoping that'd stack up their chances of surviving. There's another nine ships out there somewhere with sleepers and flinders inside, searching for planets. And who knows, maybe they got lucky.

It gives me a strange tingling, to know that there's all these men and women on the other side of the universe having adventures and seeing all kinds of stuff I can't even imagine.

We don't speak for a while after that, cos my head's spinning with all these stories.

Another little flea nip, another hour gone. I've got used to these little reminders – when they're gone we'll either have saved the ship or not. I stare at my watch and countdown cuff together – one ticking, one pulsing.

'That time when you held up your flinder and summoned the shuttle. What was you saying?'

'I wasn't saying anything, I was singing – no words. It's something we learn before we leave Homefleet. Actually, it's not the sound the shuttle picks up – you have to send it through the flinder as a thought, but it's hard to do unless you sing it at the same time.'

He hums the tune, teaching it to me. Seven notes, lilting and hanging, like the start of a hymn.

'We ain't gonna bring the shuttle here now, are we?'

He grins. 'No, we're too far away. Anyway, I'm not

projecting the song as a thought. I'm just singing it. There's a difference.'

He sees me gazing again at the chink of light at his throat, then he hands me his flinder. Echoes again. I shiver, but just at the beauty of them. Cos there ain't nothing bad about the flinder. I *know* it. And I wonder if it'd send my dreams off to them sleepers in the sky, if I'd be a true match for it. I hand it back, and feel its voices slip away into silence.

At last Peyto goes, 'Cass, can I ask you something?'

'Fire away.'

'Your mother – you don't talk about her. What was she like?'

I look at him, not answering straightaway. There was a time when I would bite back if anyone ever asked me about my mum. I didn't want no one stirring up my memories of her, forcing me to put them into words. But I can tell he's only thinking about his own mum, trying to make sense of what's happened to her.

'I don't talk about her much,' I go at last. 'Sometimes to Wilbur. He don't remember a lot about her so I try and fill in the gaps. She died five years ago.'

He don't say sorry which is what most people say, like it's their fault. A picture of her jumps into my head then – I see her laughing at Wilbur toddling along the floor of our hut, and she reaches down to scoop him up and bury her long red hair into his face.

'She was . . . strong. She made scavving, anything, like a game for us. She made out like our life was fine, that we was lucky somehow. Well, it wasn't no bed of roses, but she made a joke out of stuff that went wrong, you know? Nothing was ever that bad with her around. Leaks in the roof, flies in the summer, same food for days on end. She'd make it a laugh.'

'You do that.'

'What?'

'Making the best of it, turning it into a game.'

I don't say nothing to that cos it seems to me I don't crack jokes in the same way. Mum *really was* happy-go-lucky. I just pretend most of the time.

'She never came back from this one scav shift. A chimney stack fell in as she was chipping away at it. Things just dropped down a hole after that. Wilbur's too young to remember her but still, she ain't there for him. Dad, well, he never got over it. Days are black for him now. No amount of chivvying will ever snap him out of it.'

'What about you?'

'I don't know. I try and remember her, try and be like her, look out for everyone. Being like that, it makes me feel she ain't that far away somehow.'

That's more than I've ever told anyone about how I feel and for now there ain't nothing left to say. After a little while, he takes my hand and holds it. Which sends my ticker galloping off into the sunset. My face has got to be on red alert. I look at him, all flustered, but he don't look back, and I can see him just mulling over what I've told him, keeping it to himself. I like that, the way he listens without pushing it, the way he don't just talk for the sake of it. And slowly my face goes back to normal – well, pink alert probably. But by now the old elephant god is just a glowing ember, and the scent of the burning wood makes me ache for sleep. Which is just when my resident spiders decide to get all lively, running up and down the inside of my collar and abseiling off my hair, like they're trying to keep me awake. But I'm all in and pretty soon my eyes keep drooping. And I don't know how Peyto's keeping going but he's still wide awake, gazing at the fire . . .

And it only seems like I've dropped off for five minutes when someone rocks my shoulder. It's Wilbur. The others are up and about, yawning and stretching, and from the main chamber comes the milky light of a new dawn.

Five days to go.

ARBOR LOW WOMAN

WE CLEAR UP THE CAMP AND I STUFF THE THROWING CLUB IN MY BELT, JUST IN CASE. IT AIN'T THE SAFEST OPTION, BUT I FIGURE IT'S BEST IF WE SPLIT UP TO SAVE TIME. ME AND WILBUR start with Egypt. Erin and Peyto take Africa.

And so the search begins. I take it in at first – all the great carved faces, and lion hunts, and eagle gods, and gold beetles, and long-dead kings. The cats watch us, all jittery, cowering from my torch beam. Sometimes whole loads of them make a break for it into another room, weaving about the exhibits like floods of dark water. It gives you the shivers to think how *old* everything is – Wilbur reads bits out to me and some of the stuff goes back five thousand years, before London even, scavved from some faraway desert city. It makes my head spin with all the millions of lives what's been and gone since these things was made. Folks in a different age, yakking to each other in another language, with different worries running through their heads . . . I like the shapes of the Egypt stuff – it's all so *royal* and powerful, with all them bird-headed gods looming over you, staring out with their all-seeing eyes . . .

All the same, there ain't nothing that looks like a flinder.

Just the *dark weight* of it all – statues and headdresses and fancy daggers – it wears me out. But Wilbur, he's just lapping it up. He's still wiping the dust off plaques long after we leave Ancient Civilisations to head upstairs.

And what with all this wandering from room to room, my brain starts wandering, too. And it ain't just the question of Gramps that's getting to me. It's something about the fact that we're in a museum . . .

At last I haul Wilbur up.

'Look, if this was such a hot lead, how come it's gone all cold again? We could be here for weeks.'

'I *know* it's here, Cass.'

'Don't get all miffed – we followed you here, didn't we? It's just you said you got a tingling feeling when you was on the right track with them comics – but you ain't getting that now?'

He shakes his head.

'So maybe it was here once but it ain't now . . .' I go.

His eyes shine as he ponders this. 'No, it's definitely here. We're getting warmer, I know we are.'

Seeing him there armed with his comics and his pockets full of junk, I get a twinge of fear. Cos the ship is right. Its words about Wilbur come back to me – *His dreams of the flinder are strong. He can sense where it lies.* Somehow Wilbur does know stuff. He found Peyto at Big Ben and he's the whole reason we're on this trail at all. So maybe he is The One. But this business with the wounded ship singling out Wilbur – I don't like it one bit. Cos didn't Gramps say something about how there would be a special one who was gonna make the artefact stronger? But what does that mean for Wilbur? All these puzzles are just hovering round my head like flies, not settling.

And then something hits me. Wilbur's gone trotting up ahead along a corridor, away from the collection rooms. I hurry after him, past a bunch of 'No Entry' signs and some makeshift barriers.

'Wilbur, wait up!'

He hangs back but I can tell he's all eager to get to the next room.

'Listen, this is a museum, right? Everything's like centuries old.'

'So?'

'Well, if the flinder's here, then maybe it got found a long time ago.'

Wilbur's jaw drops open. 'What if Halina didn't leave the ship with her flinder last week, last year or even a hundred years ago when Bartlett started looking for the artefact? What if she came down to Earth in ancient times?'

'Then she's been dead . . .' We both whisper it together, 'for *thousands of years.*'

'Not a word about this to Peyto – we don't want to upset him, OK?'

But then my head just starts racing. Cos if Halina came to Earth way back when, then that means the ship's been waiting a bloody long time to wake Peyto and Erin up. Waiting for what? For The One? Why leave it so late? 'Specially when there ain't no time for Peyto and Erin to wake up all the other sleepers themselves . . . And right then it twigs. I close my eyes with the horror of it.

The Aeolus don't want to wake *nobody* up if it can help it. *It wants them all to stay asleep.*

I open my eyes and Wilbur's just staring at me, and all the colour's gone from his face.

'What's wrong? You OK?'

'I can feel it, Cass.' His voice is quiet and it raises the hairs on my neck. 'We're close, really close. It's not like the other flinders, like Erin's or Peyto's. This one, it's different.'

'What do you mean?'

'It's calling me, Cass. I can feel it.'

Then he turns and scurries off ahead.

'Wilbur, slow down!'

When I catch up, I find him standing at the edge of a large space that looks more like a warehouse than a collection room. From the skylight a sunbeam shines down onto forklift trucks and scattered crates. There's these panels that make a winding path and on some of them there's pictures and bits of writing. The scenes show a hilltop, a grass-covered ditch and some rough lumps of stone. I start to feel proper uneasy, though I ain't sure why.

'It's here, Cass,' he whispers.

He takes my hand and together we go round the maze of panels, and there at the end is a steel box on a trolley. It gleams in the sunlight, and as I move closer I see that it ain't just a box. The lid's all complicated with clamps and seals, and it's linked up with hoses to other machines.

'You reckon that's it?' I go.

'Yeah, can you feel it, too?'

'What?'

'Like a buzzing in your head.'

'No. Look, if this is giving you the collywobbles, why don't you sit over there and let me check it out?'

Suddenly he grips my hand so tight it hurts. 'Look, Cass!'

He's pointing at a bunch of stickers and official-looking stamps on the side of the box.

'Slow down – you know I can't read. What does it say?'

'Specimen: 80304. Renshaw Barrow Dig. Gib Hill. Homo sapiens, female. "Arbor Low Woman". Caution: contents at freeze-dry conditions.'

'Oh, yeah? What's all that in English?'

'It's a body,' whispers Wilbur. 'It's her. It's Halina.'

'Right, I want you to go and sit over there, OK?'

'Cass, I don't want to,' he whimpers.

'And I don't want you to see what's inside. Trust me. I'm just right here. Let me look first, OK?'

Slowly he lets go of my hand and backs away to the wall panels.

I stare at the box, just hovering there, my hand on the casing.

'Oh, God, Cass!'

I spin round, but he's only reading the wall panels.

'They found her in a burial mound that was already dug. Just by accident. She never showed up on their scans before that. And she was preserved! Normally bodies just rot away – they don't survive that long, unless they're buried in peat bogs or frozen ground. No one knows how the body lasted. She's from the Stone Age, Cass. She's five thousand years old!'

I point at the hoses and the tanks, all covered in dust now. 'Yeah, well, the power's been off since the Quark Wars so there ain't gonna be much of her left now. Anyhow, there's no way we'll ever know it's Peyto's mum. It ain't exactly got her name written on the side. Arbor Low Woman – it could be anyone!'

And I'm trying not to come across scared but my voice is all over the place. This is nuts – I must have clocked thousands of bodies but I really don't want to see what's inside. Then again, I've *got* to.

The catches on the box are loose. I lift back the lid and let it topple open. What I figure I'm gonna see is a heap of bones – something in a worse state than Oxford Street Woman outside.

What I *actually* see makes me cry out loud.

'Cass, what is it?'

'Stay back!'

But there ain't no stopping him now. He runs up next to me and leans over the edge.

It's true, Arbor Low Woman ain't much more than some bones held together with black leathery flesh, but that ain't the half of it. She's lying on her back, arms clasped over her chest – the way we lay our dead to rest. But coming from inside the skull is a pale glow, the colour of summer sky, and hovering around the cheek bones and eye sockets is a layer of dust that outlines the shape of a face. The ghost of a woman as she had once been – beautiful and young.

It gives me the chills to look at her, cos I can make out hair and eyebrows and eyelashes, like she's right there, not dead but asleep. And there ain't no getting away from it, Wilbur's right. It has to be Halina, cos she's the absolute double of Peyto. And more than that – I've seen this blue light enough times to know what's causing it.

Buried inside the skull is the missing flinder. The artefact. We've found it.

'What we gonna do, Cass? What we gonna tell Peyto?'

'We have to get him up here,' I go, trying to get a grip. 'It ain't fair to keep him in the dark. Trouble is, what we gonna do about the flinder? Damn thing's inside her head . . .'

A familiar voice stops me in my tracks. 'Well done, Cass. Now, if you would both step away from the container, I'll take over now.'

I spin round. Standing just a few metres away is Gramps. He ain't even looking at me. He's just staring at the steel box like he's blind to anything else, like his life's dream is just moments away.

'The hunt for this cursed thing is over. At last. Step back, Cass.' His voice is hard.

I blink at him. 'You can't take it.'

'You haven't got the slightest idea how long and hard I've searched for this.'

'It don't matter. You've been rooting around for it all these years but you don't even know where it's from, what it's for.'

'And you do?'

'I know that it ain't of this world and it don't belong to you.'

'*Belong?!*' He almost laughs at me. 'You think I want to keep it? All I want is for it to be gone from our city. It's caused our people nothing but misery for years. It's a curse! I want the Russians to take it away!'

'What happened to keeping it out the wrong hands?' And then, slowly, the truth dawns on me. 'You're working with them, ain't you? That's how you got across the river so quick. You just used a bridge . . . Albert Bridge is closest to Battersea Woods. You're the Vlad spy.'

'You always were a clever girl, Cass.'

'So you got here to ransack the library for the artefact. But there was always a chance it wasn't gonna be there, so you hung around for us to show up, to do your dirty work for you.'

'Bravo.' His eyes glitter but there ain't a hint of a smile.

'But how did you know we'd even get here? Ah . . . You overheard us talking about the dinghy when we came out the cellar, didn't you?'

'I'll take over from here, Cass.'

'But you don't get it. If the Vlads get hold of it, then . . .' I think of the ship spinning end over end, closer and closer to Earth.

'Then what?'

'It's curtains for everyone. A war that just don't end. Ever.'

He begins to inch towards me, and I'm trying to think of something that'll get us out of this, but I know how smart he is, how quick he is.

'Something spoke to you, Cass? What was it? Are you afraid of telling me something important?'

Wilbur presses closer to me and the poor lad is trembling. *Think, Cass, think!* For an instant, all I can picture is Gramps's mad incident map – all the pins and photos and crazy scribblings.

'Lost your tongue, Cass? What spoke to you?'

'The *Aeolus*. The voice that spoke to Morgan Bartlett . . .'

He just nods and curls his lips up into a horrid smile. And he's really close now. I can see the gleam in his eyes, all cold and *eaten up*, like he's lost it big-time, and he ain't Gramps no more. And the whole situation is so horribly wrong that I've got to do *something*. But I can't, and it's like I'm still lost in the madness of Gramps's map – all them wasted years searching . . .

'I guess you know now your map was complete cobblers – all them blind alleys. Guess you wasn't the one Morgan Bartlett was thinking of when he made all his clues . . .'

'The map led me here in the end.'

'It didn't lead you here. *We* did. You *used* us!'

'I had to do whatever was necessary. It doesn't matter *how* I did it —'

'Course it matters!' I yell at him. 'You're my grandad! You're supposed to trust us!'

'Like you trusted me?'

– 201 –

He stops just an arm's-length away, uncertain for a moment.

'Trust? You stopped caring about us a long time ago. Ain't that right? Cos you been holed up in your cellar with your clues and your crazy map!'

And just for a moment nothing else matters, cos I know what I say is true, and in spite of everything I just want him to be Gramps, the man who looked after us, when Mum was still alive . . . But there ain't so much as a flicker from him. He's a stone.

'I did what I did for the greater good, Cass. To save our people, our land.'

He shoves me aside and leans over the box for his first glimpse of Halina's ghost-face . . .

And that's when I go for it. I whip out my club and belt Gramps in the back with everything I've got. His scream echoes round the museum and it cuts right through me, but somehow that makes it easier to do what I've got to do. Cos I know it's gonna break Peyto's heart. No fannying about. No respect for the dead.

So, I look one last time into Halina's lovely face and reach up to plunge my hand into the remains of her head . . .

But I'm too late. Wilbur's there before me. He practically flips into the box on top of her, and I hear the crunch as his hand goes into her skull. I drag him out and he's got the flinder in his hand. But he ain't looking at it. He's looking straight ahead, right through the walls, and his little body's all rigid. He looks absolutely terrified.

'Oh, God, Wilbur! What is it?'

I shake him but it's like he can't see me or feel me no more, and nothing I do can wipe that look off his face.

I can hear Gramps groaning now, and in the corner of my eye I see him stirring.

'WILBUR! Speak to me!'

His voice is small and scared. 'Halina? Is that you?'

'Jesus, Wilbur, snap out of it!'

And then I twig what's happening. The flinder! It's making him see things.

So I close my fist around it, to take it off him, and several things happen at once. I can feel Wilbur in my arms, and he's crying out in terror. And behind me, someone is shouting, a woman barking orders, and boots come thumping across the floor towards us. But I'm frozen. I just can't move, it's like I've forgotten how to. And all the shouts are slowing down now, and falling behind, like I'm rushing away. Somewhere else. Diving down, into darkness.

But Wilbur's right there, too. I can feel him just a breath away.

That's it. I've blown it. I'm dead, and so's Wilbur. It's my fault. We're gonna end up a pile of bones . . .

The last place I expect to end up is *outside*.

HALINA

WE BOTH CLUTCH THE FLINDER – I CAN SEE ITS LIGHT POURING FROM OUR FINGERS. AND WE'RE CLINGING TO EACH OTHER, TOO STUNNED TO MOVE. THERE'S TREES ALL AROUND US AND THEY look so *real*! Thin birches, silvery in the sunlight, their bark peeling and dotted with fungus. Above us red leaves swish about in the wind.

'Where are we, Cass?' whispers Wilbur.

'We're still in the museum. We ain't gone anywhere,' I go. 'You can only see any of this when you touch the flinder.'

But it ain't just making us see. It's making us *feel*, too – the cold air on my skin, the springy ground under my boots. The wood is high on a hill, and I'm looking out over bare fields, but the world at the edge of the wood is hazy. Branches and leaves ripple into a half-light, a fuzz of flame and sky. It's like the wood is sunk in darkness, like them little paperweight worlds, cut off from everything else.

'It's her,' breathes Wilbur.

I follow his gaze, and there, about ten metres away, hidden in the undergrowth, stands a woman, perfectly still, like she's waiting for something. Then she steps forward into the clearing. And there ain't no mistaking – Wilbur's right – it's Halina. I just gape at her animal skins flapping in the breeze, the dirt on her skin, the black hair flowing across her face, the flinder shining at her neck. It's her, just as she was, five thousand years ago. And no word of a lie, she's just about the most all-out beautiful woman I've ever set eyes on. Tall and straight-backed and wild and alive! The way she stands there so proud and powerful, she's more like an animal than a person. Just being. Not putting on a front or a show. Just living in her skin. I'm so caught up by her that it takes me a while to cotton on to the other people behind her. They're scattered in amongst the trees, standing back, watching Halina from a distance. They're dressed like her in animal hides, and some of them have got feathers and fern stalks tied into their hair. And they're a right wild-looking bunch – thickset and lump-faced, smeared with streaks of black mud, armed to the teeth with sticks and spears and stones.

I clutch Wilbur harder and try to shrink away.

But he goes, 'It's OK – they can't see us. It's just a recording. From history.'

Then Halina speaks softly in a language I ain't never heard before. It's like verse, like singing, and it sounds so *old* and *strong*. The talk of gods, brimming and truthful, spilling out her mouth in strange and wonderful rhymes. And the maddest thing is, I understand every single word of it.

'This message is for any member of the crew who has managed to escape the *Aeolus* to search for me. As you can see, I have struck out, alone. And I have found a home. For us all. The ancients only know how long we were orbiting this ball of life – it's been here beneath our sleeping heads, spinning within our reach. I hope for my son's sake and all our sakes that I will achieve what I'm setting out to do today. Because if I fail then I expect a very long time will pass before another chance arises.

'There isn't time to explain everything. But I will try. I believe that the *Aeolus* first woke me because there was a problem with my sleeper capsule. As I was repairing it I was surprised to find that we were orbiting a planet already overflowing with life – a green haven. As sleepers we had been here for over half a billion years, slowly cloaking this world with air and water, but the *Aeolus* had chosen not to wake us. When I challenged the ship, it fought with me. There was a struggle. I tried to trigger an emergency in the hope that all of our people would be woken from their sleep, then I escaped in a shuttle-craft to the planet's surface. I hoped that it would only be a matter of weeks before my friends and my son would join me.

'You cannot imagine my shock at finding not just life here . . . but people! And they aren't here by accident. You must understand that we nurtured them, through our dreams, through our flinders. They are our children, as are all the beings of the Earth.

'I was so astounded by this world. These people, *my people*, call it the land of the blinking eye. Day and night, sun and rain, life and death. I yearned to share this place with my Homefleet companions but all my efforts to return to the ship have been in vain. The shuttle lies a day's walk from here, buried beneath the stones. The land there belongs to another tribe who will fight to the death to guard it. I must defeat them first if I am to retrieve the shuttle. These warriors behind me, they cannot understand my words, nor do they understand my task now. But they follow me and they are prepared to die with me. So it comes to this – war, the reason we left our shattered home-worlds all those aeons ago. I know now that this will be my last chance to return to the ship and free the sleepers, or I must die in the attempt.

'If you are listening to these words, then I have failed. I cannot say why the sleepers were not woken – the ship would not answer my pleas. It acts only to keep forty-nine sleepers watching over the world. It is so very ancient, and I fear that it has become twisted and locked into a secret dream of its own. For it is true, if the sleepers were to wake and take their place on the Earth, then the ship would be alone for ever. Never trust it.'

She pauses then to glance over her shoulder at the setting sun.

When she turns back, her face is wet with tears. 'If I cannot take back the shuttle now, then it falls to you to free the other sleepers. Peyto, my son, if one day you hear this message, I love you now and for all the time I have left. Goodbye, and live well.'

Halina pulls the flinder free from her neck. Behind her, the warriors raise their spears and bellow out a terrifying war cry. Then she tips her head back, opens her mouth and swallows the flinder whole. And in a moment the trees and the sunlight and the warriors have all just gone.

And we're standing right back in the museum and it's like time ain't moved on much, cos Gramps is just picking himself up off the floor.

But around us on all sides stand Vlad troops, rifles raised, their sights homing in on us.

Footsteps ring out across the floor and the soldiers step aside to make way for someone, the first Vlad woman I've ever seen in the flesh. She's dressed in black combat gear like the others, but she ain't armed and she ain't wearing a helmet, and somehow she's letting you know she don't need these things. Only one half of her face is showing in the sunlight, but that's enough to see that she is one snake-hearted female. Her hair is white-blonde, swept back and tight to her head. The one unblinking eye I can see clocks the scene, giving nothing away, still and deadly. It hits me then that she's the dark flip-side of Halina – a leader just the same, but fed on so much power and death that there ain't an ounce of her soul left. And where Halina was all heart and guts, this one looks like she'd bin half the human race just to add five minutes to her own life.

Something dawns on me then, something strange. Cos I ain't moved a muscle but I've just seen *two* crowds of warriors, and *two* chieftain women, and the gap is five thousand years or five minutes, take your pick.

Gramps stumbles forward then.

'I told you – no guns!' he cries. 'I told you I'd bring you the artefact. Now let the children go.'

He trips as he speaks and his pistol drops onto the floor. And someone opens fire.

I throw myself to the ground, dragging Wilbur with me. When I look up again, Gramps is flat on his back leaking blood everywhere, and I know by his glassy stare that he's dead.

VLAD HQ

'CEASE FIRE!' BARKS THE WOMAN.

I TRY TO HOLD IT TOGETHER FOR WILBUR'S SAKE BUT IT AIN'T EASY. I'M SO MAD WITH RAGE THAT I WANT TO CHARGE THESE soldiers down, even though I know it'll get me killed. Somehow, clutching onto Wilbur keeps me back.

His frightened voice just about tears me apart. 'They killed Gramps.'

I can't say anything. I just stroke his hair and hold him tight.

The woman steps closer and looks at us like she's working out how to do us in without getting her hands dirty. I look at those hands, in leather gloves the colour of liver.

'Stand . . . up!' English obviously ain't her first language and she spits the words out.

I get to my feet, helping Wilbur up, too, and all the while I stare at her, drilling her with my hate. But then, over her shoulder past the ring of troops, I spot a shadow flitting across the corridor.

'You give this artefact to me,' orders the woman.

Out of the corner of my eye I see that Wilbur's holding it. The light spouts from his fist.

'Hand it over, Wilbur. We ain't got no choice now.'

He shakes his head slowly.

'Hey, listen. We done our best . . .'

'They can't have it,' he whispers to me.

The woman steps forward. 'Give it to me, child.'

But Wilbur ain't budging.

'It's not yours to take!' he shouts.

She marches forward to grab hold of him. And Wilbur does something then that I can hardly believe. He throws his head back and, just like Halina, he downs the flinder in one. Then to show it's gone he opens his gob wide.

And all hell breaks loose.

The woman starts firing orders and soldiers grab us both. I wrestle and squirm and bite as hard as I can, but a sharp punch in the mouth puts paid to all that. Next thing, these boffin types are swarming round Wilbur with machines and one of them pulls out a long dagger.

'Stop!' I scream.

Another punch knocks all the stuffing out of me. As I gulp for air, I can see the terror has gone from Wilbur's face – he's just blank. It's a look I've seen before. Then his eyes start to flicker and draw up into his eyelids . . .

'Leave him alone! He's having a fit!'

The boffin rips Wilbur's clothes down to bare skin with the dagger. And I've got to do something, *anything*.

'You don't want to do that!' I yell. 'You'll lose it!'

The woman turns to me slowly. 'You should start talking or this man start digging.'

'He just swallowed it to protect it! It's alive,' I go. 'You kill my brother, you'll kill the artefact. You'll never get it, I swear!' The words just spill from me cos I've got to say something . . .

'Scan him! Is it alive? Check!'

One of the boffins holds a machine to Wilbur's belly and frowns. 'It's *gone*,' he goes in a fancy English accent.

'Gone? Where?' shouts the woman.

'It must . . . be a part of him somehow. The boy . . . He's unconscious. His heart rate is low but . . . stable.'

The woman narrows her eyes at me for a moment. 'Tell me – how we can take this artefact then.'

'He's got to give it up on his own. I can talk him into

it, but you start chucking knives and guns around, you'll scare him so bad, he'll just shut you out!'

The woman squats down to be closer to me. Her dainty nose flares for a second like she's taking in my smell, trying to sense the lie on me. Her lips curl back and for an instant I see her teeth – very white and small.

'What is your name?' she goes at last.

I try not to wilt under her gaze. 'Cass Westerby. That's my brother, Wilbur. I'll get him to give it up, I swear. But you got to give me time . . . to get through to him.'

I can see she don't trust me. But still she mutters something to the boffin with the knife and he stands back. Then she cracks out a few orders and a soldier hoists Wilbur over his shoulder like a sack of meat.

'Hey, go easy with him! He's just a kid!'

More soldiers haul me to my feet and frogmarch me towards the stairs.

I snatch a last look at Gramps slumped by the side of Halina's box, his head angled to the ceiling, eyes open and glinting in the sunlight.

As we round the corridor to the top of the staircase, I try again to pull free so I can see Wilbur behind me. And there, crouching in the shadows behind the base of a statue, I see Peyto. Our eyes lock for a moment, and I see how calm he looks. Like he's gonna get us out of this fix no matter what.

And slowly, I shove the panic down.

The soldiers march us out into the street beyond the museum courtyard to where three jeeps are parked. I get bundled into the back of one but Wilbur is carted off someplace else. I kick up holy hell about that – screaming and scrapping till they shoulder me down so hard I can barely breathe.

As the jeep pulls away, the woman's heartless face looms right up to mine. There ain't no windows in the back, and in the dark her eyes are like holes all the way through her head to the shadows behind.

'Cass, if you fight again, I order them to break your fingers. You understand?'

Not so much a threat, more like a fact.

'I seen Wilbur like this before! He gets fits some-times. I've got to be with him . . .'

'Enough!'

I stir up all my fire then, all my hatred.

'I swear to you, lady – you hurt my brother, just one hair on his head, and I'll bring the power of that arte-fact smashing down on you.'

A slight smile plays over her lips then. 'So you can do that, can you, Cass? Why not do it now?'

'I'll figure it out.' I stare at her and drag up the lie from somewhere – a way to threaten her. 'You're making a mistake, I swear. Cos it works for *us* – us alone.'

'Very interesting. Perhaps I make a deal with you.'

She turns away from me and snaps some more commands into a radio. The crackle of other voices shoots out over the rumble of the engine. And you can just tell this is a doddle for her – operations and missions, controlling people and situations, soaking up every damn detail. I've got to rile her somehow, get under her skin, give her something to fret over.

The journey is long and slow. I can't see much cos they cuff me to the wheel-arch, but I feel the jeep slide from side to side – maybe it's steering around abandoned cars in the road. And if I'm right that means we're heading further into unscavved London – probably north, further away from the river.

I close my eyes and try to think. What would Peyto and Erin be doing right now? Maybe they've found Halina's body. Peyto's bound to figure it out. He's been sure his mother is dead, but it'll be a shock all the same – to remember her young face, and then to see that she's been gone for thousands of years. I think about him peering into that box, staring at the bones, all hope for her draining away . . .

After about an hour, we come to a straight section – no potholes or obstacles, so maybe the Vlads have repaired the road. Then the jeep slows up, and I hear the tyres crunching over gravel as we stop.

They uncuff me and haul me out into a square. I'm dazzled at first by the sunlight and I can't see Wilbur. I shout his name out just in case he's come round by now, so he knows I'm there, and I get a jab in the kidneys for my trouble. Then I'm marched towards the front of a tumbledown mansion. Just once I manage to twist round to check my surroundings. Behind the jeeps is a wall of concrete defences banked up with rolls of barbed wire. The one checkpoint gate I can make out has two watch-towers overlooking the trees beyond. So we're outside of London – or maybe in one of the big parks. On either side of me bunkers are dug into the old gardens, and poking through the sandbags are machine-gun posts. So this is where the Vlads have their HQ.

There's a grand sweep up to the entrance of the house – marble steps and fancy pots, though the plants in them are long dead. Through doors carved with dragon heads we come to a gloomy hallway and more stairs covered in moth-eaten carpet. Paintings line the walls – chubby little angel kids, lords and ladies sitting on rearing horses.

Several dingy corridors and flights of stairs later I'm shoved into a room and the door slams behind me.

I stand there in the silence, all whacked out, my thoughts running ragged. The room is empty apart from a mattress, a flagon of water, and a bucket to wee in. Purple wallpaper hangs down in mildewy leaves, and above me a chandelier trails with cobwebs. At the bars of the window I look out onto an empty courtyard. But whatever is in the rooms across from me is hidden behind long curtains.

For a while I think about Gramps. He ain't even gonna end up in a crusher now. The Vlads have found their precious artefact – scavving days are over. I figure he's just gonna lie there – food for the cats and dogs and flies. I want to forget that he sold us out. I just want to remember times when he looked out for us near his hut in the woods. But it ain't easy. And though it hurts to think of him dead, no tears come for him.

The mattress is so rank that I can't put my head near it. It stinks of other prisoners, their sweat and fear. So I curl up in one corner of the room and try to go over what's just happened, how I'm gonna get me and my brother out of here. For hours and hours I think. But hard as I try, nothing springs to mind. And though I stare at the bare floorboards, that ain't what I see in the end. Cos my head's up on that ancient hill again, surrounded by trees that have long since fallen. Halina's there, looking right through me. And the unearthly glow of her flinder is rising between us, so bright now, bursting over the shadows.

THE OKHOTNIKS

WILBUR STANDS ON THE RIVER, FLOATING AWAY FROM ME, THE WATER UNFURLING ROUND HIS ANKLES. AND HE'S SINGING — SUCH A BRAVE AND SAD SONG, ANSWERING MY CRIES, HIS VOICE trembling in and out of the wind. I come awake slowly, clinging to the dream as it fades, not wanting to let it go back to wherever it's come from. And the echoes of it stay with me but it's weird too, cos I ain't never even heard him sing.

I'm hunched up, hugging my knees in a tight curl, and it's murder to stand straight. All the cramps of the night break out of me in a fit of shivering. I have to push through a layer of ice before I can drink from the flagon. I check the countdown cuff and the marks have faded so much I can hardly make them out. Only when I turn it towards the window do I see that there's just four bands left. Four days. I figure it's disguising itself so the Vlads don't notice, and somehow that gives me hope.

Outside it's a cloudless winter day and the roofs of the courtyard are dusted with frost. From overhead comes the drone of helicopters, though I can't see them. The courtyard is still in shadow, and covered not with stones but sand, raked up here and there in a figure of eight.

Then as I stare down, a horse and rider come into view. I can tell it's the woman officer by her white-blonde hair. She's swapped her uniform for riding boots, tan trousers, and a loose white shirt. The horse is a tall grey with a clipped mane and tail, a feisty creature, not at all like our nag Sheba. It skitters sideways, tossing its head, and the woman has a time settling it down. Then just as the horse falls into line, she spurs it off, racing across the courtyard at breakneck speed. It looks like a suicide charge the way they gallop towards the far wall, but then, right at the last moment, she tugs at the reins and leans into a turn. The move is so tight, I figure they're going to plough into the sand, but she judges it perfect, righting herself and pulling away harder back towards me. Now I can see her face, set in concentration, her hair flowing free. She hangs forward, perched on the stirrups, egging the grey on at a furious pace, before dipping into another turn. I watch her do maybe twenty circuits, always following the same line of hoof prints, till the horse starts slipping, making mistakes. Then she pulls up, and brings it into this slow prancing, the forelegs just seeming to float in mid-air. I ain't seen no one ride a horse like that – it's all about total control, the way the horse does her bidding.

She dismounts and then, from the edge of the court-yard, another figure appears. It's taller than the horse and it moves in powerful hops, like a monstrous bird. At first, I can't make out whether it's even human. And then I remember Fred the pigherd and his stories of machine-men. It's a girl, I realise, not much older than me, very thin, with long pale hair. But every part of her body is trapped inside a huge body-shaped frame. It's like a cage. The arms and legs are made of battered black steel, all wired up at the joints with tubes and what-not. Her bare feet dangle into armoured knees which hinge backwards, the way a bird's legs bend. Her real body is pinned up in bands of black strapping that keep her in place inside the cage. It's like she's being cradled – a rag doll waiting to be brought to life. Only her feet and her face are free.

As I gaze down, one armoured hand moves up to

push the hair from her face, and it's strange, cos a movement like that should be so carefree, so easy. And yet she *performs* it, like a dancer, so *aware* she's doing it. She reaches out to stroke the horse, but it jerks away all nervous. The woman is speaking to her but I can tell the girl ain't really listening, and after a stable-hand leads the horse away, her outstretched hand just hangs in mid-air long after anyone else would've let it drop.

More words pass between them, not that friendly from where I'm standing, then I catch the woman glaring up at me. I want to draw away from the window but I stay there, forcing myself to glare back, even as the girl disappears into the house. And to me it's as clear as the morning air – today is gonna be a duel between me and this Vlad officer.

First I dust myself down, then I clean up with what's left of the water. All the while I'm thinking hard. Cos everything's important now, from that fancy piece of riding to the girl in the frame showing up.

The guards come early, six of them armed with rifles. Just half an idea comes to me as we move through the house to the ground floor. And I'm thinking the lies I tell now have to be just perfect or she's gonna break me just as sure as she broke that horse.

I'm led into a dark room overlooking the courtyard. A fire blazes at one end where a table is laid for two. The officer is seated, togged out in her uniform and gloves now, the hair slicked back once more. She don't bother to look up as she tucks into a plate of breakfast, while a servant pours her a hot drink. The smells are proper inviting – eggs and toast and the smoky aroma of the drink, which is new on me.

'Sit down, Cass.' An offer, not an order.

I wait, wondering whether to take it up. My guts are groaning for a bite to eat, but I ain't ready to jump to a damn thing she says.

'Sit down. Eat.'

She waves vaguely at the breakfast all piled up.

I lean over and swipe the plate she's scoffing from, then settle down opposite her. She stops chewing and looks at me for the first time, just the slightest hint of respect in her eyes.

I polish off the egg and toast, and stash a couple of pastries for later. The servant pours me some of the black stuff from his silver kettle. It's bitter but good and hot, stronger than nettle tea.

When I've finished, I go, 'Where's my brother?'

'He is safe. He sleeps —'

'I want to see him.'

'Not possible.'

'I told you, the only way I can help you is to talk to him . . .'

She shakes her head. 'First *we* talk – you and I. About this artefact. I wish to know what you know.'

I shrug. 'Like what?'

She leans back, takes a cigarette from a shiny case on the table and lights up.

'Cass, let us not pretend I am stupid. You hear these helicopters today? That is a sign of escalation. You understand?'

I don't answer.

She watches me through the curls of her smoke before speaking. 'Before the wars start, before the Quark bombs, we find trail of something unknown in the connections between computers, something alive and very clever, like a voice, not human. We follow trail here to London and find one man, hunting alone. Not Russian, but a man of this city. A man called Morgan Bartlett.'

I swallow as she says the name but she don't seem to notice.

'Before dying, he speak of the *artefact*, an object of great power and knowledge – the secret of living for ever.'

Living for ever. . . I think about how the flinders have helped keep Erin and Peyto alive for a billion years. No wonder the Vlads want it so much.

I know she's waiting for me to give something away, but I ain't budging.

At last she carries on. 'Bartlett speak of some *special* one to find it, to *keep* it, to make it stronger, a person not yet born. And he speak of war coming. It seem not possible then. But wars did come. Out of nowhere, like a storm. A clash of many powers across the world. The artefact is just a story perhaps, the dream of a madman. But he made warning of the wars, no? So maybe he is not mad. It's why we use germs to attack here. To save buildings, to save this artefact. Then we come back. We search till every last piece of London is crushed to dust. Why? Because even a tiny chance we find this artefact is worth this base, these soldiers.'

I can feel her eyes drilling into me, cold and treacherous, waiting.

'Me, I did not believe this tale of an artefact. For me this posting, in your broken, dead city, far from New Russia, is like punishment.'

She twirls her cigarette, lost in thought for a while.

'But not now. Because we find *your* flying machine and *your* artefact, and now we have some things to defend. So, we bring helicopters, and new soldiers, and new weapons. Other armies of the world can hear of our discoveries here, and they come looking maybe. We must be ready.'

She waits for me to say something, but I ain't gonna be drawn.

'Who are you?' I go. 'What's your name?'

She grinds her cigarette out in the ashtray before addressing me.

'I am Commander Serov, Fourteenth Reydovik Armoured Division, Seventh Army of New Russia. And I warn you, Miss Westerby, stand in my way and you lose your miserable life.'

'I ain't standing in your way.'

'This thing – it "works" for you, you said. How?'

'It comes from another world. It's trying to get back where it came from, and it *works* for us cos it don't trust you or any other invaders.'

'It is for doing what?'

Like I'm gonna tell you. . . 'I ain't got a clue. But I guess you have, seeing as you're so damn keen to chase it down.'

She gives me a smile that in no way puts me at ease.

'A way to live for ever – a cure for death. With this secret our armies can never lose. And now the artefact joins with your brother. Perhaps he is this special one to *keep* it?'

I shrug. 'You just want to use the artefact so you can go round killing everyone.'

'Enough! Time for you to say what you know. There are others. Where are they?'

'What others? I don't know what you're on about.'

'This craft we found in the river. It is not for you to fly, I think.'

'What craft? And I ain't heard of no other people . . .'

She stands up so quickly she tips over the table, sending everything on it crashing to the floor.

'LIES! Just lies. My reports speak of *three* at the river when the craft launch away. I give you chances. You think I play a game with you? You think this whole army comes a thousand miles to hear your lies?'

Just then a door next to me bursts open. It's the girl in the frame, flushed with anger or worry, I can't tell. Up close it's so odd to see the way the outer bars surround and support her, like she's in the clutches of a giant insect. We stare at each other for a few moments. Even her face and jaw are held by a mesh of struts, but she's woven yellow flowers into her hair, and somehow you're drawn to them, not the cage that holds her together. That's what you see of the girl – the flowers and the eyes – tender and brave.

Serov says something sharp in Russian. The way the girl's jaw is so wired up it don't look possible for her to speak, but then a voice rings out from a box near her throat.

'I heard a noise, Mother. I was alarmed.'

It's strange that her lips don't move. The English is perfect but it ain't what you'd call human. Cos there ain't a trace of feeling in the voice.

Serov snaps something in Russian, but the girl's staying put, not answering. 'Go back to your room, Maleeva. This is no concern for you.'

The way Serov switches to English, it's like her daughter's won some kind of stand-off between them.

'Everything that happens here concerns me, does it not?'

'I do not ask you again. Leave us.'

Maleeva turns to me and nods, though her face is empty. And I don't know what makes me say it, but I've got to say something.

'Help me.' It's a plea out the blue and it surprises even me.

'Silence!' barks Serov.

Maleeva just watches me from the depths of her prison, and I've got no idea what she's thinking. She blinks then, and I'm sure she does it to make me see just how trapped she really is, cos without these tiny stalks that flick out and draw the eyelids gently down, she can't do it. Then the frame swivels sharply, joints creaking and whirring, as she stalks out of the room.

'What's wrong with your daughter?' I go.

Serov starts shouting commands. Instantly troops file in and surround me.

'Mistakes, Miss Westerby. This is very bad for you, very bad for your brother.'

'Look, I want to help you. Just let me see Wilbur and I'll get you the artefact.'

'You think I can just let you touch it? This thing you say works for you? I know you lie about the others, about this flying craft.'

She marches ahead as the troops bundle me out of the room towards the front of the house.

We burst through open doors into cold sunshine. Hanging in the sky beyond the walls is a whole fleet of helicopters – enormous ones with two sets of blades. And there, facing us below the steps, are ranks and ranks of soldiers. But they ain't your bog-standard soldiers. They've all got machine frames like Maleeva – but larger than hers and stacked with armour. And they all carry fearsome guns, way too heavy for any normal man. But worst still is their faces. I don't notice till we get up close. Where their eyes should be there's just holes. They all stand to attention as Serov steps forward, and I can't figure that out, cos *how can they even see her*? Then on one of them I clock a movement in the shadow under its helmet, as upwards of eight bloodshot eyes all blink at once and then glare out in every direction. Machine-men.

Serov turns to me. 'This is my Cossack elite. Okhotniks – hunter corps. Where will they go?'

All I can do is shake my head.

Then someone steps out from behind me. And there's no mistaking that trench coat. It's our scav gangmaster.

He stares at me, then fiddles with his pinky ring to stop his hands trembling.

'Elephant and Castle. That's where she's from.'

CAT'S CRADLE

I TRY SPEAKING TO SEROV BUT SHE SURE AS HELL AIN'T LISTENING NOW. ONE OF THE OKHOTNIKS WHISKS ME UP AND HARES OFF TOWARDS THE MAIN GATE. I'M PINNED AGAINST ITS armour, so close to its monstrous head that I can see each eye is a different colour. It breathes, but it's hard to think of it as human, cos there's lines of stitching all across its neck and face like it's made up of bits of wounded soldiers all sewn together. Over its shoulder-plate I can see Serov and our old gangmaster and more Okhotniks running to keep up.

As we charge through the main gate, I see jeeps and soldiers and piles of crates all gathered on the road – an army landing from the sky. We make a beeline for this hovering helicopter, smaller than the double-rotor ones. The chock-chock of the engine becomes a roar, and the gale from the blades flattens down the grass. I get bundled through the open hatch from one Okhotnik to another, then I feel the helicopter lift and tip forward. I can't move much but I spot that Serov and the gang-master are on board, too.

It's so crowded, I only get glimpses of the London buildings skating past the hatch. The Okhotniks don't say a word – they just squat or stand, waiting for orders, sometimes checking their weapons. They're there all right, but it's like they're sleep-walking, in a place where no pain, no loss, no feeling at all can touch them.

I hold it together but I'm numb with terror. It don't take brains to figure out why we're headed for Elephant and Castle. I pray that maybe Peyto and Erin have got back there and somehow persuaded everyone to get the hell out. But it's like what Dad said at the meeting house – *just where are they gonna run to?*

The flight lasts about ten minutes. I can see the gang-master pointing stuff out to Serov, then, as we come in to land, the Okhotniks bail out through the hatch and I'm on the move again. The engine dies, the blades creak to a halt, and as all the troops around me step aside, I find myself on a little hill just out the back of the village by the sheep pens. For a few moments it's like nothing's changed. Smoke escapes from the turf 'n' timber huts, a lone piglet scurries through the streets looking for shelter, gulls return to the rubbish dump. And in twos and threes, the scavs I've known all my life come outside.

They stare up at me from their little family huddles, not speaking, looking absolutely terrified. Near the edge of one group, I spot Dad, and next to him, Peyto and Erin. Seeing them is like being ripped in two. My dad, even from here, looks years older. Erin clutches her chest, rocking gently on her heels, half her face hidden behind hair. Peyto stands upright, a little apart from them, eyes wide open, not squinting like the others. I want to hug them and make them disappear at the same time.

Serov turns to the gangmaster. 'Where are these new people you speak of? Go to them!'

He trudges down, and starts to wander between groups of scavs. Everyone just ignores him, standing their ground as he checks them out. My head starts pounding when he gets close to Peyto and Erin.

And then, out the blue, someone makes a break for it. I know him by his patchwork trousers and his floppy hat. Fred the pigherd. No one else moves. I go rigid from my jaw to my scrunched-up toes. There ain't no way he's gonna make it. Serov looks at the gangmaster who shakes his head. Someone shouts, 'Fred, stop!' But he ain't stopping for no one – spooked as he must be at coming face to face with his machine-men. Serov waits till he's reached the last huts then she mutters an order.

The Okhotnik next to me lifts its rifle and fires. The shot catches Fred square between the shoulder blades and he crumples face-down into the mud even before the echoes fade. From somewhere in the crowd rises a dreadful cry and a few of the little 'uns break out wailing.

'Search!' Serov barks at the gangmaster.

Even he looks terrified now as he picks up where he left off. And he's so close to Peyto and Erin now, but he stumbles and looks wildly from one scav to another.

Serov turns to me. 'Where are they?'

My head rings with the gunshot. The way the poor old Fred lies spread-eagled, it's like he's clutching at the earth . . .

'WHERE ARE THEY?'

'There ain't no others. I keep telling you, it's just me and Wilbur—'

'If you do not give them up, I will kill everyone in this place. You understand?'

'But there ain't no one else! Honest, you got to leave

these people alone. They don't know nothing about the artefact.'

My knees are so weak I just want to drop into the mud and beg. I can't betray them . . .

'Make your choice, Cass Westerby.' Serov glances once at her watch and wipes a speck of mud from her gloves.

I look at all the villagers rooted to the spot, shoulders slumped, eyes to the mud now. They know there ain't no point in running. And they could hand over Peyto and Erin in a heartbeat, except they don't. I can't help but stare at Peyto then and he's the only one looking back at me. He passes something carefully to Erin – a tinge of blue light in the shadows between them.

And then he steps forward.

Erin moves, too, but Dad holds her firm. Peyto just keeps on walking, up the slope, right towards us, and all the while he stares at me. He stops right in front of Serov.

'My name is Peyto,' he says, his voice steady. 'I'm who you're looking for. There are no others here. I came alone. If you're clever you will leave these people be, because if you don't, I'll . . . destroy the artefact.'

'So, you are third one at the river bank . . .' Serov's lips tighten into an awful smile. 'If you speak lies like

Cass, these people all die tonight.'

She signals for the helicopter to start. I catch a glimpse of Dad comforting Erin, and in the sunlight I see tears on his face, which is something I ain't seen before, even when Mum died.

On the flight back, I feel that if I keep my eyes on Peyto, he'll be safe somehow. We're too far apart to talk. But when we're coming in to land back at the Vlad base, he mouths one word to me – 'Wilbur'. And I mouth one back – 'Alive'.

I get taken off the helicopter first and I don't see Peyto after that. An escort of four Okhotniks leads me all the way up to my prison cell where I sink to the floor and crawl into a ball. I lie there for ages, not moving, just listening to the comings and goings of soldiers and the beating thunder of helicopters. No one comes for me.

I'm so done in, so beaten that I'm ready to give up – it lurks inside me for the first time ever, the black feeling of defeat. Over and over I see old Fred fall into the mud. And I think of the villagers – Turnley and his sons, and Mabel, and Jacob Pritchard the preacher, the scavs I've known for ever, surrounded and scared. But then I feel this tickling on my wrist and out my sleeve scuttles a spider. The same one as on the ship? I'm gobsmacked there's any of them left after what I've been through, but somehow they just keep turning up from wherever they're hiding in my clothes, when I'm least expecting it. And I let it scurry over my limp fingers this way and that, till I twig that it's building a web. The threads link my fingers and thumb in a span of spider silk that wafts in and out with my breath. The more I let it beaver away, the less I want to break up what it's done. Though I know I've got to sometime. If I don't just give up and lie here for ever, that is. And it's weird, cos I *know* this ain't your average spider weaving your average web. All them spiders was changed somehow after touching Peyto's flinder back in Little Sanctuary. And this one's sticking with me no matter what. But more than that – the way it's spinning silk, it's like it's trying to chivvy me, or protect me, or *say* something to me.

So I watch it. And I try to think about the flinders, the mystery of them, what they are, what they're for. The voices inside them. The way they send out sleepers' dreams for the terraforming business. And maybe that too is like weaving a web, lines of dreaming spun out into the world. For hours the spider works, till evening comes and I can only see it by the slit of light under the door. And I can feel the strands of the web clinging to my skin, pulling the fingers tighter. Into what? A fist? Is it saying, *fight*? At last it stops, like it's run out of silk, then it heads into my jacket pocket. Job done.

I lay there staring at the shimmer that hangs between my fingers – all the tight meshings and stays, like the most beautiful cat's cradle ever. And at last I fall asleep.

I'm standing on the edge of the Thames, my feet sinking into sludge, and I catch Wilbur's singing, from miles away. But this time, he's coming towards me, standing just under the water, like before, the waves peeling back from his bare ankles. His song rises and calls to me, so that all my blood hums in time to it. And when he's nearly at the shore, he just lifts clean out the water, standing on some black hump-backed thing that sweeps over my head and right past me . . .

I wake up with a start. Shouting from the corridor outside, and heavy footsteps running down the hall. I jump up and turn to the window and nearly scream out, cos there's someone there, face pressed up against the bars! Maleeva.

Before I can do or say anything, she reaches back with one hand and punches through the glass.

'What the hell are you doing here?' I go.

'Helping you,' she says in her dead voice, lips firmly stuck together. 'It is what you asked me to do, isn't it?'

'But . . . but why?'

'Your brother. The cellar where he's being held is

heavily guarded. I can't get anywhere near him, but he's trying to reach me.'

'You mean he's awake?'

'No, he's still unconscious . . . But I know he's trying to break free. He's trying to keep the artefact safe, Cass.' She strokes her forehead and closes her eyes for a second.

'He's trying to reach you? How?'

'It's not just me. He's trying to reach everyone. Anyone who'll listen. Even soldiers. Some of them are refusing to obey orders . . . Didn't you hear it? He's singing inside everyone's dreams.'

I see Wilbur standing on the river surface, in my dream, waiting, calling out. And I remember Peyto telling me about the test, back on Homefleet, to see if you're a match for a flinder – the way it helps you share dreams . . .

'Cass, the artefact must be gone from here. Away from my mother. Only Wilbur can take it away.'

I try to take that on board – how can he take it anywhere, when he's asleep?

'You know what my mother believes?' she asks.

'No, Maleeva, look—'

'She believes that this artefact you've all been searching for can save me.'

'What?'

'This army she commands, the race for power, a way to make soldiers that can't die – she doesn't care about any of it. It's me she wants to save.'

Outside the building – more shouting, running feet. Still, I'm too gobsmacked to move. 'And can it save it you?'

Her machine voice sighs. 'I'm dying, Cass. My body is wasting away. I've got one of the new diseases – a mutant strain from the Quark Wars. Not even the best doctors in the empire could do anything for me. They say I'll be dead within six months. My mother's tried everything – she even stole from the New Russian Empire to find money for my treatments. That's why we were sent to this posting. And the artefact – well, she wishes it could save me, but I don't think it's meant for that, do you?'

Standing there then, I see that all my hate for Serov ain't that simple no more. Cos her daughter is hanging on the outside of my prison cell window, and right now she's my only hope.

'All right,' I go. 'What's your plan?'

'I haven't really got one. But it's not safe to stay – the base is on high alert, more soldiers will come for you. Now seems like a good time to go.'

I laugh out loud at that. 'Oh yeah? Hey, why don't

you come back in a week? I'll lay off the grub and just squeeze through them bars!'

She just fixes me then with her no-feeling face, and does the necessary to wink. Then she grasps one of the bars with her plated fingers, jerks back, and rips it clean out the brickwork. She hands me the bent steel before going to work on the next one.

'That's the good thing about having a commander for a mother,' she goes as the second bar pops out. 'If you have to have artificial limbs at least you get the military-grade ones.'

THE ONE

MALEEVA BECKONS ME OUT ONTO THE WINDOW LEDGE.
'QUICKLY – BEFORE THE GUARDS GET HERE. I CAN CLIMB
BETTER IF YOU'RE ON MY BACK.'

That's easier said than done, cos hanging out over this four-storey drop has just turned my bones to glue. The yelling in the corridor's getting louder . . . I keep my eyes local and take a long, deep breath. The body frame holds as I swing under Maleeva's arms and onto her back. There's a bar across the top of her chest like a second collar bone and I clutch onto that. Then, slowly, she begins to climb down. Her fingers bury themselves into mortar, and she swings down one arm at a time, using her legs just to keep her body from the wall.

Above me I hear the splintering of my cell door, and a hideous Okhotnik head leans over the window ledge, its eyes all bearing down on me.

'Maleeva, they're on to us!'

She drops away from the wall with maybe ten metres to go and I cry out cos I'm sure she's going to crash on top of me. But she bucks forward in mid-air and plants all four limbs down like a cat.

Together we scramble into the shadows. It's quiet – all the action is on the floors above and towards the main entrance.

'Now what? We ain't got long . . .'

'Your brother is in the other wing in a cellar on the far side of the square. He is very heavily guarded. Perhaps it would be better to wait here for now . . .'

'We can't just stay here! We've got to do something!'

She tries to pull me back, but I rip clear and charge out into the courtyard towards the far wing.

'Cass, wait.'

I'm only halfway across when the Okhotniks show up – four of them bursting out of ground-floor windows. They lumber to their feet, shaking the glass from their shoulders, and as I pull up, Maleeva bounds past me with giant bird-like strides. The speed she's going, I know she ain't gonna stop – she just launches into a tuck and bulldozes through one of the far windows. I try to follow but slip on the sand.

The Okhotniks blunder towards me in weird fits and starts – racing then stopping like they're seizing up. I chase around for a way out but they've got me trapped. They stagger in one step at a time, their arms flailing and clanking, their eyes flickering up and down. I steel myself, trying to pick the right moment. Two big strides and I go all out, headlong towards Maleeva, dropping my weight, charging for the gap. As the closest Okhotnik ducks down to grab me, I stamp on its fore-arm and leap. Into clear air. Then something clamps my ankle and slams me into the ground. I wriggle onto my back and I'm staring at two empty eye sockets. The head jerks and snaps at me, grinding its teeth, flinging blood from what's left of its tongue.

I sock it right in the mouth. Nothing. I might as well have punched Sheba. I try to twist free but the fist round my leg is locked shut. Then it dangles me upside down, head cocked like it can't decide whether to throw me away or eat me. More soldier-machines come piling towards us and I fall back limp then, cos the game is up. But something strange is happening. The closer they get, the slower they move – stop-start, stop-start. And I can hear all their gears grinding. They reel about in tighter and tighter circles and cables start busting off their joints with the strain of each step. Soon bits of armour and machine parts are flying off them, thudding into walls, clattering through windows, and the only thing I can do is cover my head.

It all goes quiet.

I peek out between my arms just as the Okhotniks go completely limp. Some of them keel over. Then the one holding me releases its grasp and I fall to the ground.

For a moment I'm too terrified to run. Their eyes are open, but they don't move. At last I scramble over towards Maleeva, who's still sheltering in the far wing.

'You reckon they're dead?' I whisper.

'No, just out of action. I think only their frames are damaged. The way they were moving before, it was like they were trying to obey different masters.'

As we survey the scene from the window, more soldiers rack up, proper cautious this time, though, circling their companions lying spark out in the dust. We back deeper into the house, through a warren of corridors and down two flights of stairs past about twenty Okhotniks, all busted and silent. And it's creepy, slipping past them, cos you can hear their breathing, and sometimes their eyes follow you. Half way along the basement is a steel door bent nearly in half and snapped clear of its hinges. I rush in. There's a bed on wheels – empty. Wilbur ain't nowhere to be seen.

'Don't lose hope,' goes Maleeva. 'I feel sure he is safe.'

'How the hell do you figure that?'

She holds her hand up for hush. There's a faint yelling from somewhere.

'Wilbur? Hey, we're coming!'

Further down the corridor a whole collection of broken Okhotniks are tangled together in a pile, and from deep underneath them the cries start again. Together we pull the wreckage of armour and limp bodies away, till my arms ache with the effort, and I'm so sure it's Wilbur . . .

But it ain't. It's Peyto.

He's lying there, half crushed and gasping for air. I drag him into my arms.

'Peyto! Speak to me!'

He's goggle-eyed as he takes in the sight of me and Maleeva.

'Did you see Wilbur?' he splutters at last.

'Oh, God, Peyto, he's gone – they've taken him!'

I'm right on the brink of losing it, but he reaches out to calm me down.

'Don't worry about Wilbur. I think he's the safest person in the whole building.'

'What?'

'All this chaos – it's down to him. And the thing is, I

don't suppose he's even aware of what's going on. The flinder inside him – it's stronger, don't you see? The ship was right. He *is* The One. He can make the flinder do special things. It's stopping the Okhotniks in their tracks . . .'

'I think he's trying to call them,' goes Maleeva 'To rescue him. The way they stopped and started, like they were caught in two minds.'

And only then do I remember exactly what Wilbur was singing in the dream. I've heard the notes of the song before.

I scramble to my feet. 'He's calling the shuttle! He's trying to take the flinder back to the ship. Oh, Peyto, we've got to find him!'

'The shuttle's too far away. It can't be summoned . . .'

'No,' says Maleeva. 'They brought it here for tests. I saw it arrive just before dark. It's just inside the perimeter wall, near the front of the house.'

We hurry back up to the ground floor. I peek through a window, and the courtyard's empty apart from the broken Okhotniks, hanging there in their armour frames.

'Wait here for me,' goes Maleeva. 'I'll do one circuit of the corridors. If you see me raise my hand then it's safe to come.'

With that she's off, stalking down the hallway

towards the front of the house.

'Who's that?' asks Peyto. 'I thought she was an Okhotnik when I saw her.'

'She's with us – it's a long story . . .'

I gaze at his exhausted face for a moment. Suddenly there's so much to say, but I can't see where to start. I think about Halina and her message, the one meant for him.

'Peyto, there's something I've got to tell you. At the museum we found . . . That is, Wilbur found . . . Oh Peyto, I don't know how to say this.'

He drops his eyes away from me. 'I saw the body, too, if that's what you mean . . . I know it was her.'

'No, you don't get it. I saw her, Peyto. I mean I really saw her. Like when she was alive back all them thousands of years ago. Me and Wilbur both did.'

'What?'

'The flinder was in her skull and it made all this dust hover into the shape of her face! I knew it was her cos she looked just like you . . .'

He just stares at me, completely dumbstruck.

'Then, when we both touched her flinder, she told us this message. She said not to trust the ship, and that it never woke you all up when it should've. She kicked off an emergency cos she figured that would wake everyone up. But it didn't work.'

'But why didn't the ship wake us up? Did she say?'

'No, she said it wouldn't tell her – she reckoned it was mad. Maybe it's got used to watching everything from up there, like a god. It wants all forty-nine sleepers back up there. If they just wake up and leave, it'll be alone for ever.'

Peyto's lashes turn black with tears. He grips my sleeve.

'What else did she say?'

'She said she loves you.' I throw my mind back to that green hill, the summer trees. I take his hand. 'She said to live a good life. She was trying to come back, to rescue you all. That's how . . . Well, that's how . . .' I can't say it.

I think about the warriors behind her, their war cry as she swallows the flinder. And just right then there's this mighty boom from the courtyard.

The whole front wing of the house bulges out and comes tumbling down. Through the rolling dust, I can see Okhotniks piling through the gap and firing their guns at something huge. It barges right through them, twisting and rolling from side to side. I don't cotton on what it is at first cos it's moving so fast and it's turned into this huge snake-head, thrashing about, crushing everything in its path. The shuttle.

A lone Okhotnik climbs out of the ruins. It moves unsteadily, like it's learning how to walk, turning its back towards the others as a shield. And cradled in its arms is Wilbur, still fast asleep! I can see from the Okhotnik's clumsy steps, from the way it holds Wilbur's body, that it's *treasuring* him. Whatever soul was inside that wounded soldier, it sure ain't there now. Wilbur is – sleepwalking, lost in dreams, commanding the warrior's legs as if they were his own. And there's only one place he's going. His words come back to me then. *Wish I'd been there, on the ship . . .*

I charge over the windowsill even as Peyto screams at me to come back.

'Wilbur!' I yell. 'Wait!'

The Okhotnik straightens as I run and it stares right at me. And maybe, behind them awful eyes, deep inside that battered skull, it's Wilbur that sees me. But then the shuttle rolls to a stop and opens up a hole near the nose. And I watch in horror as the Okhotnik steps inside with Wilbur. I tear across the courtyard and I've lost all fear. The entrance is shrinking when I dive at it. Mid-air I'm sure it's gonna close on me and chop me in half. It scrapes my legs but I'm through! And even as I crash to the floor, the shuttle starts rumbling.

A LOST ALTAR

I CAN'T SEE A THING, COS MY FACE SMACKS THE FLOOR AS THE SHUTTLE DRILLS UPWARDS. I CAN'T BUDGE, EVEN TO PUSH MY FACE TO ONE SIDE. THESE ENGINES ARE HOWLING ALL AROUND me, crushing me down. And something whacks into the shuttle so hard that just for a second I think we've crashed. But then all my weight jumps out into nothing and I'm peeling off the floor. It's all systems go with the alarms as the engines die down. And just to cap it all I heave my guts up and the puke shoots round in a circle and slaps me right in the chops.

The Okhotnik faces me, Wilbur still cradled in its arms. And I sure ain't getting any vibes my brother's in charge now. So I tense up for a scrap I know is gonna be over in five seconds flat. But nothing happens. Zilch. The soldier is kaput, just staring into space, mouth

- 253 -

flopped open. *Is it dead or, like them others, out for the count?*
OK, get a grip . . .

I wipe the breakfast off my face, and kick gently towards the Okhotnik. The way it bounces off the wall it looks a goner, but up close I can hear its breathing, and getting Wilbur free is murder, cos the arms holding him are *locked solid*. The way I have to tug and fight, I'm sure it's gonna jump into life any second. But there ain't so much as a flicker from its eyes. So I give up fussing and do what I have to do to get Wilbur free. And just having my kid brother in one piece after the whole Vlad army meltdown is a miracle! Yep, it's *really* him – the same jug-ears, gappy-teeth, sack-of-bones Wilbur. And apart from his do-it-yourself shiner there ain't a scratch on him. All the clues he loves to hoard come out his pockets – comics and stickers and old Navy medals . . . I'm staring at all this floating clobber when Wilbur stages his comeback.

'What's the matter, Cass? Where are we?'

He's all groggy from his marathon sleep, groping about for something to hold onto. And having him back is more than I even dared hope for. I squeeze him hard.

'Oh, Wilbur! You're back!'

'What's going on? We're . . . floating.'

I stare at him. He ain't got a clue how he's got here.

All that mayhem he's conjured up just by wanting to be here, and he's slept his way through it.

'Welcome to space . . .' I go, wondering what I should tell him.

Suddenly he grabs my arm. 'Gramps . . .'

He's all wide-eyed and you can see that things are flooding back, and for him Gramps getting shot is something that's happened in the last two minutes. And I ain't had time to deal with it myself, but in my head it was yonks ago and a hundred and one disasters have gone down since then, not the least of which is this stranded-thirteen-miles-above-London disaster that's happening *right now*.

'Look, sunshine, you've been out of it for a night and a day and then some, and a fair bit's happened . . .'

'Cass, what about Gramps?'

There ain't no way to hide it from him.

'Gramps ain't with us no more.'

I'm sure he's gonna start crying but he holds it together. Or maybe he's just zoning out on me, which is what he does sometimes when he's upset.

Then he stares for the first time at the Okhotnik.

'Don't worry, he's out cold right now . . .'

'Hunter,' whispers Wilbur.

'What?'

'It's a Hunter.' He reaches out and touches the warrior gently. 'It's . . . lost, waiting . . .'

'Eh?'

'It can't really think for itself. It's waiting for a reason to *fight*.'

'Yeah, well, let's not give it one, then.'

'Where I've been, Cass, I *saw* them.'

I think about him drumming up them warriors with just the whims inside his sleeping head. And he don't even know it. 'Where you've been is inside a Vlad prison and out for the count.'

'I wasn't asleep, Cass. I *went* places. Like where we went to see Halina. I saw how they got injured, those men, fighting in wars . . .'

'What men? Speak sense, Wilbur.'

'They nearly died but they got put back together again with bits from other wounded soldiers. That's how the Vlads make the Hunters. They've been ripped apart and sewn up again so many times their souls are broken. Now all they got is *hunger*.'

'Hunger? For what?'

'Just to carry on fighting, but they don't even know what for, and they don't even care, but they've got to, like it's the only thing that makes sense, so they live for the war and nothing else.'

All this whispering talk is giving me the creeps.

'Look, I believe you, right? But you've got a flinder inside you and so them places you been to, they ain't real like this is real. I need you here, helping me out, cos any minute now we're gonna get to the ship. And we've got to figure out how to get off it again mighty quick, OK? Cos it ain't safe.'

I pull him over to the flashing red screens and the scrolling messages.

'Can you make out what it says?'

'Where's Peyto and Erin?'

'They ain't here. Just do me a favour and read it, Wilbur!'

'Hull damage critical. Minus fourteen per cent heat shield . . . Erm, something about a one gigatonne missile strike . . .'

'OK, that don't sound good. Thought Peyto said the damn thing was indestructible.'

'We were attacked?'

'I don't know. Maybe the Vlads tried to shoot us down . . .'

'Are Peyto and Erin OK?'

I tear myself away from the screens to speak to him.

'They're all right. Well, they was when I last saw them. Erin's with Dad back at Elephant and Castle.

Peyto'll be fine with Maleeva, I reckon.'

'What's Erin doing with Dad?'

'Look, you wouldn't believe what a load off my mind it is to see you're in one piece, but I ain't gonna fill you in on everything what's happened since you went AWOL, OK? There just ain't no time for that.'

'Who's Maleeva?'

'Hey, enough! You're doing my head in! Right now we're in the worst fix ever, OK, and I'm trying to think!'

'Sorry,' he whispers. 'What's all this yellow stuff?'

'Wilbur!'

He floats clear of me, looking all set for a sulk.

'Actually, don't touch them yellow bits.'

'Why not?'

'It's . . . Never mind.'

On the screens I watch the *Aeolus* coming closer, then the docking tentacles reaching out.

'Cass, what are we doing here?'

'You really don't know?'

He shakes his head. 'I mean, I dreamt about coming to the ship, but—'

'Look, it don't matter right now how we got here. We just need to figure out how to get back, OK?'

The docking hole pops open, and just beyond it I can

see the ridged walls of the ship proper. I try to picture the layout. I try to think back . . . The *Aeolus* is silent, saying nothing. Should I try and speak to it? I figure the best thing to do is get to the bridge, keep Wilbur close – minimum of fuss. Not that I've got a clue how to reset the shuttle if we get there but I'll jump that hurdle when I have to . . .

I push through into the ship, dragging Wilbur with me. The silence, the gloomy vault, the flickering sleeper pod lights like rows of blue candles – it all puts me in mind of a church. A lost altar tumbling through the sky.

I bundle Wilbur towards the airlock hollow where the suits are stashed. Getting into them is easier than I think. But the way the helmets snap home, and the sleeves and gloves puff up to just the right size, and how the whole suit closes round you – it all puts me on edge. 'Specially cos the ship ain't saying a word. Like Erin says, it only speaks when it's got something to say. Which means it's happy for us to go to the bridge.

I touch the scab thing that works the airlock and in the blink of an eye we're on the far side facing the main shaft that leads to the bridge.

I tether up to Wilbur and drift into the passageway with its torn hull and views of the night – the dreamy silence of space. I can hear Wilbur's gasps over my helmet speaker as the curve of the Earth swings into view.

It takes a while to get to the far side cos I ain't that great at aiming the cable-gun in the suit forearm. My first few efforts glance off the walls, but finally the barbed end hits home and we reel ourselves to the busted airlock at the far end, then through the wormhole tubes to the bridge.

Everything is just like before – the burnt bits of ship flesh, the gaping hole where Halina's shuttle was docked, the hairpin tunnels and finally the bubble screens of the bridge.

I stare at the gash where Erin stuffed her arms. The innards squish about a bit. It ain't like I'm squeamish but the idea of rummaging around in there ain't exactly inviting. 'Specially when I don't have the foggiest how to do this shuttle resetting lark. I try to think back, but there ain't much to remember. Erin just went in up to her elbows and did it. So maybe it ain't that hard . . .

'Can I try?' offers Wilbur.

'No way! Stay the hell back and don't touch nothing.'

'I was just trying to help.'

'Yeah, well, you done enough helping . . .'

OK, well, might as well just go for it. I plunge both arms in. The stuff gives way, and it's sloppy and warm like offal. Which is weird, cos how would I know what it feels like if I got gloves on? But then I cotton on that the gloves ain't there no more and my bare fingers are squishing right into the gunge. In a panic I try to pull them out but they're locked fast.

'Jesus!'

'Cass! What's wrong?'

I force myself to calm down. 'It's OK. Just getting the hang of it.'

Now what?

And just as I'm getting my breath under control, something proper freaky happens. It starts with something brushing against my fingers – coming in then flitting away again. Like something wary, sniffing me out . . . Suddenly two ripples of static shoot through my arms, up past my shoulders, into my head . . . They meet there and merge, and together they make like a *shadow* in my mind – a shadow that ain't got nothing to do with me. Whatever it is, it just sits there for a bit, and I'm thinking about a million things all at once. Except it ain't really me doing the thinking. Cos it's like the shadow-thing is just rummaging through my brain, the way we scav an empty house, picking through the contents, keeping some, chucking away others. It's the ship, or the smart bit, the bit the ancients made up front before pouring it into this floating bag of flesh. Its mind or its ghost or whatever. What else can it be? And the way it races from my right eye to my left and back again, I get the feeling it's trying me on for size, checking the view . . . And by all the laws of what's normal I should be screaming right about now. Except I can't, cos my terror's all caged up and it can't get out.

Then, right out the blue, the ship speaks to me.

FOR EVERY FLINDER,
A SLEEPER

**'CASS WESTERBY, I CRADLED YOUR MOTHER AS SHE FELL.'
ITS VOICE ECHOES ROUND MY HELMET. I STOP BREATHING.
'SHE ACCEPTED HER DEATH. THAT IS RARE.'**

'Cass, what's going on?' shouts Wilbur.

I try to turn round to him but I'm stuck. *OK, be strong, be cool, just speak to it.*

'What d'you know about her dying?' I go.

'I know the faces of all those who have lived and died on the Earth. Through the flinders I have seen their dreams. I have listened to them as they called up to the sky.'

'What else about her?' I whisper.

'Cass, don't listen to it!'

'I know this. That she found comfort in the shapes and smells of trees. That she was a story-teller and treasured her skill. That she thought of her children as she gave herself up to the dark.'

Right then it goes rifling through my memories of Mum. And I know it's telling the truth.

'Cass!'

'Take it easy, Wilbur. It's all right. It ain't gonna hurt us.' Then to the ship I go, 'How do I reset the shuttle?'

'Think of the place you wish it to go. Reach out with your mind.'

I close my eyes. The innards wraps themselves tighter around my fingers. I think of London, the Thames. I picture the bridges and the black surface of the water at night, by the Jubilee tunnel – where Erin took us before.

'It is done,' goes the ship.

The ghost-shadow whips away in an instant and is gone. The innards loosen and I can feel the gloves growing back. I pull free from the hole, and tentacles of slime whiplash into my helmet.

I turn to Wilbur. He's breathing hard and he's gone all white and trembly, so I bring him close till our face-plates touch.

Then the ship goes, 'Forty-nine flinders for forty-nine sleepers. They must all return here.'

Suddenly I feel so simple and so *tiny* next to this

voice, cos it's older than the world. But I figure I've got to keep it talking while we get back to the shuttle.

'So, what's so special about forty-nine? Can't you make do with forty-eight?'

'Together they are strong. Together they are *one*. Wilbur knows.' Its voice is so calm, so cold.

I do a finger-down-the-throat sign to get him to puke up the flinder or lose it somehow. He shakes his head for a no-go. I pull him back towards the main shaft.

'You must complete the forty-nine, Cass Westerby.'

'That's what we're gonna do,' I go. 'Just as soon as we get back to London and find the others.' I can hear just how bonkers that sounds – cos how am I going to fool this ancient ship? I think about Halina battling with it, and I know it ain't just gonna let us go. Not after it's waited five thousand years to recover the missing flinder.

I swing Wilbur out through the busted airlock into the main shaft. I can see he's itching to speak but I cut him off with a look. I hold my arm out steady and aim the cable-gun towards the far airlock . . .

'The flinder must stay.'

. . . and fire. The cable loops out to the far end and . . . bull's-eye!

'All right, but how do we get it back out of Wilbur?'

'It is with him now. For all the remainder of his life.'

I clench my teeth. 'But he can't stay here. He's got a life in London.'

'The flinders cannot be allowed to fall to Earth. Disaster will reign. They must stay here, in the trail of the heavens. For every flinder, a sleeper.'

Inch by inch I reel us both in. I know there's no point in reasoning with it, cos it's got to be as mad as a box of frogs. But why is it even talking to me? That's the chilling thing. Halina said she *fought* with it. Why isn't it stopping me from heading back to the sleeper side?

We make it through the far airlock, and into the sleeper chamber. I ditch my suit and help Wilbur with his. We're nearly home and dry.

'Thing is, you ain't gonna set the sleepers free even if you repair things up here, are you? Not ever. That's what Halina said. Except you never told her why.'

Wilbur butts in, 'Cass, what about the—'

I show him a furious cut-throat sign so he buttons it.

'The sleepers will have their lives on the world. But not until the time is true.'

Suits back in their slots, nice and tidy, like we ain't really in the biggest rush ever to bail out of this floating madhouse.

'Wow, that's a bit on the woolly side, innit? So when we talking? A million years? Two million? Or just when you're good and ready?'

The ship don't answer.

I feel Wilbur's hand suddenly clench mine. And maybe he's trying to get me to go a bit more softly softly, but I can't help it – I've got to keep the *Aeolus* talking. And it ain't that far now to the shuttle entrance . . .

'So after Halina went AWOL, you sure took your time waking anyone up to find her flinder, eh? I mean, if it's so important to repair the ship and get all the flinders up here, why leave it so long?'

It don't answer straightaway. And somehow I know I've asked the killer question. Cos my scalp goes cold like the devil just touched it.

'Four thousand eight hundred and seventy-two years is not so long to find the right sleeper. The One will complete the forty-nine. The flinders will be strong again. Together we will end war, end disease, end suffering . . .'

I remember Halina's warning, *Never trust it*.

Just right then Wilbur pulls away from my grasp, and he's trying to reach a conker that's strayed out of his pocket. It tumbles away from his outstretched fingers. And even as I'm looking at him, the ship walls are moving.

'Wilbur!'

I snatch at the hem of his coat as these petals of skin sprout out the wall. He fumbles hold of the conker, and I can see the relief on his face, but now he's spinning away from me, and his smile dies.

'Wilbur! God almighty! Don't touch the walls!'

But how can he stop himself touching them?

'Cass!'

The petals rear up. They're huge and pulsing with veins, and as they fold towards him, the edges split into spiked tentacles.

'He must stay . . .' goes the ship, calm and deadly. 'He is The One.'

I'm in a frantic scramble to get to him, but I'm drifting away, so slowly, and none of my flailing about gets me any closer. The tentacles latch onto his coat, his trouser legs, his boots. And slowly, the ship gathers him in. Behind him, in the middle of the petals, a hole opens up.

'You must return alone, Cass. You must bring the last two sleepers, bring Erin and Peyto. All the flinders must be together. Or this vessel will burn. Wars will turn the Earth to dust. Wilbur must stay . . .'

'He ain't a sleeper! He belongs with me back home! Let him go!'

'Halina is dead. For every flinder, a sleeper.'

At last I brush into the far wall, and know it's my only chance to get to him. I jam my heels into the wall, coil up and spring away, and now I'm charging across the chamber towards the closing petals.

'Cass! Don't leave me!'

I slam into the tentacles. They're strong – whipping about like eels – and they mesh together like a cage between me and Wilbur. I reach in and grab his lapels. And he's looking right back at me, crying his eyes out.

'WILBUR!'

The hole closes around him.

'LET HIM GO!'

I tug at his coat with everything, but there's a ripping sound and the lapels just come away in my hands and I'm catapulted away. Just his face is free now, yelling at me. Then the hole seals shut and the petals wither away and there ain't nothing left of him.

'Jesus! WILBUR? CAN YOU HEAR ME?'

Nothing.

I clatter into the edge of the shuttle entrance. And I grab onto the lip of the hatch so I can throw myself back to where he's buried. But as I launch away, something grabs hold of my ankle.

And that's when I remember that the shuttle ain't empty.

The Okhotnik warrior is right there, all eyes wide open. Its steel fingers snip together as I try to batter my way free. Then it just flings me into the shuttle. I spin to face the chamber wall and . . .

Rushing, squealing air.

Black.

Why can't I see anything?

Pain.

Wilbur? Where's Wilbur?

Am I outside?

WILBUR?!

Breathe.

It's OK. Breathe.

Actually, it ain't OK.

It's a very long way away from being OK.

Black lumps dancing in front of my eyes. Like in the bridge.

Except you ain't in the bridge any more, you spod . . .

Sirens ripping through my head.

How come I'm in the shuttle? I don't remember being strapped into a chair harness. In a panic I wriggle free and right through a floating sheet of my own blood. My mouth is thick with it, spinning it out, like ribbons. I try to call Wilbur's name but I just choke up a load more blood and spit. And past the tightening hole of the hatch door I spot the Okhotnik as it floats deeper away into the ship. The hole closes up and even though I thump at it with everything, it won't budge. Then the engines start shuddering and rumbling, and there ain't no point in hammering at the hatch. Cos the shuttle ain't docked no more. On the screens I watch the ship grow smaller, and I can't scream or shout cos that ain't gonna change matters now. *And I can't believe I've lost him, my little brother! He's gone!*

And then I remember what re-entry is like.

And then I remember I ain't strapped in.

And then I remember the hull is busted. *Critically* busted.

I kick off the ceiling and dive towards the chair harnesses. But even as I fumble for the flailing belts, a storm punches in around me. A shrieking hurricane tearing at my skin. Somewhere near the chairs there's a pinprick of light, hot and white and shivering and swelling. The sky trying to come in. And the shuttle fighting it back.

I'm clawing myself away from the hole, but it's

getting bigger. And the shuttle is actually *shrinking*. Like it's being eaten away and it's trying to surround me. Fire and foam.

Then a cold liquid swills into my eyes, my throat, my lungs. And I think it's the sea.

THE KEY TO EVERYTHING

NOT THE SEA. TOO QUIET, TOO STILL. COLD GLUE PRESSES INTO MY MOUTH, AND I CAN'T BREATHE, THOUGH THAT DON'T FAZE ME, COS SOMEHOW I DON'T *NEED TO* BREATHE. FAR AWAY, AT THE corner of my eye, I see a rage of light but it can't touch me, cos I'm all curled up and safe. All my worries and struggles are gone. Somebody speaks but I ain't listening – the words drift about my head, never settling. And I figure this *somebody* is trying really hard to unravel me, spark me into action. But I don't want to move, cos being tucked away here in the dark where you can't even remember your own name is *bliss*. The voice ain't giving up that easy, though – it keeps picking away at me, trying different words. I know I've heard it before, riling me, chivvying me along. *Who is it?* And it's a jolt when I cotton on that I'm alone, and there ain't no one else it can be. The voice deep down inside that drives me on, no matter what, is *mine*. And all my worst terrors charge back at once . . .

Wilbur. I've *always* been the one to look out for him, to keep him safe on every scav shift, while London crashes round our ears, wall by wall, like a city of cards. *I've got to get him back!* The stab of losing him pumps my heart, and drags me to my senses . . . Then out of the darkness – wobbling amber, the crackle of flames, and a voice shouting.

Arms reach in to take me, and someone wipes the muck off my face.

It's Peyto.

I must be dreaming, cos *how is he here?* His eyes search over me, looking for signs of life. Then the struggle to breathe kicks in, and I strain for air, choking for life.

'Cass, you're OK, you're OK. I can't believe you made it back! Say something. Where's Wilbur?'

I clutch onto him and cough up some of the cold glue.

'He's still there. I've got to go back . . .'

'And we will. We'll find a way. Can you move?'

'My head feels top-heavy . . .'

I try to take in where I am. A glowing mess lies all around me and from it runs a furrow of molten earth that stretches away like a burning road. I see all this through some kind of liquid glass that slides over my face, and as I reach up to wipe it off I find that my fingers, untouched by the fire, are slathered with the same heavy stuff – and it *creeps* more than it oozes, covering my skin in slug-like waves.

Peyto is shining in the firelight, dripping in the same gloop as me, though there are wisps of smoke rising from his shoulders, and his jacket is scorched black.

'Come on, Cass, it's not safe. We've got to move.'

He pulls me up banks of smoking earth, and as the gloop falls away from us, I feel the heat for the first time – warping and roasting the air.

We tumble over the lip of the hollow and down into a pit of slurry so *shattering cold* I can't even find the breath to yell. We help each other up onto a little island and lie there gasping. It takes me a while to recognise where we must be – the maze of slag heaps and mud channels that leads to the river. The south side.

I peer back at the crater glow as it shivers up into the sky, and I stroke my face, feeling for wounds.

'I didn't even feel any heat,' I go.

He pulls at the gloop hanging from his arms. 'Thermal-protection gel – the shuttle makes it in an emergency re-entry. I had to cover myself in it before I could get anywhere near you. Without it you'd have gone up in smoke.'

'But where's the rest of the shuttle?'

Peyto gapes at me like I've lost the plot. 'There is no shuttle left, Cass. It re-assembled when the damage went critical, making the stuff it needed out of what was left. But you were burning up all the way down. You were lucky it lasted as long as it did.'

I look at the glowing mess that was the shuttle, and it hits me. Cos there ain't no way back to Wilbur now, is there? But then I remember Halina – the shuttle she came down in . . . And the way my hope hangs on a thread nearly makes me sick again.

Peyto winces as he pulls off his jacket.

'You're burned! Let me see!'

'It's OK.'

'Let me see!'

He hauls me to my feet. 'We don't have time, we have to get away from here. The whole of London would have seen you come down . . .'

He takes my hand and drags me along a trench. 'The tunnel is close by – we were heading that way to take the dinghy.'

'You knew I was coming?'

He frowns at me. 'No, how could we? We just saw

this fireball in the sky hurtling towards us. I mean, I saw it change shape and that's when I knew it was the shuttle. It was trying to make a controlled descent.'

'You call that controlled?'

I sneak a sidelong glance at him and there's a look on his face. Disbelief that I'm even alive.

'Where's Erin?' I go.

'She's around here somewhere – we were all split up in the rush to get to you. Maleeva's with us, your father, too. I can't call out – there are troops this side of the river now, lots of them. All we can do is head for the tunnel. I think it's this way . . .'

I stumble after him, trying to get my head in gear. *How long was I up there, on the ship? An hour? Two hours?* Something's not right – I feel like I've slipped through time . . . My watch-face is cracked and filled with mud. I check the countdown cuff – three bands left. Already the third band is shorter than the others. Less than three days to go . . .

'Peyto, wait! How did you get back? We must be at least twenty miles from that Vlad HQ.'

'Maleeva – she carried me on her back practically the whole way. I'd never have kept up with her otherwise. It was chaos – loads of soldiers heading back to the Vlad base. By the time we got to the scav zone it was deserted, all the bridges unguarded. When we got to Elephant and Castle we thought we'd be too late, but the Okhotnik guards were just unconscious – hanging limp in their frames. All the scavs were getting ready to leave in case the Vlads came back. We found Erin and your dad, and came here to try and cross the river again.'

'The other shuttle. . . You know where it is?'

'Not for certain. Arbor Low – that's where my mother was buried. We found maps in the museum. It's about two hundred miles north of here. Her shuttle has to be close by.'

He grabs me down into the shallows as a helicopter sweeps overhead. Its searchlights pan across the mud-holes, then it pulls away. Somewhere, over the clatter of blades, I can make out men shouting, dogs barking.

'It'll be light soon,' mutters Peyto. 'Too dangerous to cross the river. Come on!'

He snatches my hand and drags me on. Ahead, I recognise the shape of one of the slag heaps, the way it's nearly tipping over, the loops of barbed wire snagged in the overhang. The tunnel mouth is so close now – I can see where run-off water from the bog is gathering towards it.

Then the mud gives way and, as we slither down

towards the tunnel mouth, I see Maleeva and Erin and Dad all lowering the dinghy into the water.

Somehow they drag us out. Dad hovers over me, heaving with the effort, all the mud and water streaming off his coat. For a moment I only see his dark face and I figure he's livid. Cos I ain't got Wilbur with me.

But then he grabs me into his arms and hugs me so hard I reckon he's gonna squeeze the life out of me.

His voice is hoarse. 'I thought I'd lost you. I thought I'd lost you *both*.'

'Wilbur – he's alive, Dad. I know he is. And we're gonna get him back, I swear.'

'You came back,' he goes. 'You came back to me.'

There's some quip on my tongue, something about who else am I gonna come back to? Except I can't say it. And when we pull back, it's only cos we're as soaked as sewer rats that you can't see the tears. Still we stare at each other. And it is pretty bloody amazing that we've ended up here, in each other's arms. My dad and me.

And it's Erin that breaks the spell between us. 'Those troops will be here any minute,' she says.

Maleeva points back to a cluster of torch beams near the top of the slope. 'They're here now.'

THE *LODESTAR*

WE LAUNCH THE DINGHY AND PILE IN. PEYTO AND MALEEVA TAKE THE PADDLES, STEERING US DEEPER INTO THE TUNNEL. FOR A MINUTE OR SO, NO ONE SPEAKS AS WE SLIP ALONG TOWARDS the north bank. Behind us I watch the bobbing torches at the tunnel entrance but the barking gets fainter – there ain't no one following, so maybe they didn't see us or the dinghy . . .

At the far end, Peyto anchors up with the grapple hook. We all look at each other. From here it's either take our chances on the surface or carry on into the tunnel system. I look into the black reaches of the old Underground. Even with the whole Vlad army searching for us, I ain't got a good feeling about hiding out down there.

'We need to figure stuff out,' I go. 'There ain't no

point charging off into the North Wilds to find the other shuttle till we know what we're gonna do. We don't even know for sure where it's hidden.'

Erin shakes her head. 'No, first I want to know what happened on the ship.'

For a moment I stare at her, and it hits me that what she wants more than anything in the world right now is what the ship wants. Otherwise, in less than three days, all her family's gonna die. Cos the ship needs all forty-nine flinders on board to fix itself. Which means she needs Wilbur to stay where he is. She holds my gaze and I know I'm right.

Peyto goes, 'What's the matter?'

'The ship took hold of Wilbur for a sleeper,' I answer, not taking my eyes off Erin.

'It's just till the ship's repaired,' goes Erin.

'No, it ain't! It grew some tentacles and swallowed him right up, and it ain't gonna let him go without a fight. It wants all forty-nine sleepers up there full-time. It'll repair the ship and keep you all there, the way it's always kept you there.'

'How do you know that?'

'Cos it told me, Erin. It reckons with all the sleepers up there it can stop wars and illnesses and every bad thing that happens! It ain't just a bit broken, it's mad!

And while we're at it, Halina told me never to trust it neither. She was pretty bloody clear about that.'

'We have to think calmly,' goes Peyto. 'Maybe there's a way to bargain with it.'

'Oh, yeah? I can tell you, it ain't in the bargaining mood. It used the Okhotnik to force me off the ship! That don't sound like grounds for haggling to me!'

'But we can't leave Wilbur up there,' goes Peyto.

'Too pigging right.'

'Maybe it'll let Wilbur go if we find another sleeper.'

'No way. It's got some cracked idea that Wilbur's a perfect match for that flinder. It said he was The One. And now he's gone and swallowed the damn thing, it ain't exactly gonna be easy to do a handover.'

'So what do you suggest, then, Cass?' says Erin. And her voice is cold.

'We've got to fight it!'

'Are you crazy? Just how exactly are you going to win?' goes Erin. 'In case you've forgotten, Halina fought it and *lost*! If you go up against it now, then everyone on the ship will die! Including Wilbur! And what if it's right about all forty-nine flinders holding back wars? If the flinders are destroyed, your world is going to be even more terrible than it is already!'

For a moment, we're all too stunned to say a word. I

ain't on board with the whole 'end of the ship, end of the world' idea. Sounds like a smoke screen to me. To make us do what it wants. But what if I'm wrong? I've seen the flinders' power all right. Maybe if they ain't up there overseeing things, the world *will* blow itself to bits.

'There has to be a way,' says Peyto at last. 'We have to offer it what it wants. It needs all the flinders if it's going to repair itself. Otherwise it *will* crash.'

'You're sure about that?' I go. 'It ain't just bluffing?'

'Positive,' says Erin. 'There's absolutely no doubt – from a planet this size, the ship should've set the orbit at something like four hundred miles. But with the bridge damaged, the orbit must have been degrading, maybe just by tiny amounts, but over thousands of years that adds up. The ship's less than thirteen miles now – that's critically close to the atmosphere. It'll fall out of the sky unless it repairs its navigation systems.'

I look at Peyto and he nods.

'We have to find the other shuttle and go back to the ship, no matter what happens when we get there,' he goes at last. 'We've got no choice.'

Dad ain't saying a word. He don't meet my gaze. It's like he's shutting all this out, cos he's only just found out about the ship and the shuttle and Gramps getting killed. And now what with Wilbur . . . It's too much for him.

'Every second we argue about it is a second wasted,' adds Erin.

I stare at the floor of the dinghy. And I know they're right but I don't like it. Cos if we give the ship what it wants, then Wilbur ends up staying, asleep – for ever for all I know.

Then Maleeva speaks. 'We can still try to bargain with it when we get there.'

'Oh yeah?' I snap. 'Who's gonna volunteer to take Wilbur's place then?'

She swivels her head to face me. 'I will. I've got nothing to lose.'

No one says a word.

I stare at her, and of course there's no way to read her. She's a total blank.

At last she nods towards the Underground system. 'Maybe we can cross London in these tunnels, lose the soldiers, then make our way north.'

Dad shakes his head. 'We'll never make it over land to this Arbor Low in time. It's two hundred miles. Besides, the Vlads will have all the roads covered. The only way is by sea.'

I gawp at him. 'In this? I'd rather take my chances on the road.'

'We can float down the river to Gravesend. There are

trading villages I know down there. Maybe we can get passage with one of the fishing boats.'

'Then what?' goes Peyto. He pulls a torn map from his pocket and lays it out on his lap – the coastline of England. 'I mean, even if we make it round here to the top of something called . . .' he peers at the map, '. . . the Wash, it's still a hundred miles over land.'

'No, that's an old map. That's the way the coast used to be before the seas rose. London has been protected with the Great Barrier but lots of land ended up under water, especially places around the Wash. I wouldn't know where the coast is now – maybe the sea's gone in as far as Lincoln. Then by land it's maybe fifty miles, or less.'

That clinches it. It ain't exactly the most promising plan in the world but I know there ain't a better one right now. Each of us nods in turn.

Carefully we drag the dinghy up the slope to the north bank. I scout about a bit, looking for signs of Vlad troops. There's a proper commotion going on south of the river – I can see torches flickering near the water, and there's a helicopter searchlight hovering over where the shuttle crashed down. There's still a red glow rising from the slag mounds.

It don't take long to manhandle the dinghy through

the sludge to the river's edge. No one says a word. We just pile in, push out into the current and drag the tarpaulin sheet over our heads. For ages, we hug the bank, trying to blend into the drifts of junk. It's way too dangerous to go any deeper cos we'll stick out too much to the guards manning the bridges. For what seems like hours we limp downriver with the current.

Finally, as it starts to get light, I peel back the tarpaulin. We're flitting past the edge of an abandoned dock. Cliffs made from rusted-together ship containers soar above us – the nesting place of a million seabirds. The far bank is grey in the morning mist, but I can see the towers of cranes and unscavved oil refineries, and a couple of half-sunk tankers.

'No bridges,' says Maleeva at last. 'Maybe we should head to the south side before the river gets too wide to cross.'

Everyone nods, and so we paddle out to where the river is quickest, and pretty soon we're flying along with just two sticks and a bit of rubber between us and a watery grave.

I just sit in the prow of the dinghy, under the tarpaulin, looking out for danger. And it's a hairy old business just trying to keep us from tipping in the drink. A couple of times for sure I reckon we're headed for one of the huge concrete-and-steel islands that rear up ahead, but somehow we scrape a way between them.

After that the river widens right out into a clear stretch and the banks are too far away for anyone stationed there to see us. We're all wet and freezing and I'm mighty relieved when the old man pipes up that we're pretty close to Gravesend and that we should pull into the southern bank. Up ahead, for the first time in my life, I can make out the vast gates of the Great Barrier straddling the estuary, holding back the sea tides. On a rise of land to the north sit the massive power stations with their chimney stacks and cooling towers, belching steam and fumes, like castles on fire.

We steer closer to the shore where the road is mostly washed away. Up close all there is to see is a stretch of old warehouses and crumbling docks.

'Do people live here?' asks Peyto.

Dad shakes his head. 'Traders pinch what they need but they won't live in these buildings. They've built their own place where Gravesend used to be, just east of here.'

I point downriver. 'We can't get closer than this?'

'No, it's too dangerous to float near the Barrier. It's best if we go on foot from here.'

We come ashore and scupper the dinghy in the

shallows with some rocks. Then it's up onto the ruined road towards Gravesend. Dad leads the way through deserted streets up to the first stepped ramparts of the Great Barrier. I'm mighty glad we've ditched the dinghy, cos the river seems to speed up and boil as it thunders over a weir and into a cauldron of white water. Pipes the size of houses are sucking the Thames into a stairway of concrete sluices and locks and dams and towers that beggars belief. For a moment I stand there feeling the roar of the turbines and the cold misty spray on my cheeks.

We traipse maybe thirty metres up the gantries and steel ladders while all around us bits of loose foam waft in the breeze. At the top of the Barrier where the river gets dumped into the sea, I catch a sharpness of salt and seaweed in the wind. I think then about what would happen if a crack was to branch up from the river bed, if the dam was to topple. The crushers and the Vlads and the ruins would be washed away – Elephant and Castle, the meeting house, all the scav settlements . . .

Dad points to a muddle of piers built into the estuary and further on a couple of dozen round huts, caked with mud and draped with sheeting. A few of them trail smoke from holes in the roofs.

'Gravesend.' When Dad looks at me then there's just the hint of a smile, despite everything. 'I was born in one of them black-houses.'

'You think they'll help us?' asks Peyto.

'Maybe, son. They'll do what they can, I'm sure.' Dad glances at Maleeva. 'Even so, they're wary of strangers . . . I'm sorry but it's best if you lie low for now.'

Maleeva is stood apart from us, picking at the flowers in her hair. One by one she throws out the wilted ones. 'It's all right. I understand. Where shall I meet you?'

'Keep to the ruins and follow the bank. You'll come to a headland and an abandoned village called Allhallows. You'll know it by all the seabirds that live there. We'll come and find you whether we get passage or not.'

She nods and heron-steps away towards the wreckage of the old town. And never mind the bulk of her frame, she moves so easy – within just a few strides she's gone.

Down in the settlement, it's quiet – just some goats, a couple of tied-up dogs, and an old man mending nets by the water's edge.

'Where is everyone?' I go.

'Probably out fishing or on a trade run up to Medway. Stay outside for a minute. I just want to see how things lie here first.'

He ducks past the reed matting at the entrance to one of the black-houses, then a short while later he ushers us all in.

Inside it's smoky and dingy and smells of fish-heads. But, sweet Lord, it's cosy and dry! Nets and pans hang from the roof, and the fire is set in a well of cobbles and full to the brim with crackling driftwood. A beefy old dear in a shawl introduces herself as Irene and makes a big fuss of us as we file in.

'Goodness but you're soaked! Somewhere I've got some extra shirts and long-johns. Now, I'm guessing I'll have takers for bread and chowder?'

In the gloom at one end of the house, where Irene has her animals corralled up, we get changed out of our wet underclothes. Me and Erin get dressed behind some sacks of grain and she's so clueless on all the fastenings and buttons of these fresh clothes that I've got to give her a hand. When we're done she looks at me and then she tosses her flinder in the air. Right at the top of its arc, the tentacles spring out and encircle her throat.

'That's the way clothes *should* work,' she says, tucking it under her shirt.

And I smile, cos it's like she's well and truly got the hang of gravity now, but she don't smile back. She just picks up her precious ear-muffs and heads back to the fire.

I catch Peyto looking at me from behind all the bleating goats – bare to his waist, struggling to keep his balance. And in spite of everything, the sight of him tiptoeing about, hair standing on end, covered in bits of hay, makes me smile. And more than that – the way his arms and shoulders tense as he chivvies the goats out of his way makes me steal glances for a while longer.

Irene gasses on about nothing much. It seems to me she's breezing on past the sheer strangeness of us rack-ing up, though she does look happy for the company. She talks to Dad, mainly about folks he knew as a boy, but somehow she manages to steer clear of anything to do with the here and now.

Finally a silence falls over the black-house and there ain't no more small talk left in anyone, even Irene.

'You're in some trouble then?' she asks at last.

'We have to find passage to the north,' goes Dad. 'To the Wilds.'

Irene shakes her head. 'You won't find no one willing to go further north than Felixstowe.'

'Why not?' asks Peyto.

'Too dangerous, young man. Some used to head up to

fishing grounds round the Wash, but you got raiders operate them waters now. Clean you out and cut your throat. No mercy on the sea. That's why everyone goes in convoy now.'

Dad pulls out his money-bag and places it in Irene's lap.

She shakes her head. 'It ain't a question of money. If estuary people thought they could help you out they'd do it for free, but no one's gonna risk their boat chasing up north. Not without a good reason anyway.'

We all look at each other, unwilling to break the silence.

'I ain't probing,' sighs Irene. 'Your business is your business, but people round here ain't gonna go out on a limb 'less they know what's at stake.'

Peyto speaks out then. 'We don't even have a way of repaying you for the kindness you've already shown us, but you are our only hope.'

Dad steps in. 'That's enough, lad. She's said she can't help us, plain and simple.'

'But Wilbur and the others . . .'

'We'll make our own way to the north.'

'There's no time!' Peyto cries. 'They'll be dead!'

'Who's Wilbur?' murmurs Irene.

'My son, but —'

- 292 -

'Well then, you should've said so in the first place. I have a boat, the *Lodestar*, she's a pot-hauler. Not the fastest – maybe ten knots top whack, and her winching gear don't work, but her engine and hull are sound.'

Dad drops his head, powerless to argue back. 'Let me at least give you what I have.'

'You'll need that for supplies and fuel – I can help you get what you need from the chandlers downriver. My mind is set – that old boat's been tied up too long anyhow.'

I'm so gobsmacked at her generosity that I just hug her.

'Goodness, child! Wait till you see the old tub first – you might not be so free with your love then!'

'Thank you,' goes Peyto. 'This boat – I swear I'll bring it back to you.'

'Oh, so serious, young man! No promises. Not when it comes to voyages on the sea. People come back by the grace of God, and if you do, all well and good.'

She bustles us all out of the black-house and down to the pier, chatting all the while about the boat and what kind of shape she's in.

It has to be said, the *Lodestar* looks pretty rough and ready, but what do I know about boats? She's about twelve metres long – blotched with red paint and littered with junk. The wheelhouse has a cracked window and the winch on the back is fused together with rust. Still, Dad seems highly delighted. He inspects everything from the engine under the deck to the bunks beneath the wheelhouse. It ain't long before we untie the moorings and chug the half-mile or so to the chandlers. From there we load up with drums of fuel, tinned food and a barrel of water. Irene stands out on the pier to see us off.

'Don't dally now! I hate goodbyes, 'specially long ones! The Lord's speed and kind weathers to you.'

She gives us each a hug and without another word turns away, as if she's expecting us to be gone no more than a day. I can hear her gabbling on to the chandler before we've even untied. And maybe that's the best way to do goodbyes.

Dad holds the wheel and sets a course for Allhallows. It's a short journey, less than half an hour, and when we reach the headland, Maleeva's waiting there for us, gazing out to sea, while all around her seagulls swoop and cry.

FRIEND OR FOE

THAT FIRST STRETCH OF THE VOYAGE THERE'S A KIND OF LULL IN US ALL. WE'VE SPENT SO MUCH TIME FIGURING AND FRETTING AND RUNNING THAT MAYBE WE'RE ALL JUST DONE IN. UNDER THE calm, though, it's murder, cos I feel every freckle on the countdown cuff give a nip as it disappears. And as them time bands whittle away, I can't even bear to look at them no more. Cos we can only go as fast as the engine will take us. Inside I chivvy the *Lodestar* along every climb and dip, almost dragging it along, chalking off the miles as we inch northwards. The journey is dead time, but I tell myself I need it, to get strong, to get ready, for the last push.

Me and Peyto spend the first few hours dozing in the berths under the wheelhouse, feeling the chug of the engine and the sway of the waves. I wake up to find him watching me. I'm dribbling a bit so I make a joke out of it but there's a look about him that stirs me, so that the kidding about turns into a scrap of wills and we end up checking each other across the tiny space, locked in a kind of spell. Only the grim sound of retching snaps us both out of it.

It's Erin. The tipping of the deck sends her guts up so bad she's walloping over the side till there ain't a morsel left inside her. She stays at the back of the *Lodestar* with her head in a bucket, jibbing away from the very sight of the ocean. Peyto tries comforting her but she ain't in the mood to speak and she shoos him away.

It's funny how things kick off. I reckon it's being on the boat that don't help matters. Cos when you're huddled on this lump of wood in the sea your tempers and beefs ain't got no place to go.

It starts with Peyto, though it ain't his fault. I figure he's just eager to know stuff about the boat, but I don't know squat cos it's the first time I been on a proper one. So he corners Dad instead, who's only too happy to yabber on about how the engine works, and the winch, and fishing, and currents and God knows what else. And after a lifetime of having Wilbur not taking an interest in anything that ain't in a book, Dad warms to him.

At one point, I see Erin watching Peyto over the top of her bucket and if looks could strike a tree in half . . . At last Dad goes to take over steering from Maleeva.

'Getting ready to colonise, Peyto?' goes Erin. And there's an edge in her voice I ain't heard before.

'Why not? We're down here now, aren't we?'

'I just wouldn't want you to forget there's forty-seven who aren't down here.'

'What's that supposed to mean? I'm going back to the ship to get the others – the same as you are.'

'It looks as though you'd rather stay here if you had the choice.'

He walks closer to where she's huddled round her bucket. 'Well, I don't have the choice, Erin.'

'I just need to know you'll do what you have to. When the time comes.'

'Take my place as a sleeper? Even though I might end up staying asleep for a million years?'

'Or for ever,' I add.

'Stay out of this, Cass. We already know what you think,' goes Erin.

'There's no other way to repair the ship,' mutters Peyto. 'If I don't do it then who'll take my place? Not that anyone's bothered to realise I'm gambling my life to do it.'

'I'd do it for you, if it was your family.'

'It's just that you didn't even ask me. You just *expect* it.'

'The ship said we would have our time —'

'Halina said never to trust it!' I blurt out.

Erin slings her bucket across the deck and stands up. 'Halina didn't have the same problem!' she cries. 'The *Aeolus* wasn't three days from burning up when she decided to bail out!'

Peyto's voice is quiet with fury. 'She was trying to save us all when she fought the ship.'

Erin throws up her hands. 'I know that, but things are different now. Whether you trust the *Aeolus* or not, we have to be sleepers. It's our only chance for life.'

'Some chance,' I go. 'If you lay down in your pods, that crazy ship ain't never gonna wake you up! You'd be better off going up in flames – at least then you'd know what was happening!'

'Better to have certain death than a chance of life?' cries Erin. 'You don't know what you're talking about.'

'Yeah, you got all the answers, Erin!' The rage rises inside me. 'It's simple for you, innit? You ain't exactly grasping hold of a life down here cos your whole life's in storage.'

She gapes at me but her answer don't come.

'Ain't that right? But you ain't so good at seeing

- 298 -

everyone else's choice, are you? What happens if the ship don't trade Maleeva for Wilbur? Then I ain't never gonna see him again, am I? And if he wakes up at the end of the world, he ain't never gonna see me, or Dad! You never thought about that, did you?'

By now, Maleeva's watching and Dad's glancing over his shoulder at our raised voices.

'If you'd never showed up in the first place, Wilbur wouldn't be stuck up there! We helped you cos you was desperate!' I'm so riled I can't even look at no one no more. So I turn tail and head for the winch at the far end of the boat, which ain't far enough.

I wedge myself between old lobster pots to shelter from the wind, and for ages I just stare at the sea. Slowly, slowly, I cool down. It's crazy how we all got so much to lose now – different things. Erin ain't to blame – if I was in her place I'd feel the same. But still, I can't even think about being split up from Wilbur. He's a dippy spod but I don't know what I'd do without him. And it kills me to think that I can't bring him back, with us, where he belongs. If only there was a way. But every angle I look at it, the *Aeolus* will crash if it don't get repaired in time. And it ain't gonna get repaired without forty-nine flinders. *For every flinder, a sleeper*. And if that happens, it's game over. Cos I don't trust the ship – I just know it won't wake anyone up. It keeps coming round to the same problem. Sleeping's the same as dying . . .

And then it smacks me between the eyes. I'm staring at the same patch of waves but suddenly everything I'm looking at is different. My heart nearly clatters to a halt. Cos the idea that's just sprung out of nowhere is so killer that it scares me that I've even come up with it. It's desperate. A gamble that hangs on what the ship *won't* do, what it *can't* do, even if it wanted. It's all or nothing. And that's why it's gonna work. I been looking at it the wrong way – we all have. It ain't got nothing to do with repairing the ship, cos that won't cut it. But what I need to figure out is the details – that's where the devil is, as Gramps used to say. The spell of the sea draws me in then – I can't tear myself away from it. The endless pitching of tips and troughs, one wave sliding into another, like a landscape of distant mountains changing in seconds. And as the hours slip by, I play out a battle in my head, over and over again. A battle of wills.

Me against the ship.

It's bleak under the darkening sky. Peeping out under a line of cloud come the last red streaks of the setting sun, and all the shattered gold on the water. I think so hard about the plan that it seems real, like something I could see out there on the broken waves – a thing, like a blade I've polished and polished.

I'm dozing off when I hear footsteps approach. And even before I see him, I know it's Peyto.

'Friend or foe?' I challenge.

'Friend.'

He wedges himself in beside me.

'Make yourself at home, why don't you?'

'I will.'

His body next to me is warm, wriggling for space, half-fighting, half-cosying, but tense, too, like he's plain terrified. And it's uncomfortable now with him squirming about in this nest I think of as my own. But I don't want him gone.

'I never meant to say that,' I go. 'About wishing you'd never turned up.'

'Yes, you did. It's true – if we hadn't come, then Wilbur would be safe now.'

'Maybe. Except without you being there at Big Ben, Wilbur would've fallen. I couldn't've saved him.'

I don't look at him. I can't.

'We need each other maybe?' he says softly. 'The scavs and the sleepers.'

We sit like that for a bit, listening to each other's breathing. And there ain't nothing else to say. Being like that is so strange, a game of dare and double-dare, bluff and push and nerve. And all the time, all the heat swims up to my face, and I try to batten it all down, or hide it away, or lose it in the dark. I want to reach out to him, but I stop myself – how many times? I lose count.

Thing is – I can't see nothing now, unless it's through the plan. And I done my sums all right. If we play it the ship's way, chances are Peyto's going on the same long sleep as Wilbur . . . In just a few days I'll never see him again. And that makes me even more sure about what I've got to do. Except it's never that easy, is it? Cos I can't tell him. He'd argue against it. So it has to be my secret. Which hurts so bad that the only thing I can think of doing is kissing him.

The waves keep slopping about the same as ever – the dumb stuff of the world, looking on, not even taking any notice. I can feel absolutely everything – the cold, hard floor of the deck, my hair being ruffled about by the wind, the creak of the lobster pots. And just when I figure the moment's gone . . . he takes my face in his hands and kisses me on the mouth. We're lost – locked at the lips, feeling the shape of each other's teeth and grabbing breaths. And kissing is so far from *normal* that we pull apart quickly. And that makes me laugh a bit, which sets him off, too. And after, we kiss each other again, but softer this time, to hide our faces and feelings, and to wonder at it alone. We lie there for ages, and all the world goes back to being the way it was – the wind is still there, and the waves, and the moon, the same as before. Except it ain't.

My eyes droop but I fight it, cos I want to carry on feeling Peyto against me. But you can't fight sleep when it comes. And I don't dream. I just come to in a dizzy flood of daylight.

The sea is rougher, sending up streamers of spray. And my heart jumps when I remember Peyto, except he ain't here beside me no more.

LOGGERHEADS

I CAN'T TELL PEYTO, OR ERIN, OR DAD ABOUT THE PLAN. BUT I'VE GOT TO TELL MALEEVA, COS I NEED HER HELP IF IT'S GONNA WORK.

As the hours drag by, I can see we're heading closer to the coast. The land is flat and low mostly – home to the Ferals and Blue-faces, tribes I've only heard about in scav tales. I wait most of the afternoon till Maleeva is on her own, taking a turn at the wheel, and everyone else is taking a nap. She's got her back to me, hunched over something that flares with light, as I step up to the back of the wheelhouse. And as I draw nearer I twig that she's speaking to someone. She's holding what looks like a scroll of paper, except it's a screen, and on it is the face of Commander Serov.

First up I'm ready to believe she's sold us out. But

then wouldn't the troops be chasing us down by now? Serov snaps something out in Russian, and she ain't so much angry as cut up.

'I will not,' goes Maleeva.

Serov looks stung. 'Your own Russia not good for you now?'

'What is there for me in Moscow? What's the point of going back?'

Serov snorts. 'You choose to stay here – this dead island?'

'It's only dead because of war. Chasing for the arte- fact is what killed this place, its people.'

'You know nothing of the artefact.'

'I know what it did to the Okhotniks.'

Serov shakes her head and it's weird to see her face soften, just for a moment. 'You do not understand. This thing has many secrets, maybe a cure for you . . .'

'There is no cure, you know that.'

'You are angry at me, always angry.'

'I'm not. I couldn't be angry if I tried now. I'm too tired of talking it over and over. You don't listen. Just stop searching for us.'

'How can I do that?'

'It's easy. Just call off the hunt. Take your troops away from this island.'

'And then you come back to me?'

A shudder takes hold of Maleeva then. 'This cage I'm in, did you ask me if I wanted to live inside it? Did you ask me? Ever?'

Serov's face crumples – all that hard control suddenly gone. 'I need you to be alive!'

'You *need* me? And so I *must* be alive?'

'Come back to me! Just tell me where you are!'

I come nearer. I know I should just call out or make a noise but I can't help myself. I'm that close I can see the moment Serov gives up, when the words lock in her throat. Maleeva touches her fingers to her lips and passes the kiss onto her mother's face. It's final and Serov knows it, cos a gasp takes her, and then Maleeva carefully folds up the scroll from the edges in, till just the pale eyes are left, burning out of the paper, straining for a last glimpse.

I'm standing there, caught in the act, when Maleeva turns to me. She tosses the folded-up scroll through the side window, watching as the wind snatches it away.

'How long were you listening?'

'I'm sorry. I didn't mean to. I just came to find you.'

Her face is just as slack as ever but her eyes are raw, blinking away tears, and I reach out to comfort her, but she holds up her hand, warning me away.

'You can go back to her,' I urge. 'When this is all over . . .'

'And do what, Cass? And become what? You know what I want to do now? I want to run. I want to go where the chase takes me. That's all.'

I know that feeling – when it's just one stride into the next that matters, not caring where and not caring why. I try to picture what she must've been like when she'd been well and strong, a young girl, smiling.

She turns from me to gaze out at the waves ahead.

'Anyway,' she says at last. 'I'm ready to become a sleeper if I must. For Wilbur.'

I wonder at her then – she really is ready to die for us. And my blood runs quick, cos I know then she's got the guts for the plan.

'You ain't got to be a sleeper. I know a different way to win.'

She don't move. I look at her calm face, fixed like a mask in the pitch and fall of shadows. How can I be sure of her? There ain't nothing to read in her eyes, but still I've got no choice. Cos without Maleeva on board there ain't no plan. It's as simple as that.

'Just listen first, then make your mind up, OK?'

She just looks back at my reflection in the wheel-house window and nods. So I tell her my plan to rescue

Wilbur and all the sleepers. She don't make a sound, she just soaks it right up, every last detail.

For some time she stays silent, and I think maybe she's gonna wake the others up and spill the beans. I couldn't have stood in her way.

'It's risking everything,' she says at last.

'That's the only way to make the ship sit up and take notice.'

'But it's ancient and clever. How can you know what it will do?'

'Cos I know how bad it wants them flinders. It'll do anything to keep them safe. That's what matters.'

'You don't know enough – the struggle will be on its territory.'

'I know the lie of the land. I been up there twice already. Where the air is, where the breach is, the way the ship's busted, how there's only one shuttle left – it's all in my favour. It *has* to listen to me. It ain't got no choice. So then it's about whose will is stronger. That's what it comes down to. And I ain't gonna back down.'

'You are brave. But to win you must be ready to lose everything.'

'I've figured it all through. I ain't never been so sure about something my whole life.'

'But what if you're wrong?'

'Look, Maleeva, it's up to you now. Make your mind up. Either you're in or you ain't. If you go and shout your mouth off now everything's scuppered.'

I let it all sink in. I can't see if she's tipping one way or the other but I guess she's stewing about it, trying to pick out the mistakes.

'It is so powerful. What if it can know right now what you're thinking?'

'So what? Bring it on. Look, I just can't leave Wilbur up there. So there it is, if the ship's listening in right now, it can strike me down for all I care. If it's smart then it won't, cos each step we take towards Arbor Low, we're one step closer to giving it what it wants – the forty-nine flinders.'

'You've really thought all this through, haven't you?'

'Look, it's simple. It's all about the numbers. If I get there *first*, then I can burn the ship's bridges. Don't you see? It won't just be tough for the ship to win, it'll be impossible. It'll have to give me what *I* want.'

'But it won't just be the ship's bridges you'll be burning. They're your bridges too. They're everyone's.'

'That's why the plan's gonna work. Look, are you with me or not? Cos I've got to know now. When I give you the shout, you'd better be there for me or it all goes down the pan.'

She nods slowly. 'All right. I'm with you.'

'No backing out.'

I hold out my hand to her and she clasps it, the cold armour of her fingers pressing firm. And so things are set in motion. It feels right then, like me and the ship are hurtling towards each other, like nothing can stop us. And maybe it could swat me out of the way, turn the others against me, crush me from above. But what else can I do? I'm locked into the charge now.

As I back out of the wheelhouse, I see Erin on the deck staring at me. And I feel bad for shouting at her but she's the one to come over to me.

'You ain't sick no more?' I go.

She shrugs. 'There's nothing left.'

'Figured you'd be the one to find their sea legs quickest.'

'Why's that?'

'You're the one most at home floating around in space.'

'It's different. Here, I just feel . . . trapped between the sky and the sea, on this tiny boat. We can't go up or down. The two places just keep fighting over us.'

She gazes out at the waves. 'I want to belong to this world, too, you know. Peyto says we can't live here and not change the way we are. He says it's not like

Homefleet, where we just watched the stars go by. But Homefleet wasn't like that for me. This place, it's just bigger. That's the only difference I see. And pretending it's endless, like nothing you do matters, that's what makes people cruel.'

She takes her ear-muffs off and studies them for a moment, then she just tosses them overboard.

She turns to me. 'I try not to think about my family too much. It's better for me to keep them just in my heart, in silence.'

I'm so sure that my plan is the only way to save her family that I ache to tell her. But I can't. Not yet.

Instead I say, 'You're gonna be the one that wakes them up, Erin.'

'I've thought about that so many times I've lost count.'

'And then what? What happens when you wake them?'

'Don't say that.'

'Why not?'

'Because we might not make it in time. We've been travelling for countless millions of years and the saddest thing is, we might be too late, by what – a few hours?'

'Hey, we're gonna make it, OK?'

'What makes you so sure?'

A silence hangs between us then – just the slap of the hull and the wind.

She stares at me coldly. 'You're not going to tell me, are you?'

'Tell you what?'

'What you're planning.'

'What makes you think I got a plan?'

'Because you're so calm now.'

I stare back. I ain't gonna lie no more, but I ain't gonna tell her neither.

'You can trust me, Erin.'

'No, I can't,' she says quietly, and then she turns away.

The coastline inches by. For the next few hours we take turns at the wheel, and, under Dad's direction, round the coast into the Wash. The further west we chug, the calmer the water gets, till by late afternoon it's near flat, though you can make out furious currents as the tide sweeps in from the open sea, lifting us onwards in mini-surges.

I stay with Dad in the wheelhouse as he plots a way through new islands that ain't on our map. For a while, we both fuss over the charts and the compass, not saying the one thing that matters.

At last I go, 'Dad, you know you can't come with us

– on dry land, I mean. With your leg . . . You'd be too slow.'

He don't look at me. 'I know. Anyway, someone has to stay with the *Lodestar*, make sure it's safe, eh?'

We fall silent for a bit.

'Cass?'

'What's up?'

'When it comes to it, don't leave your brother alone up there.'

'That's the whole idea, Dad . . .'

'I mean it now. Promise me.'

'Promise you what?'

'That you won't leave Wilbur.'

'I promise.'

He smiles then, but his eyes are sad, gazing at the waves ahead.

For a heady few seconds, I let myself picture the future. 'Do you reckon we'll get away with it – you know, get back to Gravesend with Irene's boat, start all over?'

My voice trails off as the situation really hits me. If things go pear-shaped for us, he'll never see me or Wilbur again. I block the thought out of my head. I hug him then, trying to hold it together. And when I pull back, his face is wet with tears.

'Hey, none of that! We're gonna be gone three days

max. I got it all worked out, Dad. It's all over bar the shouting – just you wait.'

He wipes his face, angry at himself. 'Just take care of each other now. All four of you have to stick together.'

I think about my plan, and I feel cold to the bone, but there ain't no point in dwelling on it now. It's set, like nothing can knock it off course.

Outside, the light is failing again. Flat windswept islands dotted with bushes and dead trees clutter the way ahead. The channels run fast and smooth, churned brown with sand and mud. And out of the setting sun these old town ruins appear – half-bridges, roads and walls submerged into the water, bent lampposts and the craggy spike of a church tower. The sea and the land at loggerheads.

THE NORTH WILDS

THE CHANNELS GET NARROWER AND MORE TREACHEROUS. A COUPLE OF TIMES YOU CAN HEAR THE HULL SCRAPING STUFF BELOW. DAD FIGURES THE TIDE IS AS HIGH AS IT'LL GET, AND that trying to push on in the dark is pointless. So we pull into a little inlet on the east side of one of the islands, finally coming to a stop in a bed of reeds. Peyto shuts off the engine and I do my best to tie us down to an old tree poking out the water. It's shallow there – no more than a metre or so to the bottom – and sheltered on three sides by mud banks and bushes. Not a bad place to anchor up and keep the boat out of sight.

We ain't taking much with us, just some water and biscuits – no point in being weighed down with too many supplies. So we take the chance to down a bit of grub before the off. Everyone's quiet, thinking about what lies ahead.

I watch how Maleeva 'eats' hers. First up she opens this little chamber near her belly and packs it with broken biscuits. Then she takes this black bag with a tube taped to a hole under her jaw, pops it free and squeezes a load of spit over the crumbs before closing the door. She does all this without fuss, glancing at me as I chew.

'Ain't given yourself much,' is all I can think of to say.

'I don't need much. I just need it for cell repair. Nearly all my energy for moving and breathing comes from this.' She pats an armoured box that's fitted to one of her hips.

'How long does it last?' Me and my big gob.

Will you make it to the ship? How long before you keel over? Nice one, Cass.

'It depends on what I do, how much power I use up. Normally the battery lasts about two weeks before I need to recharge. I'm down to about fifty percent.'

I think about her dash from the Vlad base with Peyto on her back. This last stretch over land is gonna cost her.

At last we're ready, and there ain't no point in hanging about. Dad ain't big on hugs so he shakes hands with the others, but you can see he's choked. Finally, he takes me in his arms.

He whispers in my ear, 'I love you, Cass. Come back to me. Come back with Wilbur.'

I nod, but I ain't able to say a thing. I just hold him for a bit, drawing in the smell of his old jacket – scav dust and toil. Then I clamber off the *Lodestar* and into the shallows. The last time I turn I see a lonely figure on the deck, his arm stretched out in farewell.

It ain't easy to see in the gloom, but we strike out for the tallest clump of treetops, hoping that's the mainland. We have to wade in places but most of the time it's pretty easy-going. In fact, it's harder when the tide goes out, cos then the channels are just pure sludge and there ain't no water to hold you up. I keep thinking about when's gonna be the best time to make my move. I figure I'll wait till we suss out where we are on the map. Maleeva has to be thinking all this, too, but she never catches my eye. We just slog onwards in silence, trying to pick out the shadow of the land against the darkening sky.

It takes us about an hour to reach what we hope is the mainland. The bushes and trees here are proper rooted down and there's the remains of a road, too, all cut up and loaded with plants, but the white lines are still there down the middle. It leads roughly westwards, winding through the forest, rising and dipping with the lie of the land. After a mile or so we come across an old road sign facing back the way we've come, half buried under brambles.

Peyto reads it out. 'Twenty-two miles to Lincoln.'

'So we passed it in the boat, then?' I go.

Ahead of us, Erin calls out. 'There's a village up here!'

We hurry along the road to what's left of an old settlement. Lumps of concrete and slate lie about, covered in moss and ivy. It ain't till we're on the far side of the place that we find out exactly where we are. There's a 'Please Drive Carefully Through Our Village' sign, then, a little further on, the name, Darlton.

'We're here,' goes Peyto, casting a lighter flame over the map. 'On the A57 road. It's maybe fifty miles to Arbor Low.'

Erin checks her cuff. 'We've got just over twenty-one hours.'

'It's going to be tight,' mutters Peyto.

I glance at Maleeva but don't say nothing. It ain't the right moment. But maybe I'm stalling, kidding myself. Cos when exactly is the right time to betray your mates?

We hurry on at marching pace, following Peyto's

directions onto a smaller road, checking the village signs along the way, past the odd rotted down car or truck, and, in places, grey tangles of bones – probably copped it from Quark bomb radiation. Tuxford, Broughton, Ollerton, Edwinstowe. We trudge through the night, slowing up with each mile. Only Maleeva looks fresh – bounding ahead now and then to scout for trouble.

Towards eleven at night, she goes missing for a good twenty minutes and I start to worry. At last she comes striding firmly between the potholes towards us, but when she spots me, she waves at us to get off the road. We scramble through a ditch and into the woods proper.

'What is it?'

'There's a camp up ahead.'

'What? Are you sure?'

'Yes. It's on the edge of a built-up area – Mansfield maybe. They're wild – Ferals.'

'This is not good,' mutters Erin.

'What are they doing?' I go. 'How do you know they're Ferals?'

'Who else are they going to be?' groans Erin.

'I mean, did you get a good look at them?' I ask, ignoring her.

'Whoever they are, they look dangerous. And we'll have to be careful skirting around them because they're not asleep,' goes Maleeva. 'They've got a big fire going and they're roasting a deer or something, and they're all hooting like they're drunk. Some of them are just wandering about in the woods singing.'

'How many are there?'

'Hard to tell – maybe a hundred. I don't think it's where they live – there's no huts or shelters, just the fire and their horses.'

'They've got horses?'

'Yes, there's about twenty of them tied to logs and trees.'

I stare at her, waiting for her to guess what I'm thinking.

'Oh, no, Cass. It's too dangerous . . .'

'Are you kidding? It'd be rude not to! Listen, you said yourself they're all half-cut. It'd be a cinch. We need to make up the distance . . .'

'You're crazy,' goes Peyto. 'Me and Erin, we can't ride horses!'

'You don't need to. Look, we only need to nick one. You can ride with me, then Maleeva can carry Erin. We'll be there in half the time.'

'Unless they catch us snooping around!'

'No, Cass is right,' goes Erin. 'It'll save time. Walking's just too slow – we'll never make it.'

Maleeva is still staring at me, probably trying to fathom out how all this changes the plan. But it makes perfect sense to me.

'How far ahead are they?' I ask.

'About a mile. You hear them before you see them. Cass, I can't go anywhere near horses – I spook them.'

'That's all right. I'll do it. You just guide the others past the camp. I'll meet you further up the road, where it's safe.'

'This is insane!' complains Peyto.

'Look, you're out-voted three to one. It'll be a breeze, don't worry.'

Maleeva takes Erin by the hand and leads her away from the road, north into the trees. Peyto hangs back, then he leans towards me and grabs a kiss.

'You're wasting time,' I whisper. 'Just keep going, I'll catch up with you. Go!'

But when he's disappeared into the undergrowth, I linger there in a daze, suddenly shocked at the idea of being totally on my jack.

I creep onwards, keeping the road in sight. Maleeva is right – I hear the Ferals long before I spot them. The drumming comes to me over the wind, a scary clatter of beats and bellowing. I slip from tree trunk to tree trunk, my legs all weak with fear. The woods give way to a concrete clearing and some old factory buildings. A hardcore of Ferals are gathered around a huge bonfire, kicking up holy hell. God knows what they're on but they're completely wild, charging about half-naked and screeching at each other in a frenzy. They're all men – no women or kids – like a hunting party, or maybe they're just bandits. And they're all daubed up in splashes of blue, the paint glistening in the firelight. A smell of cooked meat reaches me through the trees and I can make out the remains of a big animal on a spit. By this time I'm pretty terrified, cos being this close, you can see they live up to their name all right. Some of them are smearing themselves with meat juice.

As I'm trying to make out where the horses are tied up, I realise I'm a tad too close for comfort. No more than six metres away in the undergrowth are a couple of bodies snoring gently. I whip out my knife, but they carry on snoring just the same.

I edge closer. They're sentries, I reckon, fallen asleep on the job. One of them is on his back, his belly rising and falling with each breath, a great hunk of half-eaten meat resting on his chest. The stink of him makes me gag. His mate is curled up sideways, groaning in his sleep, cradling an empty glass bottle. There's a niff of that, too – not booze so much as chemicals, like paint stripper. It's the North Wilds all right.

I creep past them, trying to be sure of my footfalls, feeling out for twigs and stuff that might make a noise. The horses are tethered up further on – shuffling about half-asleep. I make a soft clicking noise so as not to alarm them as I approach and hold my hands out to the nearest ones so they can get used to my smell. They feel me out with their muzzles, all wet and warm and friendly, whinnying at me softly. So far, so good. I get in amongst them and stay there for a good ten minutes, patting and stroking and calming them down. I choose a fairly big one – brown with a white streak on his bonce. Most of the others are bareback, but this one's got a saddle and reins, all togged up and ready to go. The only problem is, the horse I've picked is hobbled. I duck down to get busy with my knife when a great holler freezes me to the spot. The horses shift about all nervy, snorting and stamping. Between their legs I can see a great oaf of a Feral crashing about in the bushes, howling away to the moon.

I think about just cutting my horse free and going for it, but if this Feral raises the alarm I'm stuffed. No, I've got to sweat it out. Trouble is, it don't look like he's going anywhere in a hurry. He sways about for a bit, then he drops his tattered trousers and starts going for a dump. I can't believe it! The way he's straining away, I'm set to be there for hours. As I drop my head, I catch sight of a stone and start grubbing it up out of the mud. It's a big old cobble but I don't trust my aim, so there ain't nothing else for it – I've got to creep up behind him.

First I cut my horse free and take the rope. There are just ten or so paces between me and my squatting target. I can see his great pale bum cheeks in the firelight shuddering away to another gargantuan fart. That seems to be my cue. To hell with stealth. I just charge him, swing back my stone and clobber him on the back of the head. He pitches over without a peep, leaving behind a great pile of steaming turd. Quickly I tie his hands and feet with the rope, then gag him with the piece of rag he's been using as a belt. I make sure all the knots are proper done up, and bury him under a load of dead branches.

Then it's back to the herd to lead out my horse. I coax him through the trees, and round in a big circle past the camp to pick up the road again. Then I'm in the saddle and kicking on – just a gentle canter, nothing too hectic.

About a mile on, Peyto comes flying out the trees

waving his arms. When I see him grinning from ear to ear, my heart dives, cos I know I've got to give the shout to Maleeva soon enough. Not yet, I reason. Get some distance between us and the Ferals.

I think Erin is quietly impressed. She don't look at me, but she smiles and makes a fuss of the horse. I help Peyto into the saddle behind me, and Maleeva hoists Erin onto her back. We're away. Maleeva goes loping ahead and I keep about ten lengths behind with Peyto clinging to my waist.

That's how the night passes and I try to block everything from my head, settling into the ride, staring into the tunnel of trees, their branches clacking overhead in the wind. And I can feel Peyto's body resting warm against my back. There ain't no more thinking to be done – the plan is set as sure as a loaded sling and the only question is when I should let it fly.

But with each canter stride north, the waiting just gets harder, till every breath is heavy, and the thought of breaking away from Peyto makes me sick to the soul.

BETRAYAL

IT'S A LONG NIGHT AND WE REST ONLY TO TAKE WATER. WHEN THE GREY LIGHT WASHES IN, WE FIND WE'RE IN OPEN HILLS. STREAKS OF MIST FLIT OVER THE RUINS OF FARMHOUSES AND broken walls and bare hedges. I glance at the only band left on my cuff, growing ever shorter. I count up the freckles. There's just eight hours to go.

It nearly sends me off to sleep watching Maleeva's swinging strides ahead of me – so regular, like a pendulum. But as the mist thickens, I see her slow up, and I know her batteries have got to be running down now. It ain't a sudden thing, but the bounce goes out of each thrust forward, and for the first time ever I see her stumble.

As the morning wears on, the hills grow steeper around us. There are ravines and rivers and nestled villages – all quiet, home only to tiny birds that burst for cover as we come near. I grow dizzy for sleep. My horse is down to a walk, head bowed, clopping through the mud. The mist closes right over us. Then the rain sets in, straight as stair rods, but I'm too done in to care now. Only the cold trickles down my neck are keeping me awake.

'We've got to rest,' goes Peyto at last.

'No time.'

He jumps down and stares up at me, squinting in the rain. 'No, listen. We're nearly there but we have to be alert now – in case the Russians are up here. There's another village up ahead, see? Let's put our heads down, just for an hour or so.'

With him off the horse there's a golden chance to do what I've got to do. Maleeva has stopped up ahead and I can see her poised waiting for the signal. But still I hang back. I'm so cold and wet through that the idea of getting out the rain is too tempting.

And when Peyto grins up at me, I feel the guilt as a sting inside, rearing up from my chest, looking for a way out.

He goes, 'Look at you – you're so tired you can't even speak!'

He calls out to the others and so we cast about for

somewhere to lie down. I don't even ask what this place is called but it's the biggest settlement we've come to for ages. There's a sorry-looking parade of amusement halls nearby and we break into one of them through the window. It's fusty inside but fairly dry – dust covering all the fruit machines and video games, but no reek of bodies. We're all so whacked out we don't even speak – we just cosy up to each other, Peyto in the middle, me and Erin on the outside. Maleeva is stood stock still in the doorway gazing out at the street or maybe she's asleep already, slumped in her frame. For a while I stare up at the drapes of old spider webs near the ceiling, then I feel Peyto's hand gently seeking out mine and the guilt rises hot inside me again. This is the last leg, the time for choices that'll make or break us all, and I can't go soft, not now. But still, lying there with his fingers cupped in mine, I can dream for an hour at least that things are gonna pan out, that we'll pull it off. And so I shove the guilt away and turn to my enemy, the ship, and all the details of my plan bubble up, until sleep takes me down. And I dream of the ship sailing silently through the black sky with its cargo of sleepers, waiting, waiting . . .

I'm alone on the floor when Maleeva wakes me, her caged face just above mine.

'Just when are you going to do it?' she whispers.

'Hey! Back off! When it's the right time I'll let you know.'

'What are you waiting for?'

I look over her shoulder towards Peyto and Erin who are talking by the entrance. Peyto glances over at us – is that a worried look on his face?

'Look, I've got it sorted. We need to be close to Arbor Low before everything kicks off.'

'Not so close that the whole Russian army can track us down. You don't suppose this thing will happen quietly . . .'

'We don't even know the Russians are up here.'

'And we don't know that they're not. Cass, you're waiting too long, letting your feelings . . .'

I sit up sharply. 'My *feelings* ain't none of your business, right? I'll give you the shout when it's the right time and not before. I don't want anyone stranded in the middle of nowhere while we do the necessary, OK? Everyone's got to be where I can find them or this ain't gonna work.'

Maleeva's head nudges forward in its frame, slipping out of the stays that keep her cheeks in place. I guess she's lost a load of weight for that to happen, and even in the hour I've been asleep she looks worse. Her movements have slowed right down, even the assisted blinking, so that her eyes are raw and moist. Almost straightaway I feel wrong for snapping at her and I start to say sorry, but she waves it away.

'I'm sorry, too,' she goes. 'I just want it to be over now.'

'Before we get to Arbor Low, I swear.'

And so after sharing the last of the food in our packs – just a few broken biscuits and some water – we set off again into the rain.

We try to step up the pace but after an hour we're flagging. Maleeva has the map and keeps stopping to check signs and roads more often, and I know we've got to be close now. I check the cuff – there's just two freckles left. Less than two hours . . .

It's Peyto who spots the danger first. We're picking our way along a narrow road clogged up with bushes and brambles when he clutches at me and points through a gap in the branches. Across the field, maybe quarter of a mile away, is a clump of trees on a hill and gathered around it is a small encampment – men and trucks and tents. A crane is being winched into position near the top of the hill and there's a scar of earth and bare rock splitting the slope in two.

'Soldiers, it has to be,' breathes Erin.

If it is the Vlads, it's just a small unit – no helicopters, no Okhotniks. And that's strange, unless they're camped in force elsewhere.

Maleeva checks the map. 'It's Gib Hill.'

'Where Halina was buried,' I blurt out.

And Peyto stiffens on the saddle behind me.

'It was all written down at the museum, where she was found,' mutters Erin. 'It makes sense that the Vlads would come here, too.'

'But what are they looking for?' goes Peyto. 'How can they know there's another shuttle?'

'They don't know,' answers Maleeva. 'They're just digging to see what they can find.'

'Then what are we waiting for?' goes Erin. 'We've got to summon the shuttle now!'

I feel the moment close around me. It's now. Or never.

When I speak, my voice is flat, stone-cold certain. 'The shuttle ain't there.' I think about Halina speaking to me down through the ages. 'It's buried under some stones.'

Erin stares at me. 'What stones? How do you know?'

'From the message in her flinder.'

'You never said.'

'I didn't think we'd make it.'

'That means they're digging in the wrong place,' says

Maleeva, pointing at the map. 'The stones – that has to be the circle here at Arbor Low. She tried to reach it, but she died in battle. They must have buried her where she fell . . .'

It's hazy, but I half-remember the photos and displays at the museum. On the map, the stone circle is set to one side of Gib Hill but very close, perhaps within sight from the trees at the top of the slope.

Maleeva and me stare at each other. There ain't never gonna be a better time.

'Now!' I snatch at the word, feeling the threads of everything draw together.

Maleeva drops her shoulder and topples Erin, pinning her to the ground. Peyto scrambles out of the saddle to help her. Erin squeals and wrestles, but Maleeva holds her firm with just one arm.

'What the hell's going on?' cries Peyto. He tries to reach Erin but Maleeva checks him with her free arm. He whirls to glare at me.

This is gonna be the worst part – the explaining. But they've got to know certain things or it all goes belly up.

'Me and Maleeva are going on alone,' I say.

Peyto starts towards me but I pull the horse clear, ready to spur away if he gets too close.

'Are you crazy?!' Erin bucks and spits and throws

herself at Maleeva, but there ain't no budging from that grip.

'No, I ain't crazy,' I go, trying to keep my voice level. 'We're going up there to bring back Wilbur, and all the other sleepers. But the only way that's gonna happen, is if you and Peyto stay right here on Earth. You can't come with us.'

I'm pretty calm then, all things considered, cos the plan is so utterly clear, like a road unwinding ahead of me.

'This is madness!' screeches Erin.

'I'm sure Cass is going to explain.' Peyto's voice has gone deadly quiet now.

I look over at Gib Hill. I can't just sit here and tell them the full story. The soldiers might rumble us at any moment.

'But we *all* need to go!' shouts Erin. 'The ship needs all forty-nine flinders to stop it crashing!'

At last Peyto closes his eyes. 'You're not going up there to repair the ship, are you? You're going up there to confront it.'

'You can't!' cries Erin, beating at Maleeva's solid pillar of an arm.

'I ain't leaving Wilbur up there. End of.' I hold my hand out to Peyto. 'I'm going to the ship without you.

– 333 –

And you're gonna give me your flinder so I can get there.'

Peyto shakes his head. 'But what if it won't listen?'

'Just hand over your flinder, Peyto.'

But he ain't budging.

Erin's nearly choking with the effort to break free. 'Why don't you trust us? We were all going up there to save Wilbur . . .'

'The ship thinks he's the perfect sleeper. It ain't gonna let him go. Not unless it's forced to.'

'But if the ship refuses . . .' goes Peyto. 'You won't have Erin's last flinder with you – the ship will crash. And wars will sweep across the world. Everyone will die, including you.'

'I don't care. If the ship repairs it won't wake anyone up – not for centuries, maybe never. It's mad. I ain't leaving Wilbur up there.'

'What makes you think you can defeat the ship when my mother couldn't?'

'Cos your mother didn't have a plan, and I do. That's why. I'll be making the ship a deal it can't turn down. As soon as I'm there, the shuttle can't come back for you and the last flinder, unless I reset it. So the ship *can't* complete the forty-nine the way it wants. It'll let the sleepers go. It has to.'

'What if it can't let them go, Cass? What if it won't?

You're holding everyone on board to ransom – Wilbur, too.'

'The flinders are too precious. The ship won't let them or the sleepers die.'

'But you would?'

There's no answering that. The whole thing hinges on what I would risk, what I'm prepared to do. I wait for his flinder.

Erin gives a strangled cry, a last-ditch attempt to wriggle free. 'You and Maleeva can't *both* go back to the ship! It'll dock on the bridge side where there's no air and there'll only be Halina's suit in the shuttle . . .'

'I've thought everything through. I need Maleeva up there in case the Okhotnik shows up, but one suit's enough.'

'There is no other way.' Maleeva states it as plain fact. 'Give her the flinder, Peyto.'

'No! Don't do it!' Erin cries.

He nods very slightly, maybe working it through in his mind, and a sad smile rises to his lips. 'When did you figure all this out, Cass?'

'On the boat.'

'Well, maybe you haven't thought through every-thing,' he goes.

'What's that supposed to mean?'

'It's not just a question of numbers. It's the identity of the sleeper that matters. How the flinder *chooses* you, remember?'

I stare at him and the tears come to my eyes at last. 'I ain't got time for this.'

'No, I suppose not. But you think about it when the time comes. Because you're a match for this. More than me. We both know it.' And with that he reaches under his collar and pulls out the flinder. It sparkles blue in the gloom, a light hovering between our outstretched arms. Then he puts it in my hand without another word.

IN TANDEM

ERIN BEGINS TO WAIL AS I SPUR THE HORSE FORWARD, DUCKING THROUGH THE HEDGEROW BRANCHES, OUT INTO THE OPEN. MALEEVA COMES BOUNDING UP ALONGSIDE ME – HER STRIDES ragged and off-balance. I know there ain't no point in stealth – we've got to go for it. It's a straight race to the stones of Arbor Low now.

I keep my head low, almost against the mane, feeling the horse strain forward, and ahead of me the field slopes upwards into steep banks of turf – the edge of the circle? I blot out thoughts of Peyto and Erin. Only getting to the *Aeolus* matters now. I charge to the top of the slope and the horse rears up, spooked by the sudden dip that lies over the edge. The circle stretches below me, sheltered on all sides by great banks of earth, like a crater. I slide out of the saddle and pull the horse down, trying to soothe him. Back towards Gib Hill I can see men scurrying about in all directions, headlights firing up, and over the wind comes the sound of engines and shouting.

I watch in horror as Peyto and Erin stumble out into the open field, trying to catch up with us.

'Come on!' cries Maleeva. 'We can't help them! Do what you have to do!'

She drags me down into the circle. Here, protected from the wind, lies a ring of maybe thirty stones, fallen and half-buried in the ground. They're all misshapen, covered in splashes of lichen, weathered and broken. It's a forbidding place, and somehow I know it's unimaginably old – old even when Halina had been queen of her tribe. I'm dazed at being there at last – the place where she'd come to Earth all those thousands of years ago . . .

'Cass! Hurry! Call the shuttle! Do it now!'

I pull out the flinder and stare at its pulsing surface. I think about how I reset the shuttle, just with thoughts. Then I close my eyes and sing, reaching out with my mind, and sending out them seven simple notes. But nothing happens. Maybe it's buried too deep. A scream rises to my throat – I feel it lodging there, building up. All this way for nothing!

But then a grinding starts deep under my boots, like boulders being crushed. I step back out of the ring and I'm suddenly showered with dirt and stones. Then, thrusting out of the earth, comes the dark, gleaming head of a shuttle, shrugging off cloaks of grass, like an animal desperate for air. A hole opens in the hull surface, blasting mud into a fountain. But the shuttle don't stop. It writhes out of its burial chamber and ploughs right through the outer bank of the circle like it's diving into a wave. I scramble after it, through the ruins of its wake and back towards Gib Hill. It disappears for a moment, corkscrewing into the ground, kicking up a fan of dirt.

Over the fields jeeps bounce towards me, headlights spiking through the storm darkness, and there, at the edge of the road, are Peyto and Erin, not moving any more, closed on all sides by soldiers pointing their guns and shouting. But high above the drone of distant engines I hear the sound of Erin calling, chanting, summoning the shuttle. I've stopped singing, so it's going to her instead . . .

Something thuds into me and scoops me up. Then I feel the hard, alien movement of Maleeva running – chasing the surge of bursting earth ahead of us. To free up my hands I stuff the flinder into my mouth, and it's hot under my tongue, knocking against my teeth. I claw at Maleeva's frame as her head flops inside its cage. A rocket fizzes through the rain, snaking in low, blasting into the side of the shuttle, and it's so close I hear cinders hissing into the grass. One gigantic stride – maybe that's all she's got left. All the gearings of Maleeva's frame go loose and we're sailing towards the shuttle as it banks away from the jeeps. She hits it on all fours, locking to the surface, and I tumble away, flailing for the entrance hole, feeling it shrink as I snatch at the lip with my fingers. The shuttle careers sharply to one side and I'm sure the thing is gonna capsize and crush me into the ground, but somehow it stays upright and I throw myself in through the hole. Above me, Maleeva's arms reach for the opening, skittering off the hull, and I grab at her, knowing I'm too late, that the hole is too small to let her in now. That's when I gob the flinder into my hand and hold it back up towards the open sky. It's just blind action. I ain't got a clue if it'll stop the closing hatch or if my hand is gonna be snipped clean off. But as I stare at my fist trembling against the grey sky, the hatch suddenly sweeps open again and Maleeva crashes in on top of me. And I feel the roar of the engines gather, swallowing me up as we thunder skywards.

There ain't no time to strap in – we both get dumped to the floor. I can't even see Maleeva, cos I'm wrenched over so hard I figure my spine's gonna push through my ribs. Finally, the engines die away and gravity lets go of us and I splay out into weightlessness. It's only then that I can see if our gamble has paid off or not cos it's gonna be curtains if we get up there empty-handed. I spin round and round trying to see it. Nothing. Then wafting out of the shadows like a drowned ghost comes the thing that's gonna keep us both alive – Halina's suit.

Peyto's flinder drifts past my face. It reaches out its two tentacles and gently clasps me round the neck. And it's my flinder now . . . I feel it choose me – the way the tentacles brush my skin as they reach together. Then I think about what I've just done – how Peyto and Erin have probably been captured by now.

Maleeva grabs the suit. 'Hurry, Cass.'

Her voice box cuts in and out. Her skin is wet and pale. I try and blot out what's happening on Earth. There ain't nothing I can do. I've got to get my head straight – in a few minutes the shuttle is gonna dock and the hatch doors'll open on the bridge side where there's no air.

And so the first part of my plan is put to the test. There may be just the one suit but if it's like the others

– 341 –

it'll change to fit the size of the body that puts it on. And so me and Maleeva become one. I embrace her so her head's resting against my chest. Then she clutches me, leaving my arms free. I jam my feet into the stork-like joints of her frame, and in tandem we wriggle into the suit. I hinge down the helmet, snap down the seals and wait for docking. I've got to hold tight to my plan, stay sharp. Cos when I set foot on the ship it's all gonna kick off straightaway – all-out war.

I whisper to Maleeva, 'Can you breathe OK?'

Little patches of mist collect on the inside of the helmet from my breath.

Maleeva don't answer straightaway and from the moment she speaks I know something's badly wrong. 'I was b-born in a village near Gori at the f-foot . . . of the Caucasus Mountains,' she slurs.

'What? Hey, Maleeva, hold it together!'

'My father was a t-trader – a man who brought goods . . . from the B-black Sea ports.'

'Maleeva! This ain't no time to flake out!'

'M-my mother was a general's . . . daughter, a hunter, t-trained from an early age to kill . . .'

There's a jolt as the shuttle docks, then the hatch opens and there's the bridge area, with its tides of litter, like the hold of a sunken boat. I scan for the Okhotnik.

'I had t-two brothers. B-both joined the . . . New Russian Army – they were . . . killed in the first w-w-wars to protect our land from . . . people in the east . . . invading Mongols.'

Her voice slows down – it's her battery packing up. The last push to get onto the shuttle has finished her. She's dying.

'Hang in there, Maleeva! You hear me?'

As I thrust into the ship, her grip around me loosens.

'When I-I was a ch-ch-ild my mother took me hunting . . . in the mountains. We stalked bears and d-deer . . . s-sometimes sleeping under the sky . . .'

'Don't go to sleep! Come on, fight it!'

I fling myself through the passageways of the bridge. I don't know what I can do for Maleeva now – there ain't nothing to do but stick to my guns.

The *Aeolus* don't say a word. Maybe it's pondering choices. But right now choices are few and far between. Halina may have fought with it but she'd have been too scared to try and destroy it outright. The lives of all the sleepers, including her son, would've held her back. But me, I'm going all out.

'You know I ain't gonna reset the shuttle until all the

sleepers are awake,' I go at last. 'And you can't reset it on your own. Which means you can't get Peyto and Erin up here to make them sleepers. And without Erin's flinder, you can't repair yourself. It's over. You got to do what I say.'

Then the ship speaks to me. Its calm, sad words fill the helmet.

'You have come, Cass. But this is not the way.'

'OK, listen up,' I go, trying to keep my voice strong. 'I'm coming to get Wilbur and if I so much as get a sniff of that Okhotnik on the way I'm gonna bail out into space with my flinder.'

'I will not harm you but you cannot take Wilbur.'

'Nope. Wrong answer. And I ain't just here for Wilbur. You ain't got no choice – you've got to free everyone, let them return to Earth. Cos if you don't, your precious hoard of flinders is gonna go up in smoke with you. You've held them with you too long to let them die with the sleepers, ain't that right?'

'If I die . . . it is of no consequence. But the flinders must not be scattered on the Earth. It is too soon. They must become strong. They must become *one*. They must watch from the sky. Together, through them, the sleepers can throw out a net of dreams to heal this world, banish the ills that plague it.'

'Everyone's coming to Earth, or we all die up here. It's up to you.'

'Wilbur cannot leave. His command of the flinder makes the forty-nine *strong*. Wilbur *will not* leave.'

'He weren't never meant to be up here in the first place. He's got a life and a family back on the ground. You *forced* him to be a sleeper.'

'Sleepers cannot be forced. They must choose with a free will.'

'A free will?' It really is all-out bonkers. 'You snatched him out my arms and swallowed him up! How's that his choice?'

'I had to let him see. I had to show him the dream of the ancients. The flinders must become *one*. He knows.'

For a moment, I remember the flinder echoes, the spiders weaving together, the web pulling my fingers together. *The flinders must become one.* It's like the spiders was trying to show me something. A *weaving* of flinders somehow . . . like the flinders are shattered parts of something . . . something *stronger*. And I think about Wilbur – how his head never was in the real world, the world of scavs, how he was always up in the clouds, buried in stories and dreams and things from London what happened years ago. I think about him giving himself that black eye the night we first crossed the river. And the way he clung to the minute hand at Big Ben . . . Maybe he did choose the life of a sleeper – to travel through time, like Captain Jameson, but forwards instead of backwards.

But then Halina's words come back to me. *Never trust it.*

I clamber through the honeycomb of tunnels to the main shaft that leads to the sleeper side. A ray of Earth light punches in from the hull breach as I hang back, trying to see if it's clear ahead. Gas streams past the edge of the hole where the littlest torn threads are glowing like bulb filaments. The ship swings round a backdrop of stars and in the wheeling light there are things like chunks of ruby, uncut, the size of fists.

'Once we g-got . . . caught in a b-blizzard and we made a snow-hole to shelter . . . sc-scooping out a space just big enough for the two of us . . . like winter animals . . .'

'Maleeva, we're nearly there. Hold on!'

But the truth is, I ain't got a clue what I can do for her when I get across to the sleeper side. Without a battery she's never gonna make it.

'Cass, I will not let you endanger this vessel and its cargo. I have seen your plan. I watched it grow in your mind.'

'But that don't matter, does it? Cos you can't stop me.'

At the edge of the shaft I try to line up the cable-gun on my forearm. It ain't easy – Maleeva's gone as limp as a wrung chicken and my body feels too chunky, what with the both of us stuffed inside the suit.

I fire the cable, watching it trace out a line to the far airlock, and out of nowhere my view ahead gets blocked by a sight so awful I start yelling. The Okhotnik! It looms up like it's going to grab me and I chuck out my arms to fight back. But then it just hangs there like a busted puppet and I cotton on at last. It ain't got a suit on. It's frozen solid, twinkling in the Earth-light rays – covered in a fur of blood crystals, spikes of flesh bursting out of its eye sockets and mouth. I try and get my breathing under control. What the hell's it doing here? An accident? Did it top itself? Did the ship egg it on?

I feel Maleeva's head stir. 'I-I awoke first, pushing through the snow. It was calm, c-clear . . . so c-clean. A hare hopping through the s-snow below me . . . white fur . . .'

And then it twigs. The Okhotnik's frame has got to work like Maleeva's. I can save her! I latch onto the gently somersaulting body and start rooting for the battery. It's in the same place – an armoured box strapped to its thigh. I fiddle with the catches and rip it free.

'Listen to me, Cass,' goes the ship. 'You cannot win. You will not win.'

But I ain't listening – I just reel myself in towards the airlock. And as I reach level with the hull breach it's like a dream, cos I've run through all the ways this can pan out.

'You must send back the shuttle for the last flinder,' it warns. 'Already the atmosphere is too close. You must do this or you will die, your brother will die . . .'

I wriggle my legs, trying to snap Maleeva into life. 'Come on. You was on the mountain in a snow-hole with your ma. You saw this white hare. What then?' But Maleeva's gone silent on me now.

And in the deep quiet of space, I feel another nip from the countdown cuff. There's only one tiny freckle of time left. One hour to go.

At last I reach the airlock, untether the cable-gun, and wait for the bubble to let me through to the sleeper chamber. All the while I watch the walls for tentacles. But there ain't no hitches. Maybe I got it worried now. Cos it must know – one hint of an attack and I'm off into the great outdoors and there ain't no way to recover my flinder once I've gone. It's got to play by my rules.

Once I'm safely on the sleeper side, I rip off the suit and pull Maleeva clear. She looks terrible but she's still alive – I can see the ribs of her frame gently working each breath. I fumble with her dead battery. Out with the old, in with the new. It snaps home perfect.

'Maleeva! Can you hear me?'

Nothing. Her wasted body nudges against the tethers of the frame. Her eyes are open but there ain't no one home . . .

'Maleeva?'

I reach out to touch her face.

And then the stalks on her head-frame blink for her. Her fingers flex . . .

'Jeepers creepers, you had me squitting it there. You OK? Can you hear me? Maleeva?'

She seems to gaze at me for a moment, except maybe it's just the way her head's angled, cos it's hard to tell if there's any life in them eyes.

Her voice box crackles into life. 'You saved me, Cass . . .' The words are so flat, she almost sounds disappointed.

'Yeah, good job that Okhotnik was floating about, eh? Reckon you shouldn't go nowhere without a spare.'

'What?'

'Your battery pack – it was running low. I swapped in a new one from the warrior – he ain't gonna need it any time soon . . .'

'He was dead?'

'As a dodo. Just spinning about near the hull breach without a suit on . . . which was pretty handy when you think about it . . .' My words trail off as it dawns on me how that's just too good to be true. Like it was planned.

'Oh, Cass . . .'

And I'm looking right into her eyes when the ship strikes. A tentacle shoots past my shoulder and slams into Maleeva's forehead. It pulses as it latches onto her, spreading its skin over hers.

'No! Maleeva!'

I try to pull her clear of the tentacle but it's stuck firm. Then her chest heaves and I can hear air rushing into her lungs.

'I can feel it, Cass. The ship – its spirit. It's coming for me . . .'

'Hold it back! Fight it!'

But I remember the way the ship rummaged through my thoughts, the way it peered out my eyes, like it was looking out the windows of a house. I know its spirit can *move*. From one shell to another . . . I tear at the tentacle but it grows between my fingers, sending out blue veins that race across her cheeks, into and under her skin. It spreads so fast, snaking round and round her head, under her ears, over her lips, into her nostrils. And all the while the tentacle pulses and pumps and glows with a dim blue light.

'Maleeva! Hold on! I'm gonna get you free!' But even as I say it, I feel the ghost of the ship rippling past my fingertips, ancient and *hungry*.

She looks at me then and for the first time I see life in her face. *Proper* real life. Cos her eyes *move* in their sockets to find mine.

'Remember me, Cass,' goes the voice box. 'When I'm gone.'

A great spasm shoots through the frame and all the little motors in her joints whir at once. Then everything goes loose in my arms. Like she's dead.

'Maleeva!'

I stroke her cheek. It's all scaly and cold where the tentacle skin has spread across her face. Two tears of blood leak out of her eyes. The red runs round her eyelids and off the ends of her lashes.

And then her lips move. The words of her true voice call out, lost after all this time. Except it sure ain't Maleeva doing the speaking.

'I am reborn – the *Aeolus*, ninth pioneer ship of the

Homefleet. Maleeva is mine until the forty-nine are complete.'

I'm too stunned to move. I watch as the tentacle stretches then snaps, leaving two little horns glued to Maleeva's head, twisting and writhing.

'Where's Maleeva?' I gasp. 'Jesus! What have you done with her?'

'She is . . . with me still.' The eyes gaze at the steel-clad fingers as if for the first time, as they reach up to stroke Maleeva's forehead. 'In here. Inside this vessel of bone.'

'You've stolen her body?'

'Borrowed, not stolen.'

It flexes Maleeva's fingers, like it's testing their strength.

'Forgive me,' it goes.

'What?'

'You leave me no choice. It is just a small hurt. But I must . . .

Then it brings the armour-plated fists together and swipes upwards. The attack is slow, like it's deliberately taken the pace off. But even though I see it coming, there ain't no way to dodge it. Cos I'm floating there – a sitting duck. The punch lands. Straight into my chops . . .

Crunch!

Spinning . . . over and over . . . the lights streak past . . . no sound . . . no pain . . .

No, wait. Here comes the pain. In jagged waves.

Then nothing.

Black 'n' grey 'n' buzzy.

Like a hornet swarm gathering in the summer. Man, how long ago was summer? When things was just normal . . .

As my eyesight comes back it's like I'm looking through a wodge of frogspawn. But slowly it clears.

My tongue's all warm and it feels *wrong*. Bits of broken glass in my gob. I cough. And out comes a tooth – in pieces – together with a whole wad of blood 'n' spit. The hole at the back of my jaw feels hot and slushy.

And then I remember Maleeva. Except it ain't Maleeva no more, is it? It's the *Aeolus*. And it's gone. But gone where?

I just float in a haze, staring as the chamber walls pass me by, all speckled and veiny. I'm trying to think but I'm as slow as a slug race. And the blood on my cheeks is all dry and flaky . . . Dry? That means . . .

God, how long have I been out cold? I look at the countdown cuff – the marks are all gone now. So less than an hour left. It's just minutes now, but how many?

Slowly, bit by bit, my poor battered bonce works it out. And the pieces of my shattered plan fall down around me. Cos if the ship's got a body now, then there's only one place it's gone. The bridge. I twist round in search of Halina's suit. It's nowhere to be seen.

That's it. I've lost.

If it's gone to the bridge, then it can use Maleeva's hands to reset the shuttle. Which means the shuttle's going back for Erin – and the last flinder.

For a moment, I gaze at the living walls around me – just empty flesh now that the ship's soul has escaped into Maleeva. It just waited for us to come.

At last my elbow nudges against something solid. And as I turn, I see Wilbur's face – peaceful and waxy white – buried deep inside Halina's old pod.

THE LAST SLEEPER

A SHIVER RUNS THROUGH ME. I STEEL MYSELF. THERE'S STILL TWO SPARE SUITS — I STASHED THEM IN THE AIRLOCK SLOTS WHEN I WAS LAST HERE WITH WILBUR. THAT MEANS I CAN GET to the bridge. I picture the *Aeolus* inside Maleeva's body, resetting the shuttle, climbing through the hatch, hightailing it to Earth . . . But maybe there's still time. Maybe I can reach the bridge first . . .

I thrust against the wall, and its surface feels hot . . . A stink of cooked flesh hangs in the air. We must be close to burning up in the Earth's atmosphere. I push towards the airlock and seal myself into one of the suits. I'm about to hinge down the helmet, when there's a sharp noise overhead. Something has docked sleeperside. Then a hole punches through the dock wall, and three figures appear.

First Erin, then Peyto, and, lastly, Maleeva's hijacked body.

I know it ain't Maleeva, cos it still has them two horns stuck to her head curling round and round, like they're sniffing the air for something. The sharp joints of the frame poke the suit into odd bulges at the knees and elbows, like swellings.

Erin and Peyto stare at me silently. They seem horribly shaken by something.

'Do what it says,' urges Peyto. 'Please, Cass. There's no time. The ship will burn up any minute now!'

I think of all the Vlad troops pouring across the field towards the stones of Arbor Low, surrounding Erin and Peyto.

'How come you got away from the Vlads?' I whisper.

'Serov was there,' breathes Erin. She glances at the *Aeolus*, at the body it's stolen.

'I threatened to end Maleeva's life,' says the *Aeolus*. 'Serov had no choice.'

I feel the *bite* in them words. It's testing me, sowing doubt. And it knows now what I'm relying on, the secret I've figured out, it *has* to.

Smoke rises out the ridges in the ship's walls.

'Don't fight it any more,' pleads Peyto. 'You can't win.'

The *Aeolus* speaks at last. 'Erin, take your place as a sleeper.'

'Erin,' I whisper. 'Don't do it – you don't have to. Listen, it can't force you.'

She looks at me and shakes her head. 'I'm sorry, Cass. I must. It's the only way.'

She kicks towards the last two empty pods. And I ain't got the heart to try and stop her. Cos right now, for her, even if she's too late to save her family, sleep is the bliss of not even knowing. Sleep is a desperate hope. She'll either go to ash without feeling it, or she'll wake up in some future heaven on Earth with her family beside her. I stare at the grid of sleeper pods and wonder then, for the first time, which of them hold her loved ones. She looks at me just once before climbing inside her pod. She's utterly wrecked – covered in mud and trembling. But she fixes me with a curious stare, all her anger and fear gone.

'Goodbye, Cass,' she says simply.

I nod at her. And when her pod is sealed shut, I feel my body sag like the fight's gone out of it. Cos there's just one pod left. And that means it's either me or Peyto.

Just right then there's a massive shudder in the walls. It ripples down one whole side of the ship and a column of fire bursts into the chamber. The *Aeolus* pulls Maleeva's helmet down over her head, and Peyto charges clear of the docking hatch towards where the last suit is stashed . . .

The hole seems tiny at first. But then anything not tied down funnels towards it in a great rush. And a thin scream of air cuts through the chamber. I slam my helmet shut and snatch out for a handhold, cos I can feel my legs being dragged back towards the hole. But I'm floating free and there ain't nothing nearby to cling to. Only as I start to slide back do I think of the cable-gun on the suit's forearm. No aim. I just fire, and jerk to a stop with the storm all around me.

Just beyond my flailing legs I see Peyto struggling his way into a suit, but then I lose sight of him. The last puff of air squeals out the hole and everything drops slack. In an instant the chamber is silent apart from my heaving breaths. I unclip the cable and throw myself into a spin to see if I can spot Peyto. The hole in the ship wall yawns huge and white-hot. The edges buckle apart without a murmur. Arcs of light break past me, eating up the inside surface now – cracks tearing through the hull. As I stare at the hole, trying to take in the fact that there ain't no air left, something nudges against me. And Peyto is there, safely inside his suit, just a face-plate away. *Thank God . . .*

He takes me by the shoulders.

His voice crackles through the helmet speakers. 'Cass! Can you hear me? You can still save the ship!'

'What?' I look at him in a daze.

And then I cotton on to what he's saying. The cold truth sinks in, and the dread of it makes me lose all hope. Peyto couldn't be the last sleeper now even if he wanted to be. Cos the final flinder is with me, inside my suit, and there ain't no air left. Either I go into the last pod alone. Or I stay here with him till the ship catches fire.

'Cass, you know there's no other way. You have to be a sleeper. If you climb into that pod, you can repair the ship. You can save yourself, you can save Wilbur. There's still time!'

'What, go to sleep for ever and leave you behind? I can't. No way.'

Then the ship speaks in its stolen voice – the voice of Maleeva. And, even now, with human lips and human breath, there ain't a speck of emotion in its words.

'Cass Westerby, this is your final chance. Take your place as the last sleeper.'

I gaze at Peyto and I start to cry. I can't help it though it makes me mad, and I can't even wipe away the tears as they sprinkle free. It's too much, to leave him, after everything I've been through.

But then it's like the tatters of my plan come together. Cos there ain't no forest of tentacles springing out to drag me into that last pod, is there? The *Aeolus* was only telling half the truth when it said a sleeper can't be forced. The whole truth is that *it can't do the forcing*. Even when it took Wilbur from me, it didn't harm him, it didn't make him become a sleeper. It couldn't. And it's desperate to complete the forty-nine now. But it can't without me . . .

'You will not let every soul on this vessel perish,' goes the *Aeolus*. '*You will not.*'

And that's when I know for certain what's going to happen. I've wondered over and over, when push comes to shove, if I'll have the guts to do it. To let myself die, and Peyto, and the forty-eight people who now sleep on this ship. My own brother. Erin and her family. Maleeva, too – though God only knows whether she can see or hear any of this now. I've always figured the ship would back down rather than lose its precious flinders. And now I'm sure. Cos it's got no choice.

Then for a moment I waver. What if all the sleepers together can hold back wars on Earth? I've always figured that was a lie to keep them up here with their flinders. But what if I'm wrong? Maybe the Earth will end unless forty-nine sleepers are allowed to sleep and sleep. Except I can't possibly know, can I? . . .

Never trust it.

The truth is, I just want my brother back.

And the only way I'll ever get him back is to risk it all.

So to hell with it.

'No,' I whisper. 'I ain't giving in. Let the sleepers go. You have to, or they'll die.'

'They must not wake. Without them watching over the Earth, wars will rage.'

'They'll have to find a different way, a new way to protect the world. I *know* you can let them go. If you can snatch Maleeva's body from her, if you can sprout tentacles whenever you want, then you can set them people free. Do it.'

The ship's walls blur and shudder.

At first Peyto just gapes at me, not believing what I've just said. But then he reaches out and holds me, squeezing me tight. Cos he knows I ain't gonna budge, not now. And the fire's gonna take us any moment.

The *Aeolus* don't say a word. But then, just when I figure it's too late, as soft as dandelion heads lifting into the breeze, the first pods lift away from the walls.

A FIGHTING HEART

HUNDREDS OF BARBED TAILS SPRING OUT FROM THE WALLS. THEY
GLOW AND SMOKE, BUT STILL THEY MOVE AS ONE, LIKE GRASS
STEMS BOWING IN THE WIND. AND THEY LIFT THE PODS ONE BY
one towards the shuttle hatch.

'Come on!' yells Peyto.

He snatches my hand and leaps towards the pro-
cession of pods. We latch onto the back of one and
scramble through the gap into the shuttle. Already
there's hardly any space left – it's rammed with body-
shaped cocoons, like tightly wrapped corpses. The last
body to enter is Maleeva's. Deep down, behind the
helmet visor and the struts of her head-frame, her dead
eyes stare back at me.

The ship is a furnace now. Sheets of white fire rip out
into space as bright as lightning. And beyond them I

can't see nothing but stars. Then the hatch seals shut and the pods snap together around us, as the shuttle blasts away from the ship.

Then gravity kicks in. I clutch hold of Peyto. 'We're gonna burn.' My voice ain't no louder than a croak. I just ain't got the strength to be scared no more.

'No, the shuttle's much tougher than the ship, remember?' He pushes away from me and tries to force his way past the sleeper pods. 'But right now there's nothing steering it!'

'What?'

'The ship's breaking up! The bridge has gone – there's no way to reset the shuttle! If we don't do something we're going to crash! Help me!'

I try to reach out to the pods, but it's no use – they're locked around us and by now we're falling so hard I'm pinned flat. I can't even move my arms . . .

But then Maleeva's body stirs next to me. It jerks into life and heaves the pods to one side. Then it grabs me by the helmet and drags me towards the edge of the shuttle.

'Peyto, help!'

Them mighty machine arms hurl me down, then one fist reaches back, punches right through the shuttle wall and comes up with a handful of torn cables that spark and jitter about.

Maleeva's limp face thrusts towards mine, and the girl's voice hisses out, 'You have a fighting heart, Cass. Prove it again now.'

'What?'

I stare back at this jumble of creature and machine, and I ain't got a clue what it can truly be now – a ship's mind inside a girl inside a frame. Layers of metal and skin, and at the heart of it a ghost, spun together by people over a billion years ago . . . It stuffs the frayed cables into my arms. They leap and wrestle like a net of live eels. And I can *feel* the surge of the shuttle engines. They thrum against my chest and beat into my ribs. And then the flinder round my neck starts to burn.

'I am just human flesh and blood now,' goes the ship. 'I cannot command the shuttle. Only the power of your flinder can save us. Take control.'

I feel helpless. 'How?'

'Steer it, Cass!' yells Peyto. 'You're the only one who can do it! Use your flinder.'

And my mind flips. It feels like when I rammed my hands into the innards of the ship and set the shuttle on its way. Like when I called up Halina's shuttle from the ground at Arbor Low. It's the same. I shut my eyes and just let go. I picture the Wash, and the racing tide, and the sunken buildings of Lincoln, and the *Lodestar* bobbing at anchor. And I picture Dad.

We're hurtling through the wind, scudding over waves, slamming through spray, skimming from crest to crest like a flat stone.

The flinder closes tighter round my neck and it scalds into my skin, but I don't let up. I just hug them leaping cables and fly.

The sea roars around us.

Then a hole opens up above me and a gale of air blasts in from outside. The cables in my arms go dead. The roof of the shuttle peels right back and the seawater floods in.

'Peyto!'

He's out of reach, trapped by the sleeper pods, and, as the weight of water collapses in, he gets sucked further back. I dunk my helmet down into the bubbles, and it goes dark as we plummet further down. Great clouds of silver air mushroom past me as I dive deeper.

There in the green gloom I see a hand and I snatch at it. Then something yanks me from behind and I tear up through the currents and out into the dazzling bright air. Peyto bursts out next to me.

It takes me a few breathless moments to figure out what's happened. It's Maleeva's frame that's saved us from dropping to the sea floor. The *Aeolus*. It holds us both, one in each fist. We dangle there by the suit collars, water coursing down our helmets. It dumps us like landed fish onto some kind of raft. It ain't that stable – I can feel myself pitching about on the logs, ready any second to topple back into the drink.

It's only then that I twig that these ain't logs. The raft I'm lying on is made of forty-eight floating sleeper pods – seven by seven with a gap in the middle – held together with knotted tentacles that slither over each other like bronzed serpents.

I rip back the seals, toss away the helmet, and drink real air down into my lungs.

Next to me Peyto's done the same. We look at each other for a moment, scarcely believing we can still be alive.

The *Aeolus* don't say a word. It rips great fistfuls of Maleeva's suit away and launches her helmet into the sea. Then it just stands there astride the pod-raft with outstretched arms. And strip by strip, the suit flies away from the frame into the wind. Maleeva's beautiful face sits on top of the tower of scaffold that holds her together, like a hovering angel. And I wonder where her soul has gone, if she'll ever come back.

I watch Peyto then as he struggles out of his suit, but I'm too plain knackered to even move. He heaves the suit over the side and it drops away into the deep. When he stands up, he shields his eyes to the sun and starts laughing.

'What's so funny?'

'Good navigating, Cass!'

I look over to where he's pointing. And there, in the distance, is a church spire rising from the water. The sunken town we passed in the Lodestar.

The tide sweeps us along then, tipping us into furrows of current, closer and closer to the islands that dot the coast. I figure we're rudderless, the way we spin and lurch, but then the tentacles at the edge of the raft start to work together, dipping and pushing, so that at last our course steadies.

Peyto helps me out of my suit and I stand up with him to balance on the creaking pods. I gaze at all their faces – the sleepers that have found their home at last. Near the front of the raft is Wilbur, and next to him, Erin – both of them still locked in their dreams. Suddenly it hits me proper that scavving is over. It has to be now the artefact – Halina's flinder – ain't buried in London any more. For all the Vlads know it's lost in space now, out of their reach. And that means the scavs are free. The crushers of London won't ever be heard again.

Soon there's islands all around us, and, at last, nestling in the lee of the tide, I spot the *Lodestar*. I can see Dad scrambling to the edge of the deck and he's hooting at the top of his lungs. Peyto grabs hold of me and lifts me off my feet.

'You did it!' he whispers to me.

'We *all* did it,' I go. 'Joint effort, I reckon.'

'No, Cass. You were ready to risk it all. I'd never have had the guts. That was the maddest, bravest thing I've ever seen anyone do.'

'Brave? I just had to stick to my guns. You don't get it, do you? I *knew* it would back down. It *had* to.'

'What?'

'I figured it out, Peyto. The ship's secret.'

I glance at the *Aeolus* but it ain't even looking at us no more, like it's zoned out, staring at a world it's only seen through people's dreams.

'It can't harm people. Remember what you and Erin told me? It's alive but it ain't a creature. Humans can kill. I can and you can. But it can't. Its only reason for being alive is to create life, to nurture it. So it couldn't stand by and watch all the sleepers die. It had to set them free.'

He draws away from me, and looks at the sleepers that make up our raft.

'But you *were* ready to let us all die.'

'I had to be. The *Aeolus* wouldn't have backed down otherwise.'

He turns back to me and grins. 'I don't care what you say, Cass Westerby. Mad, brave, headstrong . . .'

I grin back. 'Headstrong's about right. Worked though, eh?'

Then I start proper belly-laughing.

'What?'

'I don't know – you wait a billion years for something to happen and then it all kicks off, eh?'

And I feel strong being on that raft as it bobs ever closer to the *Lodestar*. I reach up to my throat and there's a searing mark where the flinder burned me – *my flinder* now. But I don't care no more. Cos I feel something then – something beautiful about all the flinders being together, like the way this raft of pods is knitted together. *The flinders as one*, the *Aeolus* said.

Peyto hops about on the front edge of the raft, yelling and whooping with Dad, as we bump into the prow of the *Lodestar*.

Then he turns to me with a smile and goes, 'Now what?'

ACKNOWLEDGEMENTS

Cass's voice is a mix of many sources but the main ones are three generations of women in my family: Elsie Quinn, my nan; Terry Webb, my mum; and Sophie Malcolm, my sister. Thanks for helping my writing come to life!

I want to thank my wife, Rebecca, for her support, patience and priceless sanity-checking of early drafts.

Many thanks also to Veronique Baxter who first rescued my manuscript from the slush pile and encouraged me to make it better!

Everyone from Chicken House has been a delight to work with and learn from, in particular Barry Cunningham and Imogen Cooper who saw the potential in my complex tale and gave me enormous support to complete it.

There are lots of people without whom my efforts would have been remained so much scrap paper. So: Tony Webb, Chris Quinn, Clare Telford, John McCrone, Paul Vincent, Lorna Harty, Davey Fraser, Mark Proctor, Chris Tones, Graham and Caroline Parker, Anthony Fennel, Mark Lee, Katherine Pascoe, Natalie Davies, Alex Potterill, Suzanne Beishon, Olivia Boertje, Mario Constantinou, Claire Barber, Heather Swann, Kate Turnough, Clare Brown, Corey China, Joe Ungemah, Kerry Hedley, Tracey Sinclair, Kara May and everyone on the Goldsmiths writing course, Laura Windley, Frankie Pagnacco (for the race), Jane Butterworth, and Mave and Al Bilham-Boult – thank you all for your advice, encouragement and feedback.

It would take a lifetime for me to list all the artists and writers who managed to fire my imagination into strange and wonderful places. So here are just the ones who helped inspire *Six Days*: George Lucas, Arthur C Clarke, Stanley Kubrick, William Gibson, Iain Banks, Margaret Atwood, James Cameron, Danny Boyle and Robert Louis Stevenson.

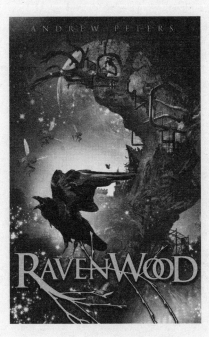

THE MAZE RUNNER
James Dashner

When the doors of the lift crank open, the only thing Thomas can remember is his first name. But he's not alone. He's surrounded by boys who welcome him to the Glade, an encampment at the centre of a bizarre and terrible maze.

Like Thomas, the Gladers don't know why or how they came to be there, or what's happened to the world outside. All they know is that every morning when the walls slide back, they will risk everything to find out – even the Grievers, half-machine, half-animal horrors that hunt the Maze's walled corridors.

A dark and gripping tale of survival set in a world where teenagers fight for their lives on a daily basis.
PUBLISHERS WEEKLY

Paperback, ISBN: 978-1-906427-50-4, £6.99

Available August 2011:
The Maze Runner 2: The Scorch Trials
Paperback, ISBN 978-1-906427-79-5, £6.99

 Find out more about Chicken House books and authors.
Visit our website: www.doublecluck.com

F WEB